THE
GYPSY MOTHS

GREG F. GIFUNE

JOURNALSTONE
YOUR LINK TO ARTIST TALENT

ISBN: 978-1-950305-67-4 (sc)
ISBN: 978-1-950305-68-1 (ebook)
Library of Congress Catalog Number: 2021951448

First printing edition: December 3, 2021
Published by JournalStone Publishing in the United States of America.
Cover Design and Layout: Mikio Murakami
Edited by Sean Leonard
Proofreading and Interior Layout by Scarlett R. Algee

JournalStone Publishing
3205 Sassafras Trail
Carbondale, Illinois 62901

JournalStone books may be ordered through booksellers or by contacting:
JournalStone | www.journalstone.com

For my father

"I wished I knew what nature's way was, because all that was happening in
our family did not seem to be natural or normal."
—Richard Ford
Wildlife

THE
GYPSY MOTHS

PROLOGUE

MUCH LIKE THE evil that sometimes fosters it, madness is a thief. It comes as shadow, memories blurred and twisted in an exhausted mind, a vague scent on a night wind or hidden within the soft laughter and whispers of those we love. It hunts in darkness, unnoticed, stealing gradually, silently and without remorse. When it's gone, only sorrow, anger, and the unsettling realization of having been violated remains, forever haunting those who never saw it coming. Those like us. Those like me.

I suppose it's possible that madness stalked my father prior to that spring of 1977, but I never saw any indication of that. Instead, it happened suddenly, and took him down quickly. The rest of us were collateral damage. Until then I had mistakenly assumed that might lessen the carnage for us, but soon learned victims of collateral damage often sustained as much loss as the original target.

The schoolyear was almost over and summer was already underway. I was an eighth-grader, just shy of my fourteenth birthday, and as much as I was looking forward to summer, my last before entering high school, I didn't feel much like a kid anymore. Without warning, the roles in our family had been drastically and cruelly altered, and I knew even then we'd never get them back to the way they'd been. Wasn't possible, my father had become someone else.

There was no going back. Not from that.

That particular day, the one I often think of when those old ghosts come looking for me, I'd been home for little more than half an hour. The entire time my father stood at the glass sliders off the den, watching the woods beyond our small backyard. It was late afternoon, and he was disheveled, unshaven, and still in his bathrobe. He hadn't left the house in weeks, and I couldn't be sure when he'd slept or showered last, but it was at least a few days.

"*Dad*," I said for the third time. "Come away from there now, okay?"

"It's out there," he finally answered in an unusually rough and raspy voice. Staring straight ahead, he remained entranced by things only he could see and feel and touch and know, or even begin to understand. "They don't think I know what's really happening, but I *do* know."

For a few weeks now, stories of a peeping tom had swept through town. Apparently a few women had called the police after seeing someone lurking near their windows, and since we had very little crime in town, it was a sensational situation everyone was talking about. The latest victim had been the music teacher at the elementary school, a single woman who lived only a few streets over from us. I assumed this was what my father was referring to, but due to his bizarre behavior of late, I couldn't be sure. I couldn't be sure of anything.

Using the moniker the local newspaper had given him, I asked, "Who is, the Peeper?"

"No."

"What then?"

Unsure if he hadn't heard my question or simply had no intention of answering it, I said, "I could make some grilled cheeses if you want."

"Not now, son."

"Maybe you should try to get some rest."

"Can't," he muttered. "It's there. It just doesn't want you to see. Not yet."

"What's there?" I followed his gaze to the trees. "What do you mean?"

"Don't be fooled."

"Dad, there's nothing there."

"When you see it, then you'll understand."

"There's nothing to see, I—"

His eyes, bloodshot and saddled with black bags, glared at me with such intensity that I stopped mid-sentence. I thought for a moment he might explode into a rage and spend the next several minutes ranting and raving like the lunatic I was terrified he'd become, but instead, his demeanor changed, as if something had occurred to him just then. Maybe he felt sorry for me. Maybe he was just scared and confused. I like to think that in that strange moment he remembered how much he loved me, because as quickly as it arrived, his anger slipped away. "When you see it," he said, "*then* you'll understand."

I nodded wearily.

"You don't know what's happening," he added. "But you will."

Sighing, I sidled up closer to him.

"I wish you didn't have to know," he said, voice cracking with sorrow and helplessness. "I never meant for any of this to touch you. Please believe me, Frankie Boy. I never wanted this for you. Not you, never you."

I put an arm around my father's shoulder and watched the woods with him a while. Although he was a few inches taller than I, and outweighed me by at least forty pounds, for the first time in my life he'd begun to seem small to me, fragile. "It's all right, Dad," I told him. "Everything's going to be okay."

"You wouldn't think so if you'd seen it too," he said.

I gently rubbed his shoulder, hoping to lessen the tension in his muscles. After a moment, against my better judgement, I asked, "What does it look like?"

"Nothing friendly," he whispered, as if fearful it might hear him.

"What's it doing?"

"Watching the house, it—it's just watching. For now…"

"Why is it watching us?" I asked.

My father looked at me with those sad, crazed eyes, a phantom now, fading like a memory, aloof and slowly vanishing into a netherworld of shadow and dreams. "It's waiting."

"Waiting for what?"

"You, son," he said grimly. "It's waiting for you."

CHAPTER ONE
~2017~

HE COMES TO me like the ghost he is. Moving gracefully from behind a cluster of trees, my father stands before me. He's been expecting me.

I wait, knees trembling, my throat dry, heart racing. It isn't possible for him to be standing here looking so alive and vibrant. Or perhaps it's not possible for me to be there. Either way, we remain quiet for what seems a very long time, our eyes locked as memories and nightmares pass between us. Good, bad, and everything in between, all of it important and relevant, all of it necessary. We're alone, my dead father and I, in this dark and foreboding forest, standing in a time and place from very long ago.

My father looks like he has something important to tell me, so I wait for him to speak. But he just smiles a sad little grin of regret and affection.

They did things to us, son.

His words come to me like thoughts.

Without warning, he throws back his head, his eyes roll to white, and a blizzard of tiny winged creatures erupt from his mouth.

Fluttering and swarming around us, they form a living cloud uncontrollably drawn to flame.

But there is no flame.

There is only me, only my father, and that dark forest.

Through the writhing mass, I hear his voice, but cannot make out what he's saying. The moths have already begun to gnaw at our flesh, intent on devouring us like defenseless leaves dangling from slowly dying trees. I can hear them eating him, feel them eating me.

I try to remember the things we used to say to each other, those things fathers and sons sometimes say. But I also think about the things we left unspoken, then and now.

In the end, I wonder if there's much difference between the two.

Maybe there's not supposed be.

With memories of the dream still fresh and replaying in my mind, the same dream that first came to me just days after his death and has haunted me ever since, I adjust my position in the chair, fiddle nervously with my cocktail napkin and watch the door. Although I hadn't experienced it in a few years, the dream retuned to me the night before, perhaps because this meeting was on my mind, or maybe because wherever he was, my father was still trying to communicate with me. I gave up trying to figure these things out long ago, and have done my best to convince myself I've moved on to become one of those well-adjusted but elusive people you hear so much about but never actually encounter. In the end, I suppose we all lie to ourselves about how safe and sound we are to some extent. There's nothing particularly noble at play, just basic survival along with an intrinsic desire to keep hopelessness and madness at bay. The key is to pick your spots, because like everything else in this life, it boils down to a balancing act between a tolerable, sustainable state of existence, and a wasteland of utter oblivion.

I find myself in a dive bar in Samoset, Massachusetts. Named for the first Native American to make contact with the Pilgrims of Plymouth County, Samoset is the small coastal town where my friends and I grew up. I now live in the city of Syracuse, New York, several hours away. This is the first time I've been back. Like much else in town, Milo's, Samoset's most infamous watering hole, is largely unchanged. A staple in town, it has served as the preeminent stomping ground for twenty- and thirty-somethings for three generations. Going to Milo's was a rite of passage for townies, the place you went once you hit legal drinking age, a hangout you haunted on Friday and Saturday nights with your friends or on dates. A place that pumped out watered-down booze, cheap beer, and the tastiest bar pizzas in the area, it wasn't unusual to find locals arguing or even brawling in the parking lot, before drunkenly staggering back inside, arms around each other and friends once more, ready for another round. When I was younger, everyone knew each other here, and there was a kind of tacit camaraderie in that, a bond that united us, including those that didn't get along. Like a family, we could fight and terrorize each other, but if anyone else tried it, they answered to all of us.

I have my share of memories of Milo's, good and bad, and while there are other places in town better suited to more mature patrons, this seemed a fitting place to meet, especially after all these years.

Being late afternoon, things are still fairly slow. Only a few stools at the bar are occupied, and except for mine, and another on the far side of the room where a young couple chat and flirt incessantly, the tables between the bar and pool table area are empty.

Sipping a Cutty and water, I watch the young couple, careful not to be too obvious. A man my age already stands out here, I don't need them thinking I'm some sort of pervert. Truth is, the older I get the younger everyone else seems to be. People in their twenties look like teenagers to me, and teenagers look like little kids. At fifty-four I'm not exactly old yet, I'm just not young anymore. But here I am, watching this couple, zeroing in on the woman and thinking she's on a one-way trip to getting her heart broken. I can tell by the way she looks at him that she's in love, or thinks she is, and ready for the long haul. Because I don't see the same thing in her boyfriend's eyes, I want to warn her, tell her to dump the sonofabitch now and save herself the heartache. I have no children of my own, so it's not exactly a parental thing, more likely just the teacher in me. I've taught high school for nearly thirty years, and every year, while I get a little bit older, the kids—it seems to me—get a little bit younger.

If nothing else, the couple serves as a welcome distraction from the fear that's been rising in me since my return to town. Fear that has never truly left me, but I've convinced myself I had under control for a very long time now.

With a squeal, the door to the front entrance opens, spilling sunlight into the otherwise dimly lit bar, and for a moment, the old terror recedes.

Through the glare, a silhouette appears. It remains still for a second or two, then moves through the doorway and steps inside. As the door closes and swallows the sunlight, the silhouette becomes a middle-aged man with a trim build, meticulously styled short gray hair, and a closely cropped gray beard.

It's been forty long years, but I recognize him immediately.

All the joy and sins of the past fall around us like rain, and suddenly, if only for a moment, Max and I are kids again.

A little under average height, he wears designer sunglasses, a tan linen jacket over a button-down shirt, white cotton slacks and a pair of brown huarache sandals. Slung over one shoulder is a black leather satchel. Draped in an air of unconscious importance and clothes too stylish and expensive for Milo's, he casually removes his sunglasses. Pale blue eyes scan the area, and as they settle on me, recognition dawns in them.

Despite our shared nightmares, I feel myself smile.

Max strolls through the tables until he reaches mine. "Frankie Boy," he says, voice whispery and a little deeper than I remember.

I stand, put my hand out. "It's good to see you, Max."

He shakes my hand. "I'm just so sorry it's like this."

"I know," I say. "But here we are."

"Here we are indeed."

We stand there awkwardly a moment, then finally embrace.

Max smells of sandalwood soap and heady cologne, and in that moment, I lose him. The boy I knew so well is gone, replaced by an imposter, a middle-aged man from some other place and time.

I wonder if he thinks the same of me.

"It's lovely to see you," he says. "But if you don't let go soon, people are bound to talk."

And just like that, the old Max returns.

"Fuck 'em," I mutter.

"But it's so much better when they go fuck themselves."

I release him and, holding my smile, drift back to my chair and sit.

"It really is good to see you, Frankie Boy." Max casually pulls the satchel from his shoulder and places it on the table. Taking the chair closest to mine, he positions it just far enough from the table to have sufficient room to comfortably cross his legs at the knee. "Does anyone still call you that?"

No one's called me *Frankie Boy* in a long time. It feels good, though. My father never called me anything but. "It's just Frank these days," I tell him.

"Of course, that makes sense," Max says through a wide smile, his once uneven teeth now capped and perfectly straight. "But you'll always be Frankie Boy Molinari to me."

And to me he'll always be Max Gilligan, the short, chubby, blond-haired kid with the quick wit and acerbic humor who, despite his small stature, never hid who he was and never once backed down from anyone. He'd been ahead of his time in many ways, and I'd always respected that.

"Then Frankie Boy it is," I say. "I mean, that's who I am, right?"

"Sure, although we do change, age, evolve. Well, *hopefully* we evolve."

"Not always a sure thing these days, but yes, I'd like to think so."

He gives me a quick wink. "Just the same, deep down we're still those boys in a way too, don't you think?"

"I hope so."

Max's smile fades, but his eyes never leave me. He doesn't have to say anything more. We know all too well what we're feeling. And it's all right. For now, in this old bar, in a town neither of us has set foot in for years, it's all right.

After finding out what he'd like to drink, I head to the bar for a refill on my Cutty Sark, and a vodka and cranberry juice for Max. When I return we pretend there aren't deeper, more pressing issues at hand, and instead engage in small talk, forcing as many pleasantries as we can stand. Whistling past a graveyard, certainly, but that's exactly what's necessary just now.

Though it played out very differently, like me, Max escaped our past by going to college. I went to a small school. He got into Princeton. A successful investment banker in Manhattan for decades now, he lives in a luxury apartment in Tribeca I've never been to, with a husband of twenty-five years I've never met. None of which I knew until we spoke on the phone a few days before.

"I was glad to hear you're still teaching," he tells me.

"High school," I say. "English and American Lit."

"I'm sure you're wonderful," Max says, and means it.

"I do my best."

He replies with an air of sorrow we both understand all too well. "You always did."

I want him to be right, but who can be sure of such things?

"How're your parents doing?" I ask.

"Honestly? I'm beginning to fear they may be immortal."

I give a quiet, obligatory laugh.

"They're in a retirement community down in Florida. Costs me a fortune, but I suppose they're happy as can be expected." Max shrugs. "How's your mother? Are you still in contact?"

I knew the question was coming and was prepared for it, but it's still a difficult topic. Death always is. "She passed away a couple years ago."

"I'm sorry." Max's mouth becomes a thin grim line. "I know your relationship with her was always, well…let's go with *complicated*."

"She bounced around for years before she finally settled down out in San Francisco," I tell him. "Spent the last twenty years of her life there, but struggled with an opioid addiction until the end. A neighbor found her body one afternoon. Apparently she'd been dead a few days. The coroner listed her death as an accidental overdose."

"How awful," he says gently. "I'm so sorry."

"Thanks. I hadn't seen her in a long time, but we talked on the phone now and then. She was never really a part of my adult life, such as it is." I sip my drink as a means of rescue, then change the subject as gracefully as I can. "I'm glad to hear your parents are still with us. And you, happily married, huh?"

"I'm very blessed," he says in a cautious tone.

"Living in Tribeca no less, must be doing quite well for yourself."

"It's truly amazing what money can do. I listened to my parents' religious nonsense for years about how I was destined to burn in Hell. I got into Princeton, graduated at the top of my class, while Lenny barely made it out of high school, yet he was the golden boy and I was the evil *fag* disgracing the family. Nothing helped. That is until I started to pull a high six-figure salary. Lenny's job as a mechanic, while admirable and honest work, wasn't about to pay their bills now, was it? So suddenly, just like that—praise the lord and pass the biscuits—all was forgiven."

I try to think of something witty to say, but it eludes me.

"Are *you* married, have any children?" Max glances at my hand, searches for a ring. "Dare I say *grandchildren*?"

"No." I leave it at that, hopeful for now that he'll do the same.

He does. Max always was the smartest of us.

"What about you? Got any kids?"

"A daughter," he says proudly. With remarkable speed he locates a photograph of a bright-eyed young woman on his phone and shows it to me. "Dana Marie. She just turned twenty, graduates from Julliard next year, can you believe it?"

"Wow, that's wonderful, Max, really."

"Isn't it, though? Dustin and I couldn't be prouder." He shuffles through more photographs, settles on a shot of him with another man roughly the same age, good-looking with a bright smile and kind eyes. "That's Dusty. Without question the sweetest man alive. He puts up with me, after all."

"I'm happy for you, man."

Max smiles at me fondly then puts his phone away. As he sits back and looks around without subtlety, his smile slips away, as if he's only now realized where we are. "My *God* this place is every bit as depressing as I remember it."

"We had some good times here though," I remind him.

"Did we?"

"*Didn't* we?"

Max sips his drink and seems to think it over a while. "Has there been any word from Shawn?"

"Nothing since we spoke on the phone."

"I can't imagine he was easy to find."

"Apparently he's been living in a little desert town not far from Vegas for a while now."

"Finally putting down some roots, is he?"

"Much as someone like Shawn can, I guess."

Something similar to suspicion drifts across Max's face. "What's he up to these days? Staying out of trouble, I hope."

"I don't know a lot about his life." I look away, ashamed. When you're a kid you think the friends you have will be the people you're closest to for the rest of your life. It never occurs to you that could change, until decades later, when you come to understand just how wrong you were. It's lost— *they're* lost—and you along with them. You can't even remember how or why. It just happens. But all those years ago I couldn't imagine life without

Max, Shawn, and Alex. It seemed impossible for us to ever be anything other than close friends. "We didn't talk long," I add. "I let him know what was happening, that's about it."

Max absently strokes his beard. "You're sure he'll come?"

He knows better, but I answer anyway. "He'll be here."

"How's old Ronica holding up?"

"Haven't seen her yet, but I imagine as well as can be expected."

"I think of her sometimes." He says this with a droll smile.

"I'm sure we all do. She is a legend after all."

"That girl was a force of nature."

Images of Ronica fire across my mind's eye, but those fond memories are quickly replaced with one more recent. "When she called me," I say softly, "I knew. The minute I realized it was her, I knew."

"When you called, I knew what you were going to say too," Max says. "I can't believe Alex stayed here all these years. I can't imagine…"

I nod but say nothing more. The fear reminds me it's never far. I try not to let Max see me shudder, but those old ghosts are back, rattling their chains and screeching at me from the dark.

"I'd been waiting for that call for years, if you want to know the truth." Max stares down into his drink. "I knew it was Alex. I'm just surprised it took this long. I never expected him to make it out of his twenties. I was never sure any of us would. Isn't that an awful thing to think, much less say?"

Maybe, but I understand exactly what he means. And *Max* damn well knows it. We do the dance anyway. It's what old friends do. We go through the motions and let the memories come. We say the words and think the thoughts and play the games, because what else is there? Sometimes the only way out of the fire is straight down. And even when you know what's waiting just south of Perdition might be worse, you go anyway.

Nobody grows old in Hell.

CHAPTER TWO
~SUMMER, 1977~

MOONLIGHT FELL ACROSS the slowly breaking waves and along the lengthy stretch of beach leading to the house on the cliff. There was a full moon that night, so we hid in what darkness we could find, huddling down next to a long stone jetty a hundred yards or so from the house.

"For the record," Max said, dropping to the sand and leaning against the jetty, "this is a really bad idea, especially with the Peeper running around town."

"Of course it is." Ronica smiled that dazzling, treacherous smile of hers. "The best ideas always are."

With the smell of the ocean and the warm night all around us, I tried to remember how we'd come to be here. It seemed like only moments before we'd been at Ronica and Alex's house, down in the basement listening to records, sneaking hits off a joint Ronica had managed to get hold of and laughing our asses off. And now we were clustered in the dark like assassins, watching a house beyond the jetty that looked like something out of the movies. People like us didn't go beyond this point, we weren't welcome there. The jetty separated the public beach from the private, and all the fancy homes the wealthy in town lived in. It was like an invisible barrier existed, and everyone agreed to it. If you were in that neighborhood, you better be working or have good reason, or the cops would come down on you without mercy. The older folks were fond of saying everyone knew their place in Samoset, whether they liked it or not. If you tested that, you found out quickly what a bad idea it was. In those days, few questioned such things. I don't know why. Maybe because that part of town and those people were alien to us anyway. They were an oddity, like some rare creatures you only caught a glimpse of now and then and weren't entirely sure what to make of. They didn't want us around, and we didn't want to be around them, so it wasn't much of a loss, far as I could tell. Besides, why waste time worrying about it? Not like those things or people were going to change anyway.

"You're sure she's in there?" Shawn asked, the glow from his cigarette the only indication that he was even there. He'd found a patch of deep darkness in all that moonlight. If anyone could, it was Shawn.

"She's babysitting," Ronica said, gazing up at the house. "By now the little ones should be tucked in their beds, so she's all by her lonesome downstairs."

Shawn puffed away, the orange dot burning like a tiny beacon in the night. We all snuck a cigarette now and then, but he and Ronica were real smokers. "If you say so," he muttered.

"What exactly did Tracy do to deserve this again?" Max asked.

"You mean besides being dumb enough to tell me she'd be here alone babysitting tonight?"

"Yes, Ronica," Max said with a sigh, "besides that."

"Last week of school she turned me and Cindy Wayne in for smoking in the bathroom." Ronica stomped her foot, made a cartoonish frown, and imitated Tracy in a voice that sounded an awful lot like a Shirley Temple impersonation. "'They're smoking *cigarettes* in there! It's *so* gross! G-R-O-S-S—gross!'"

"Holy shit, does she really sound like that?" Alex asked.

"I shit you not. That goody-goody's the biggest narc in school."

"This is going to scare the hell out of her, you know," Max said.

"That's the whole point."

"Seems cruel," he said, "and kind of unnecessary."

"That's how practical jokes work, darling."

"Oh, is that what this is, *darling*?"

Ronica turned away from him, her long chestnut-colored hair blowing in the warm sea breeze, her breasts barely contained in a white bikini top. I stayed quiet and watched her, certain I'd never seen anyone so beautiful.

"You can sit it out or go home any time you want, Maxie," she said.

"What-the-fuck-ever!" Shawn growled, tossing his cigarette to the waves and stepping into the moonlight, his ice-blue eyes darting back and forth between us. In a sleeveless t-shirt, jeans, sneakers, and a red bandana tied around his head that barely contained his mane of dirty blond hair, he was lean and cool as ever. He looked dangerous. "Are we doing this or not?"

"Yeah," Alex said, "if we're on, let's do it. I'm getting tired of this standing around shit."

The truth of the matter was that, other than Ronica, none of us really knew Tracy Davenport. Like Ronica, she was sixteen—two years older than we were—and already in high school. We'd gone along because Ronica wanted to do it, and because with the exception of her younger brother Alex, we were all madly in love with her in one way or another. For Shawn and me, it was likely more lust than love, but we all worshipped Ronica. She was smart and beautiful. She had a body we drooled over. She was tough, sexy, cool, funny, and fearless. There wasn't a whole lot not to love. Even Max adored her, just not like Shawn and I did, and not even like Alex did. He and Ronica had their own thing, which was probably why Max was often able to call her on her bullshit when the rest of us wouldn't dare. Their relationship was a duel of sorts, but there was no mistaking the bond between them. As for Alex, he looked up to his big sister. He was a good kid, sad and kind of lost and lonely even when he was around us, but a loyal friend who was always there when you needed him. He had a slight build, a mop of unruly brown hair, sad puppy-dog eyes, and an oddly spiritual aura about him. But between the two of them, Ronica was the star attraction, and everyone knew it, even Alex. Maybe especially Alex, because unlike the tempest that was his sister, he was generally the quiet brooding type, and usually had his nose buried in a paperback novel, pro wrestling magazine, or comic book. Still, they were close and rarely argued like other brothers and sisters did. For the rest of us, having an older badass girl like Ronica around, even though she only hung out with us now and then, was about the coolest thing that could've happened.

"It's getting late," I reminded everyone.

"Frankie Boy's right," Shawn said. "Let's get this show on the road."

Ronica reached into a pillowcase she'd brought with her, pulled out the cheap plastic Halloween clown masks she'd gotten at the drugstore downtown earlier that day, and passed them out. "Discount bin leftovers from Halloween," she explained. "What's scarier than clowns wandering around in the dark?"

As Shawn and Alex debated the answer to that question, I put my mask on. The eyeholes were uneven and restricted my vision, and the mask itself had a chemical smell and was so tight I could barely breathe. I tried adjusting it three or four times, but nothing helped. "I can't see or breathe for shit in this thing," I said, voice muffled.

"It's worth it," Ronica said. "Trust me."

I did. We all did.

Slowly, we made our way around the jetty and crept along the sand to the dunes leading up to the house. It was an enormous structure, the front all glass and lit up bright as could be. I'd seen houses like that in movies or magazines, but had never been inside anything so extravagant. Stumbling up the dunes with the others, I did my best to keep my balance until we reached the summit and found ourselves crouched behind a short cement wall. On the other side was a large patio area with a pool and Jacuzzi built right in.

And then, the house, the entire first floor, including Tracy, on display through all that glass and awash in brilliant interior light. It all looked so pristine and perfect it didn't seem possible anyone could actually live there.

Sitting on a plush couch and wearing white painter pants, clogs, and a blouse, Tracy was all blonde hair, braces, and big eyeglasses with plastic frames. Watching TV, she absently nibbled her fingernails, still unaware of our presence.

"Perfect," Ronica purred beneath her hideous mask. "This is *perfect*."

Quietly, we climbed over the cement wall and drifted toward the glass before us. Once there, we stood side-by-side, silently watching Tracy and hoping she'd look up at some point and notice us.

When she finally did, Tracy cocked her head and squinted, as if she couldn't be sure she'd actually seen something. But then a slow dawning came over her, and her face twisted in terror.

Screaming, she toppled from the couch, one of her clogs sailing through the air and slapping the glass with a dull thud. Scrambling back to her feet, she tried to run but slipped, frantically regained her balance, and then, still screaming as she went, bolted across the room in a frenzied whirlwind of flailing arms and blind panic. A urine stain, followed by something much worse, suddenly bloomed and spread across the back of her white pants.

We all burst out laughing, but it was short-lived, because Tracy quickly reached the wall phone and began furiously dialing, screaming for the police even before the call could've connected.

"Shit," Shawn said, "she's calling the cops!"

We all looked to Ronica.

"Run!"

None of us moved.

"Run!" she screamed again.

This time, howling with laughter, we charged back over the wall and down the dunes to the beach below. Running hard and fast as I could, once I hit the sand I blew by the jetty, back onto the private beach, and continued on toward the parking lot in the distance.

I was well out ahead of everyone else, or so I thought, until suddenly Ronica appeared at my side. Passing me easily, she slowed only long enough to look my way, stick her tongue out, and laugh. As she left us all in her wake, I marveled at how impossibly fast she was, this petite girl just a little over five feet tall, in her cutoff jean shorts and bikini top, bare feet slapping the wet sand as she sprinted through the moonlight. In that strangely wonderful moment, I was certain there wasn't anything Ronica couldn't do. She wasn't just powerful, she had the ability to make us all feel invincible and alive in ways we couldn't quite get to without her.

"She's magic," Shawn would always say, "nothing but magic."

And God help us, she was.

We all made it back to her car, a junky Volkswagen Bug, and piled in.

"Hurry up!" Max said as he squeezed in between Shawn and me.

"Go! Go!" Alex slapped the dash. "Go!"

In the cramped backseat, I pulled my mask off. Breathing heavily, I looked out the little window at the night and the section of beach from which we'd come. As Ronica pulled out and sped away, I secretly wished I could stay in that car with them all night. But I couldn't. I was already out later than I should've been and was probably in trouble. I felt terrible about frightening Tracy Davenport to the point where she'd messed in her pants, though I believed even then we hadn't meant any real harm. I guess the only thing I knew for sure was that I was free of the things I had to deal with at home, and I wanted to keep it that way.

"Did you *see* her face?" Ronica said, still laughing as she reduced her speed so as not to draw attention.

"She shit her pants," Alex said. "We're talking a serious piss, too."

Shawn shook his head. "Never seen anybody haul ass and scream like that outside of a horror movie."

Ronica's sultry dark eyes lifted, found mine in the rearview, and held my gaze a moment. Something passed between us, I was sure of it. I smiled at her, but she was already gone, eyes back on the road.

"Remind me never to get on your bad side, Veronica, dear," Max said.

"Don't be silly, you could never be on my bad side, Maximillian, *dear*."

Our chatter died down, and it was quiet in the car, the only sounds those of that old VW Bug doing its best to drag us along.

Not thirty seconds later, flashing blue lights cut the darkness. A police cruiser flew by in the opposite direction, followed by a second, and as their lights faded into night, we all laughed again. I couldn't be sure if it was because we found genuine humor in what was happening or if we just didn't know what the hell else to do. I suppose it didn't really matter.

* * * *

I lived in a small single-story house on a short and quiet street lined with other small single-story houses, all of which more or less looked the same. Our street was within walking distance of the public beach, so ironically, despite my desire to prolong our outing, I was the first one Ronica dropped off.

When I snuck in through the backdoor, which landed me directly in our kitchen, I was surprised to find my mother sitting at the table, alone and in the dark. The only light in the room came from a small bulb on the stove several feet away, which left her almost entirely in silhouette.

I froze, unsure of what to do, but she didn't say a word, so I closed and locked the door behind me, and with uncertainty, moved closer to the table.

My mother had been to the hairdresser since I'd last seen her that morning, as her hair was a bit shorter, styled fancily and sprayed into place. She had more makeup and jewelry on than she normally wore, and was decked out in a tight, low-cut black dress I hadn't seen before. I never knew her to use heavy perfumes, but I could smell a strong and sweet scent wafting from her that made my eyes water. Sparkling glass droplets dangled from her ears, and a beautiful string of pearls my father had given her two Christmases ago adorned her neck. Her stockinged feet were tucked under her chair and crossed at the ankle, and the black high heels she'd taken off at some earlier point were positioned neatly together on the floor. On the table before her sat a tiny black purse, a plastic ashtray, half a glass of whiskey, a gold-plated lighter with her initials engraved on it, and a pack of cigarettes. She smoked slowly and deliberately, the bracelets on her wrists clacking together each time she brought the cigarette to her lips.

Through the shadows, I could see her eyes.

They looked empty and distant, hopeless.

"Mom," I said, "what's wrong?"

"You startled me," she said, though she didn't seem startled at all. It was more like the sound of my voice had awakened her from a trance of some sort.

"Sorry."

"I didn't see you come in. I must've closed my eyes a moment."

I couldn't tell if that was true or not, but I knew then she wasn't waiting for me. She was just...there.

"I assumed you were in your room, I only just got home myself." As she took another drag on her cigarette, leaving a smear of lipstick on the white filter, I noticed her fingernails were polished and glossy and painted blood-red. "What time is it?" she asked.

I looked to the clock on the stove. "Almost ten, I—"

"You're not allowed to be out this late," she said, as if it had just then occurred to her. "You're only fourteen years old. I won't have my son running around at all hours like some juvenile delinquent."

My birthday had been the week before. Neither she nor my father had remembered. Later that evening, it apparently dawned on my mother that she'd forgotten the anniversary of the birth of her only child. When she came home and found me in my room, she kissed me on the cheek and handed me a card. There was a smiling cartoon dog on it holding a birthday cake covered in candles. Inside, it read: *Have a Dog Gone Good Birthday*! In pen she'd hastily written *Love, Mom and Dad* at the bottom and there was a twenty-dollar bill inside. She apologized, said she'd been busy at work, that she loved me and that there was a cake in the fridge from the grocery store. Then she wished me happy birthday and went to bed. My dad never mentioned anything about it. I still had the twenty tucked away in a book in my room, and I never touched the cake. It hadn't been in the refrigerator for a few days, so I assumed my mother threw it out.

"I was over at Alex's house," I told her. "Guess I lost track of time."

"There's something wrong with that Nelson boy." She scratched at the corner of her mouth with the tip of a pinky nail, causing her diamond wedding band to twinkle in the sparse light, as if mistakenly. "I can't put my finger on it, but there's something *off* about that kid."

My mother rarely approved of my friends, so I was used to hearing these things from her. Experience had taught me it was best to remain quiet.

"Don't you ever stay out this late again without my permission," she said flatly, sipping her whiskey and watching me over the lip of the glass. "Do you understand me?"

"Yeah," I said.

The ice cubes in her glass clinked as she returned her whiskey to the table. "Whatever happened to the word *yes*?"

"*Yes*, I mean. And I'm sorry I stayed out later than I should have, okay?"

"Don't be so sorry all the time," she said in the same strange monotone, pushing her bottom lip out and exhaling a thin stream of smoke toward the ceiling. "People think they have a limitless supply of apologies. They don't. In fact, the genuine ones run out much faster than we realize, so it's important to take particular care not to waste them."

I knew my mother was drunk, but I'd never seen her that way before.

"Just don't do it again," she said. "Okey-doke, cowpoke?"

She'd used that expression with me regularly when I was a little boy, but I hadn't heard her say it in a very long time. "Okey-doke," I said, responding as she'd taught me to all those years before.

"Now get to bed." A long ash fell from her cigarette. "I don't want to have to harp on you to get up for school in the morning."

It seemed impossible, but I could tell she was serious. "School's been out for a couple weeks now, Mom," I said. "And anyway, tomorrow's Saturday."

"Of course, I wasn't thinking," she said, her voice shaking suddenly, like if she said anything more she might cry. "I'm very tired."

I didn't want to embarrass her further, so I craned my neck and looked into the den instead. It was dark and quiet like the rest of the house, adding to the feeling that it was much later somehow, more like the middle of the night than only ten o'clock. "Where's Dad?" I asked.

"He's in bed. I think. I haven't checked on him yet."

"Maybe he's finally getting some sleep."

"Let's hope so."

"I don't think he's had any in a while now," I said.

"No, he hasn't."

Smoke from her cigarette filled the air and curled around us like snakes.

"Mom, why are you sitting here in the dark all by yourself?" I asked.

"I'm unwinding. Adults need to do that sometimes."

"You look nice," I told her.

A smile touched a corner of her mouth, gone so quickly I nearly missed it.

"How come you're all dressed up?"

"I had to attend an awards banquet for work," she explained.

A year ago, not long after my father lost his job, my mother had left her position as assistant manager at a local gift shop she worked at for years, and took a better paying job as an office manager for a small insurance company in town. I didn't know much about insurance, but it sure seemed like they had an awful lot of business dinners and liked giving each other awards.

"Dad didn't go with you?"

"The way he's been behaving lately? Don't be ridiculous. It's more than a month since he's even left the house."

I knew I shouldn't, but I asked anyway. "Is he going to be okay, Mom?"

"Your father's having a difficult time right now. We all are."

"Why can't he get a job?"

"Look at him. Is it any wonder?"

"But he always worked. He wasn't always like this."

"No," she said, "he wasn't."

"I don't even think he's trying to get a job anymore."

"I imagine he assumes there's no longer any point."

"Did he do something wrong, Mom?"

"You shouldn't ask so many questions," she said. "Eventually you'll land on one you don't want the answer to."

Her response worried me, so I tried to steer the conversation in another direction. "Did you have fun at the banquet?"

A tiny burst of laughter escaped her, as if by accident. It was a bitter laugh, a sad and angry little laugh that made me feel naïve and foolish, like a child whose question was so inane it couldn't possibly be answered any other way. "Go to bed, Frankie Boy," she said through a heavy sigh. "It's late."

Rather than leave the room, I stayed where I was.

"What is it now?" she finally asked.

"Are *you* all right?"

"Happy as a peach," she said, then seemed to think about it. "My mother used to say that to me when I was a little girl. It's silly, doesn't make a lick of sense, but it sounds nice. Doesn't it?"

"Mom," I said softly, "are you sure you're all right?"

"I'm fine. I'm *always* fine."

I stood there staring at her. There seemed nothing else to do.

"Like a great many things, you'll understand when you're older," she said, rescuing me in the only way she could. "Now go to bed."

When I kissed her cheek, it felt strange and unnatural against my lips, as if I were kissing something covered in all that powdery makeup that wasn't quite alive, or perhaps never had been. "Goodnight, Mom," I said. "I love you."

Crossing the room, I hesitated in the doorway and looked back.

The same as I'd found her, she sat there in the dark, quietly smoking her cigarette. While I didn't know it then, in many ways my mother was already away from us, already gone. I could no longer be sure of her, and that was terrifying.

Later, lying in bed and staring at the ceiling, I tried my best to make sense of things. My life was no longer as safe and secure as I'd once believed. I knew I had to come to grips with that, I just didn't know how. My father was losing his mind, and my mother was so unhappy she seemed barely able to function. My parents were my only family, our house the only security I had, all I'd ever known. Yet it was all becoming unrecognizable to me. Our home was now a peculiar and uncertain place, occupied by strangers that had once been Mom and Dad.

I was afraid, and had never felt so powerless, so horribly alone. Maybe that's why I tried instead to remember what happened at the beach that night, how beautiful Ronica had been in the moonlight, and how we'd all laughed as we ran across that sand for the car, free and mischievous and alive in ways we'd never be again. Because rather than laughter and such wonderful abandon, that summer became more about tears and things we were about to lose that we could never get back, the deaths we were about to die, the mysteries and nightmares we were about to find ourselves trapped in, and the fallout we'd have to live with for the rest of our lives.

In the end, despite his madness, my father had been right all along.

There really was something out there.

And nothing would ever be the same again.

CHAPTER THREE

LIKE MOST GUYS my age in 1977, I woke up nearly every morning with a raging hard-on and Farrah Fawcett smiling down at me from my bedroom wall. As usual, I focused on the poster and let my eyes sweep across her face, that dazzling smile, and then the rest of her. Still groggy, I fantasized about our sordid sexual escapades together until I was no longer tenting my underwear. Afterwards, I sat up, swung my feet around to the floor, and cleaned up with an already crusty and disgusting towel I kept hidden under my bed. I tried to avoid the instant waves of guilt, but being Catholic I failed miserably, so I said a quick Hail Mary and hoped for the best.

I easily could've gone back to bed for a few hours, but my plan was to get out of the house before anyone else was awake. We were in for a hot day, as it was still early morning and the humidity was already on the rise. After a quick search for some clean clothes, I threw on a Rolling Stones t-shirt, a pair of gray cotton shorts, white gym socks, and my Puma sneakers.

Cautiously, I opened the bedroom door and listened a moment.

The hallway was empty, the house quiet.

Slipping from my room, I crept down the hall to the bathroom. I peed for what seemed an eternity then washed my face and brushed my teeth. A quick inspection in the mirror revealed tired eyes and tousled hair, which I wore at a length just shy of my shoulders. With a sigh, I convinced myself I didn't look too bad, all things considered, and after straightening my hair, opened the door to leave.

I walked directly into my father.

"Jesus!" I said. "You scared the— I didn't expect to see you there, Dad."

I had hoped he'd slept the night before, but he looked as exhausted and troubled as ever. In his summer robe and pajamas, both wrinkled and stained, he still hadn't bathed or shaved, and his eyes were bloodshot, his face covered in thick salt-and-pepper stubble that was quickly becoming a beard. His chapped lips moved as if he was speaking, but he made no sound.

I wondered if he was searching for the right words, or perhaps had already found them and simply couldn't bring himself to say them aloud.

"What's the matter?" I asked.

He looked down the hallway then back at me, as if to be sure it was just the two of us there. "You need to come with me," he whispered. His breath was sour and smelled of stale coffee and cigarettes.

"Why, what's going on?"

"You'll see." He shuffled away, the belt from his robe dragging on the floor behind him like a tail. "Come on."

Wearily, I followed.

The shades in the den were drawn, and the drapes over the sliders were pulled closed, leaving the room in near-darkness. Several tattered notebooks my father had been scribbling in for weeks lay scattered across the coffee table in front of the couch. Next to them was a single burning candle, a cold mug of black coffee, a plastic ashtray overflowing with spent cigarette butts, and a small wood board displaying letters and numbers, a heart-shaped planchette sitting atop it.

"You remember what that is?" He motioned to the board with one hand while nervously scratching at his neck with the other.

"Yeah, it's my old Ouija board."

"I found it the other day at the back of the hall closet."

I vaguely remembered getting it along with some other board games for Christmas when I was still in elementary school. After the initial novelty wore off, I never really played with it much. Packed away and forgotten for years, I didn't even know we still had it.

"Something told me I had to find it." He looked around again as if fearful someone else might hear our conversation. "I couldn't get it out of my head no matter how hard I tried. Then I started dreaming about it. That's when I knew."

I wanted to cry. I loved my father dearly, but I was becoming afraid of him. "Where's Mom?" I asked.

He squinted, as if he might be losing sight of me. "What?"

"*Mom*," I said again. "Where is she?"

"Asleep. She was up late last night."

"Should I go get her?"

"Why would you do that?" He seemed genuinely baffled.

"I don't know, I—"

"Son, don't go getting goofy on me, all right? I need your help."

"With what, I—"

"Sit down," he said, hustling me over to the couch.

As I did, he took the stool across from me. "Dad—"

"This thing," he said, motioning to the Ouija board. "It's more than a silly game. I thought that's all it was, but it's not. It's real. The goddamn thing, it—it actually *works*, do you understand?"

I shook my head no.

"It's been talking to me. It knew about that...*thing*. It knew."

"Dad, you got to—"

"Somehow, it knew."

"Y-You need to get some help or something," I stammered, heart racing. "You can't live like this. This isn't right."

"Did you hear me? It's *telling* me things, son. It's not like it talked to me the way we're talking now. I didn't hear it. Not with my ears, anyway, I—I heard it in my head, you know what I mean? Like thoughts, only they're not mine. It's putting them there, in my head. I don't know how it does it. I don't even know what's behind it, but there's something communicating with me through this Ouija board, and I need to know what it is."

"Jesus, Dad, I—"

"It works better with two people."

"What does?"

"The board, aren't you—come on, son—aren't you paying attention? This is important." He rubbed his eyes with the base of his palm. "It works better with two people, so I need you to do it with me."

I wanted to run, to get away from this and out of the house, but that felt cruel, like I'd be abandoning him, and I couldn't bring myself to do it. Instead, I searched my father's face, failing in my attempt to recover even a trace of the meticulously groomed man he'd once been, the man in a freshly pressed shirt and tie, a briefcase in one hand and thermos of coffee in the other, smiling as he left for work each morning. I still believed that man existed—I had to—but feared he was buried so deeply inside the broken soul before me that any chance of resurrection might have already been lost. "Okay, Dad," I said softly. "Sure."

"Good." He reached across the coffee table and gave my knee a quick pat. "Good boy, you—you're a good boy. You've always been a good boy."

We placed our fingertips on either side of the planchette.

"Keep your touch real light," my father instructed. "And don't push or move it on purpose. Just let it go on its own."

I nodded. I remembered playing with the Ouija board a few times years before and being thoroughly unimpressed, but I did as he asked. It was oddly quiet in the house, so I focused on the slight wheezing sound that emanated from my father every time he exhaled.

"Whoever's there," he said softly, "tell me what you told me before."

Despite my embarrassment for him, I did my best to concentrate.

The flame from the candle flickered, sending shadows along the walls. As they caught my attention, the planchette began to move. I was puzzled, and a bit frightened, because I knew I wasn't pushing it. In fact, my fingertips were barely making contact, yet it was slowly gliding across the board. I assumed my father must've been doing it, albeit unknowingly, since he was staring at it intently and awaiting its answer.

"You see?" he whispered. "There it goes."

Slowly, the planchette moved to the letters and slowly spelled out: I AM WATCHING

A chill burst across the back of my neck and shot up behind my ears. I pulled my hands away. "Jesus, what the—"

"I'll be a sonofabitch," my father muttered. "That's exactly what it told me before, but I was afraid since I was alone maybe I did it wrong or didn't read it right. I told you, Frankie Boy. I wonder if it's that thing."

I looked at him. "What thing? The thing you said was outside?"

Instead of answering, he said, "What does it want? Why is it here?" He looked to the ceiling, as if whatever he believed was communicating with him might be found there. "Why me, why—why did I see it? Can you tell me that much? What does it want with me?"

After he gave me a look, I returned my fingers to the planchette and sat there quietly for a while, waiting for the board to answer.

"Concentrate, son."

"I'm trying."

The planchette didn't move.

We took our hands away then tried again, but still, nothing.

"Damn it." My father deflated, his shoulders slumping. After a moment he removed his hands, stood up and began to pace over by the door. "Why won't it answer now?"

"I'm not sure how any of this works."

He looked over at me, his eyes filled with helplessness. "I don't know what to do, son. I'm sorry, I'm supposed to, I—I'm the father, right? The father's always supposed to know what to do. But I don't."

I knew he was trying, but he was lost in his own head, and I had no idea how to bring him back. "Maybe if you went to a doctor," I said softly.

He frowned. "You think I'm crazy too, Frankie Boy?"

"No."

"No?"

"I think you're tired and just need some help to sort things out is all."

He nodded slowly, as if I'd made sense to him. "Never been so tired, I..."

"A doctor could probably help you, Dad. Maybe give you something so you could sleep, you know?"

"There are things happening you don't know about," he said. "It's still out there, Frankie Boy, still watching. It doesn't want you to see it, not yet, but you saw what the board said. It's not just me. And there's more. Something's coming, son, the Ouija board told me so. A *swarm*, that's the word it spelled out. I don't know what the hell that means, but I think they're connected somehow."

I didn't know what to say.

Luckily, he motioned to the planchette, so I didn't have to come up with anything more. "I need to ask it one more question," he said.

Lightly resting my fingertips on the planchette, I looked across the board at my father and nodded. "I'm ready."

He placed his fingers across from mine. "Who are you?"

I closed my eyes.

"Will you tell me?" I heard my father ask.

The planchette began to move.

Opening my eyes, I nervously watched as it spelled out a single word.

NO

I pulled my hands away, recoiled from the planchette like it was a hot burner. "Jesus, Dad, this is creepy as hell," I said, standing. "Are you doing that? Seriously, are you moving it?"

"Of course not," he said, glaring at me.

"*Of course he is.*"

My mother stood in the doorway to the den wearing a nightgown and slippers, her hair mussed. Except for some smears around her eyes, the heavy makeup from the night before was gone.

"We're busy in here," my father said, standing and turning towards her. Nervously straightening his robe, he looked like an anxious child about to be reprimanded. "Can you give us a minute, please?"

"No, I can't. Snuff that candle out before you burn the house down."

He leaned over and blew it out. "Okay? Anything else I can do for you?"

"You could try bathing," my mother said with a level of disgust I'd never seen her display toward him before. "You're beginning to smell, Paul."

"I need to get going," I said, moving out from behind the coffee table. "I'm meeting the guys this morning."

With a final harsh look in my father's direction, my mother left the doorway and headed for the kitchen. I stood there a moment, looking at my dad. He gave a shrug and a little smile. He looked so sad it broke my heart.

I gave him a hug, kissed his stubbly cheek. "It's going to be okay, Dad."

He patted my back quickly but didn't return the hug. "You better scoot," he said. "Your mother's mad enough already. She doesn't understand what's going on. No one does. But that'll change."

I nodded like I had some idea what he was talking about.

"Be careful out there, son," he said.

"Yeah, I will."

"I mean it. Keep your eyes open, understand?"

"Yeah, I understand."

He motioned to the door. "Go, before she comes looking for you again."

"I'll see you later. I love you, Dad."

Rather than answer or acknowledge me, he focused again on the Ouija board. As he dropped back down on the stool, he took up one of the notebooks and a pen and began scribbling something down on one of the pages.

I could've already been gone. In a way, I suppose I was.

After grabbing my birthday money from my bedroom and stuffing it in my sock, I found my mother in the kitchen making coffee. She glanced at me while pouring a scoop of grounds into a paper filter. "Did you have breakfast?"

"No, I—"

"Sit down. I'll make some eggs."

"It's okay, I'm not really hungry."

"How about pancakes, would you like that?"

"Thanks, Mom, but I got to go."

Her back to me, she ran the water in the sink, filling the carafe for the Mr. Coffee we'd gotten a year or so before. My mother had seen the commercial on television with Joe DiMaggio and mentioned it, and a couple days later my father came home from work with one. Rather than concentrate on the tension in the room, I remembered how surprised she was that day, and how excited she and my father were over some silly coffee maker. "Don't pay any attention to your father's nonsense," she said flatly. "It's best if you just ignore him."

"What's wrong with him, Mom?"

She placed the full carafe on the counter, but kept her back to me.

"Is he crazy?" I pressed, voice shaking.

"Your father needs to see a doctor so we can find out what's wrong."

"That's what I was trying to tell him."

"May as well save your breath," she said. "He won't listen to you any more than he listens to me."

"Why won't he go to the doctor?"

When after several seconds she still hadn't responded, I knew an answer was not forthcoming, so I quietly told my mother I loved her and that I'd be back later. Then I slipped out the kitchen door in the hopes of escaping the shadows and darkness for sunshine and fresh air, even if just for a little while.

But what I didn't know then was that just because I couldn't see the darkness didn't mean it wasn't still there.

CHAPTER FOUR

I LIVED ON Beach Street. Shawn's house was two streets over on Marion. Until a few months prior I'd have ridden my bike, but for reasons I never fully understood, at some point the whole bicycle thing became uncool. Since we were still a couple years away from getting driver's licenses, and apparently only little kids rode bikes now, guys our age had no choice but to walk everywhere. Cool guys walked, and at fourteen, cool was paramount. So I set off on foot.

The quickest route to Shawn's house was to go to the top of my street, cut across a couple backyards and then over onto Marion Road. It was only a three- or four-minute walk, and I hadn't gotten far when I noticed no one else was outside. In fact, most of the houses were still dark, and the neighborhood seemed unusually quiet for eight o'clock on a Saturday morning, particularly in summer. This, of course, only helped to make the world seem even more off-kilter, as things I'd previously taken for granted suddenly felt peculiar, if not vaguely ominous. Nothing was quite right, and with the exception of my friends, it seemed as if my life had been secretly replaced with something similar, an imposter doing its best to fool me.

The normal population in town was right around four thousand people, but in summer those numbers increased by several hundred. You noticed things were a little busier, there was more traffic, and you started to see people around town that didn't look familiar. There were few employment opportunities beyond some service, retail, and menial positions, and those offered by the town itself. The only large employer in town was the Samoset Paper Company, which produced various products ranging from hot dog holders to napkins and paper placemats to the little red and white baskets restaurants put fries or onion rings in, and all other sorts of commercial paper-based products. They employed a little over three hundred people, and until a year or so ago, that number had included my father.

At eighteen, his flat feet made him ineligible for service in the Korean War, so he went to work at the Samoset Paper Company as part of the mailroom staff. In less than a decade, he'd worked his way up to a supervisory position in the production department. A few years later he became a highly regarded middle management person, and although he took numerous business courses at the local community college over the next several years, he never earned a college degree. His lack of formal education prevented him from moving any higher up the ranks, but for a high school graduate, he'd done very well for himself, and likely would've worked there until his retirement. Instead, he'd gone from that unlikely success story to the even more unlikely mess he'd become, stumbling around our house in his bathrobe like a madman. And no one could tell me why.

You shouldn't ask so many questions.

My mother's words echoed in my mind.

Eventually you'll land on one you don't want the answer to.

I wondered. What could my father have possibly done?

I'd never known him to hurt anyone. He was a decent, gentle man that went to work five days a week and came home every night. On weekends he did things around the house, spent time with my mother and me, and went to mass every Sunday at Saint Mary's. He was never in any trouble I was aware of, rarely drank, and was a happily married family man. He'd become annoyed now and then, but not once had I seen an outburst of anger from him, and I could count on one hand the times I'd even heard him raise his voice. I'd always known him as a fair, smart, curious, and abundantly patient man, a good father who loved his family and believed in hard work and that doing the right thing paid off. He believed in justice and equality for all, loved adventure novels and all sorts of movies (though comedies were his favorite), had a terrible sweet tooth and adored Italian food. He was the more demonstrative parent, always there with a hug or kiss, and showed emotion with no reservations whatsoever. Although my mother had become distant recently, she hadn't been like that prior. She was just more reserved, while my dad wore his emotions on his sleeve. They'd always been something of an odd couple, I suppose, as unlike my father, my mother had left Samoset for a time, was better educated (she had a liberal arts degree from NYU) and came from a family of professionals. Upon graduation, my mother lived in Boston for a year and worked as a buyer for one of the high-end shops on Newbury Street before eventually returning home and marrying my father. The people on my dad's side were all working-class, few of them educated beyond high school.

So there had always been differences, but we were happy, all of us, and I wasn't wrong about that. I couldn't be.

My thoughts shifted to the Ouija board. Had my father moved that planchette? Had I? Could I have done so without realizing it? Or could it be possible that some entity from the spirit world really *had* spoken to us?

Until that point, even though I'd been raised Catholic, I wasn't sure I believed in a spirit world. I always loved horror movies, EC Comics, ghost stories and the like, but that's all I ever considered them to be: stories, fantasies conjured in the minds of flesh and blood human beings. Maybe that's what I'd gotten wrong. I could no longer be sure, and while I wasn't convinced, in some ways, that was enough.

I arrived at Shawn's house, a modest ranch with a small front yard and an attached one-stall garage, to find his father out front loading tools into the back of his van. Darren O'Hara worked as a laborer for the town in the Department of Public Works. A little over six feet tall, with long sandy brown hair he wore in a ponytail, and a walrus mustache that hung well below his jawline, he was slim but muscular, a wiry guy without an ounce of fat on him. Between his love of comic books, horror movies, and playing electric guitar and jamming to many of the same bands we listened to, he was considered the coolest of our parents by far. While my father was in his mid-forties, and Max's dad was even older, Alex and Shawn's dads were closer to my mother's age, which put them just shy of forty. Yet they seemed significantly younger. When you're fourteen, you consider everyone beyond high school old, but in reality, in the summer of 1977, Shawn's dad seemed young because that's exactly what he was.

"Hey, Mr. O'Hara," I said as I approached the base of their driveway.

Bent over and rummaging around in his van, he looked back over his shoulder and peered at me over a pair of dark aviator sunglasses. "Frankie Boy," he said, smiling. "What's happening, youngblood?"

"Nothing much," I said. "How's it going?"

He quickly finished what he was doing in the van and slammed closed the back door. "You can go on in if you want," he told me, strolling to the middle of the driveway to greet me. "Shawn's getting dressed, he said you'd be by."

"Yeah, we got to go get Alex and Max too."

"What are you maniacs up to today, huh?" Mr. O'Hara pulled a box of Marlboros from his shirt pocket and shook a cigarette free of the pack. "Chasing girls and causing trouble?"

"I don't know," I said. "Beach, maybe?"

"Wish to hell I could go with you guys." He stabbed the cigarette into the corner of his mouth and lighted it with a zippo that had a skull engulfed in flames emblazoned across it. Unlike my dad, he was too young for the Korean War, but he was in his early 30s and still eligible for the draft to Vietnam in 1969. Due to a high lottery number and the fact that he was married and had a young child, he'd been exempted. "Good day for it," he said. "Weather guy said it's supposed to be hotter than Cheryl Tiegs out here today. But I got to get to work."

"How come you're working on a Saturday?"

"Emergency situation," he said, exhaling a stream of smoke. "Believe me, I'd rather be at the beach too, but we got a full-scale invasion on our hands, pal."

"Martians?" I asked with a grin.

"*Martians*," he said, chuckling. "That'd be cool. But nah, unfortunately I'm talking about gypsy moths."

"What's that?"

"You'll see them around town if you ain't already, the little bastards are everywhere. They got these blue and red wart-like things running down their backs. That's how you tell they're gypsies. Went to the library, got a couple books, been studying up on them. Got to know your enemy, youngblood, you know what I mean?"

I didn't, actually, so I asked, "But if they're just moths, what's the big deal?"

"Well, that's the thing, Frankie Boy. These ain't your normal moths." He took another pull on his cigarette, exhaled through his nose. "These are badass kamikazes, dude. A bunch of little *Jaws* with wings, eating everything they come into contact with. If we don't get them under control and stop them, they could defoliate the whole damn town. Thing is they're not easy to handle, they show up in this huge swarm."

The word *swarm* hit me like a baseball bat to the shins.

There's something coming. The Ouija board told me so.

"They can take out huge areas," Mr. O'Hara continued.

A swarm, that's the word it spelled out.

"It's crazy, man. They cause all kinds of damage, and— You all right?"

"Huh?"

"Look a little freaked out there, youngblood."

"No, I—I'm cool," I said as nonchalantly as I could, the word *swarm* continuing to repeat in my head.

"No reason to be upset about it, we'll stop them. We have to. They got the power to screw up the entire ecosystem, as it were."

"What do you do about them then?" I asked.

"We're gonna take them down, bet on that. We'll use pesticide sprays mostly, and we got to wrap some trees too, they especially like oaks. Whole thing's gonna get messy, and it ain't exactly fun work, especially in this heat, but what the hell you gonna do? That's the job, right? Least I'll be pulling some good OT. Anyway, don't worry about it. Me and the rest of the boys at the DPW been assigned to handle it, and we will."

"Okay," I said.

"Hey," he said, poking me gently in the shoulder. "Read the new *Conan*?"

"Not yet."

"It's awesome, dude, he finally gets off that—well—I won't ruin it for you."

"I'll probably grab it today. New *Captain America's* out too."

"Yeah, I got it, just haven't had time to read it. Shawn did though, said it was real good." He took another drag on his cigarette then dropped it to the pavement and stepped on it. Cocking his head, he looked to the sky. "I best boogie, don't wanna be late."

"Good luck with the invasion."

"Thanks." He headed back toward his van. "You guys have fun, all right?"

"Okay, seeya." I started across the small lawn to the front door.

"Hey!" Mr. O'Hara called after me.

I looked back.

"Next weekend I'm taking Shawn to the movies," he said as he climbed into his van. "We're gonna catch a matinee of that new flick *Star Wars*, up the Dartmouth Mall. Looks pretty cool, you wanna come along?"

"Definitely," I said. "Thanks."

"Right on!" From the stereo in his van, Foghat's "Fool for the City" suddenly blared to life. "Catch you later, youngblood!"

As he pulled away, I tried to ignore the fear rising in me. The whole swarm coincidence, if that's what it was, was freaking me out. I kept it under control as best I could, climbed the front steps, and through the screen door saw Mrs. O'Hara clearing dishes from the kitchen table.

Sheila O'Hara, a nurse in the maternity ward at the local hospital, was pretty and petite, with long blonde hair and the kind of look and figure usually only found on vixens sprawled across album covers. Because his mother was so attractive, Shawn took a lot of crap from other guys about it. While I found her as sexually enticing as anybody else, I always kept that to myself. On this morning, she moved around the kitchen tidying up, clad in short-shorts, little white Keds, and a tight tank top, sans bra, that left virtually nothing to the imagination. On the counter, a small radio played a Doobie Brothers song. Absent-mindedly, she sang along, dancing her way across the kitchen floor.

Before I could say anything, she caught me standing there gawking at her like the little pervert my raging hormones had left me. "Hello, Mrs. O'Hara!" I said with forced enthusiasm, as if this hopelessly awkward and desperate attempt at redemption might somehow save me. "Good—Good morning!" I added, my voice cracking as a hot wave of mortification surged through me.

"Hey, Frankie Boy," she said, waving. "Come on in."

I pulled open the screen door, stepped inside, and joined her in the kitchen, but remained on the far side of the table. *God*, I thought, *she probably thinks I'm the Peeper now.* "I wasn't sure—I mean—I was just about to knock—"

"It's okay," she said with a sly smile, her amusement at having let me twist in the wind written all over her face. "Have you had breakfast, honey?" She placed the last of the dirty dishes in the sink. "Just cleaning up, but I can make you something real quick if you want. It's no bother."

"Thanks, no, I—that's really nice of you—but I'm not hungry. Thank you, though, I—thanks a lot." I cringed, realizing I'd thanked her three times.

"You're welcome," she said. She smiled at me like I was a precocious toddler just too adorable for words. "Shawn's in his room. You can go get him."

I turned to head for the hallway just as Shawn came bounding into the room, his golden retriever Thor happily following behind him. "Hey, man," he said, sweeping past me and over to the counter where there were a few pieces of leftover cooked bacon on a paper towel. "What's up?" He grabbed a slice of bacon, chomped on it. "You just get here?"

"Yeah," I said, crouching to pet and say hello to Thor.

"Shawn, if you're going to eat some more then sit down," Mrs. O'Hara said. "In a chair. At the table. You know, like a normal person."

"Can't, got stuff to do." He gave his mother a quick kiss on the cheek. "Thanks for the bacon, Mom."

"Be home for dinner."

"Yeah, all right," he said, turning to me. "Come on, man."

He gave Thor a pat on the head then pushed by me, the screen door slapping closed behind him.

"Bye, Mrs. O'Hara," I said, giving a little wave.

"Bye, Frankie Boy," she said, noticeably amused and smiling with the same ice-blue eyes Shawn had. "You two behave yourselves now."

"Yes, ma'am," I said. "Bye, Thor."

I hurried after Shawn, and by the time I got outside, he was already on the street, pushing the hair from his eyes then fastening his mane in place with the red bandana he always used as a headband. "C'mon," he said, tying it in the back. "Let's go."

"What's your rush?" I asked, jogging over to him.

"What do you think?" He slid a pair of mirrored sunglasses into place, then pulled a pack of Camels and a lighter from the back pocket of his cutoff jean shorts. "I'm having a nic fit, man."

"It's only a matter of time before you get bagged," I told him.

"That's why I'm careful." Figuring we'd gotten far enough from his house, he took a quick look back just to be sure then lit up. "In another couple years nobody's gonna give a shit. But now?" Shawn exhaled a cloud of smoke before looking back over his shoulder. "My mother catches me smoking I'm dead."

"You really think her and your dad don't know you smoke?"

"How could they?"

"You smell like an ashtray most of the time."

Shawn stopped suddenly. "Dude, seriously?"

"Don't worry," I told him. "The constant stench of piss covers it up good."

He slumped with relief, laughed lightly, then playfully pushed me as he walked by. "Fucking asshole," he muttered.

"I do what I can."

We continued on until we reached Max's place. His was a big red house with black shutters on the corner a few streets over. Like the others there, Max's yard was always perfectly mowed and manicured. Though not even a mile from ours, the neighborhood was more upscale, the houses and yards bigger, and the cars in the driveways a little nicer, newer, and more expensive. The inside of his house reminded me of a museum. But for Max's older brother Denny's room, it was always meticulously clean and neat to the point where it looked as if no one actually lived there. It had a sterile, cold feel to it, and parts of it looked more like a religious shrine than a home. Houses, the neighborhoods they formed, and the lives led within them, were like people and their personalities: everyone's was different. While Max's neighborhood was certainly foreign to us, he often seemed even more out of step with it than we were.

Neither of us wanted to go inside, so I suggested rock, paper, scissors.

Before we could start, Max came out and joined us on the street. We all knew Max's parents held radical religious views, and we all knew Max was embarrassed by this and their constant need to push them on anyone within the sound of their voices, so it wasn't unusual for him to stop us before we could get inside. As usual we were grateful whenever he did so, and that morning was no exception.

"So, what's on the agenda?" he asked cheerfully.

Shawn looked him up and down, taking in the Ray-Bans, neon yellow tank top, cuffed khaki shorts, and brown leather sandals. "Jesus, dude, what the *fuck* are you wearing?"

"Oh, relax. We can't all look like roadies for Lynyrd Skynyrd, Shawn. Just be grateful I didn't go with a speedo and my summer clogs."

"You sure you don't want to go back inside and get a parasol?"

"One, I'm pleasantly shocked to learn you even know that word. And two, fuck off." Max turned to me. "And how are *you*?"

"What's up?" I said through a wry smile.

"No fashion critiques this morning?"

"I think you look fine. Hell, if you were a chick I'd probably take you out."

Max groaned and rolled his eyes. "You really need some new material."

I really didn't give a shit what Max or anyone else wore. I figured people should wear whatever they wanted, but in those days it took a lot of guts for a kid Max's age to leave the house dressed like that, and to be as open and secure in his sexuality as he was. Truth was, I respected the hell out of him for it. We all did, and although he was forced to endure shameful amounts of flak for it, Max was who he was and didn't give a flying fuck what anyone thought. Sometimes the rest of us took grief for being his friend and defending him—in fact, we'd all been in fights having Max's back over the years—but to us, Max was just Max, the same kid we'd known all our lives. He was one of us, and like siblings, we could shit-hammer each other but never allowed anyone else to get away with it. Whenever Max was hassled he could handle himself just fine, but no one was going to go after him or anyone else in our little circle physically without also having to deal with the rest of us. People weren't exactly shaking in their boots over that prospect, though it did help us survive, because in most cases there *was* strength in numbers. The bottom line was we needed each other, and in our own ways loved each other. At fourteen, we didn't always know how to show or say that, so we just did the best we could.

"Let's get out of here," Shawn said. "Grab Alex and decide what's up."

As we made our way down the street toward the other part of town, still unsure of exactly how we planned to spend our day, I couldn't shake my father's warning to be careful and keep my eyes open. I didn't necessarily believe the other things he'd said, but if the Ouija board had somehow been right about the coming swarm, wasn't it possible there could be some truth to the rest? At that point all I wanted to do was try to have some fun with my friends, forget about the rest, and eventually go home that night and assure my poor father there was nothing to worry about.

Unfortunately, I never got that chance.

CHAPTER FIVE

THE HEAT CONTINUED to rise as we crossed the old train tracks and ventured over an incline, through the tall grass on the far side and down a rocky slope to the street below. A neighborhood on the literal outskirts of Samoset, right near the state highway, not a lot of people resided out this way, and those who did were poor and as largely forgotten as the part of town they lived in. Other than a small liquor store that also sold basic groceries, the neighborhood was mostly littered with businesses long-closed, and was home to numerous commercial properties, vacant and rotting. The only thing that thrived in the area was BAD COMPANY, a notorious hardcore biker bar that had been there for years and was frequented by an array of unsavory characters, including lots of transients in the summer months on their way back and forth from Cape Cod.

With all the infamous tales of what had allegedly taken place inside that windowless shrine to the unknown and dangerous filling my head, stories the whole town knew and that only served to foster a reputation and legend that was likely far worse than reality, we tramped across the lot and filed by the dark bar to the dirt road beyond.

It led to a row of four single-story clapboard houses shaped like boxcars set back a hundred yards or so from the street. In the 1920s, the buildings were constructed as barracks for railroad workers, and later for the families of those that worked the station. In the 1960s, they were renovated and converted into single-family homes, then rented out as government-funded affordable housing. The second unit, a pale-yellow house, was Alex's place.

Ronica's old Volkswagen Bug was parked out front, alongside a pristine white El Camino that belonged to their mother's longtime live-in boyfriend Rafe. Alex and Ronica's real father took off when they were both toddlers and was supposedly living somewhere down in Florida. Neither of his children knew him, and hadn't seen or heard from him since he'd left. Rafe—despite looking like something straight out of the band Sha Na Na— was a few years younger than their mother but had been on the scene from the time both Ronica and Alex were in elementary school, and while neither were terribly close to him, he was the only thing even approaching a father figure they'd ever known.

When we arrived, doo-wop tunes were playing from a transistor radio sitting next to a lawn chair on the small cement patio to the side of the house. Rafe was cutting grass and weeds around the foundation with a scythe, leisurely swinging it back and forth, a Lucky Strike hanging from his mouth and a pair of dark sunglasses hiding his beady, rodent-like eyes. Despite the heat he wore cuffed jeans, a t-shirt with his cigarettes and lighter rolled into the sleeve instead of in the pocket, and the same pair of scuffed black boots he always had on. A slight but muscular man with a hawkish face, pock-marked skin, and rubber-tire black hair slicked into a pompadour and held in place with generous amounts of pomade, he mostly kept to himself and rarely spoke. In those days, few people sported tattoos, but Rafe had several along both arms and on his chest and back. Many had to do with his years in the Marines, which along with his general aloofness gave him a strange mystique, at least to the rest of us. Alex said he'd been a sniper and killed lots of people in Vietnam but never talked about it, and while it was difficult to image him in that role, we had no reason to doubt it. No longer in the service, he and Alex's mother Lara lived on her income as a cashier at the local A&P, and the odd jobs he did around town. Mostly, Rafe was just sort of there, always doing something on their property. You never saw the guy sitting around, he always had one project or another going, and in those rare instances when he didn't, he spent his time obsessively washing and waxing his pride and joy, that white 1969 Chevy El Camino SS. Max often joked it was worth more than the house, and he may have been right.

"Hey, Rafe," Shawn said as we got closer. Normally we referred to parents as mister or missus, but Rafe was just Rafe, and always had been.

Without breaking his swinging rhythm or uttering a word, he acknowledged Shawn, Max, and me with a slow tilt of his head. Returning his attention to the weeds, he exhaled streams of smoke from the nostrils of his beak-like nose and smiled so subtly and quickly I almost missed it.

Before we reached the patio the wood screen door swung open with such force it slapped back against the house, the springs squeaking as Lara Nelson emerged from inside. "Ronica's taking a shower," she announced in her usual gravelly voice. "So you little perverts just keep your asses out here." The door bounced closed as she plopped into a lawn chair on the patio, a cigarette in one hand and a glass of clear alcohol in the other. "Alex's coming out in a minute."

We all stopped and stood there awkwardly, just shy of the patio.

Wearing only a lightweight imitation-satin robe belted at the waist that barely reached her knees, Mrs. Nelson was barefoot, the soles of her feet black as coal and the polish on her toenails cracked and peeling. She looked as if she'd just rolled out of bed, but was obviously already more than a little tipsy. She was the kind of person my mother described as "rough around the edges." Still, Mrs. Nelson had been beautiful once, and it was clear Ronica had gotten her looks from her mother. But unlike Ronica, she was usually drunk and mean. Her life had not been an easy one, and it showed in every line on her face, every glassy blink of her eyes, in every weary sigh and in every snide comment.

I could feel her glaring at me. She didn't care for any of us, but had a particular dislike for me, which I never understood since I'd always been polite to her. I gazed out at the expanse of land between here and the bar and tried to focus on that rather than her death-stare. I couldn't see the highway but could hear the cars rushing by in the distance just beyond the slope of a hill perhaps a quarter of a mile away. This area was so bleak it always gave me the creeps, especially the few times I'd been out this way at night. It was as if it had been plucked from some other place—a faraway desert village on the other side of the country perhaps—and dropped here at the edge of town. It didn't fit in with the rest of Samoset, not just because it was so depressed, but because things were more serious in this desolate part of town, more dangerous, maybe. That which separated the alleged safety of our little cocoon of a town from all the crazy things you heard about going on *out there* didn't seem to apply here.

"What are you gawking at?" Mrs. Nelson said suddenly.

Max pointed to his chest. "Me?"

After a gulp of booze, she threw her head back and let out a loud, bawdy laugh. Then she sat forward and pointed a finger directly at Max. "*Me? Me?*" she mocked. "You little sicko, I thought you were a fag! I'm old enough to be your mother, looking at me like that!"

Max smiled politely, turned away and sidled up next to me. "Okay," he whispered, "the cunt's *really* drunk this morning."

Biting my bottom lip so I wouldn't laugh, I kept looking out at the road as if he'd said nothing, and thankfully heard the screen door open again.

Alex came out in sneakers, a pair of shorts, and a t-shirt, a ratty knapsack he sometimes carried slung over his shoulder. "Hey, guys."

We all acknowledged him subtly, and Shawn gave him his best *we need to get out of here right fucking now* look.

"Hey," Mrs. Nelson snapped as her son stepped off the patio.

Alex looked back, annoyed. "What?"

"You get over here, give your mother a kiss and say goodbye before you go running off like some stray dog, that's what."

With a sigh, Alex walked back, leaned over and gave her a peck on the cheek. "Bye, Mom."

"You sure Rafe don't need your help with anything today?" she asked.

Alex drew a deep breath, let it out slowly. "Rafe," he called, "you need my help with anything today?"

Still killing weeds, Rafe shook his head no and waved us off.

"All right," Mrs. Nelson said, her eyes panning slowly from Shawn to me to Max. "Don't get in any trouble, you hear me? I plan on having a nice quiet day off, don't need you little pukes ruining it for me."

A minute later we were crossing back over the train tracks.

No one said anything about Alex's mother. We were used to it, and we all knew she embarrassed him, so what was the point?

"What's with the knapsack?" Shawn asked. "We hitting the Grill?"

"Why the hell not?" Alex said, his unruly hair hanging in his eyes. "Couple new wrestling magazines out, plus they should have the new *Fantastic Four* and *The Defenders*."

"You know it's only a matter of time before we get caught," Max said. "I can't believe we've gotten away with it this long."

"That's why we got to keep rotating it," Shawn said. "Who's up?"

"Me," Alex said. "But if I go, I got to do it cold, I got no money."

"Too dangerous, we did that last time," Shawn said. "If you guys want to go back to my house, I got about thirty-five bucks in my lawn-mowing jar, I can grab some of that."

"I'll do it," I said. "I got twenty bucks on me, no problem."

"Where'd you get twenty bucks?" Alex asked.

"Don't worry about it."

"Who said I was worried?"

"It's leftover birthday cash," I told him.

"Cool. We'll pay you back."

"No you won't," I said, elbowing him playfully in the ribs. "But who cares?"

"Shit, man, get something for yourself," Shawn said. "You shouldn't spend birthday money on us."

"What the hell else am I going to spend it on?"

We moved down onto the street and in the direction of the Samoset Grill, a small restaurant closer to where the rest of us lived that served breakfast and lunch to most of the working-class folks in town. They also had the largest and best magazine and comic book display in town. We'd been ripping the place off in one way or another since fourth grade.

To the side of the building, just beyond the small dirt parking lot and beneath several tall trees that provided some cover from the relentless sun, we huddled at one of three vacant picnic tables and shored up our plan.

"Okay," I said, wiping sweat from my brow. "Looks packed in there, so let's keep it simple. Four cheeseburgers, cool?"

Everyone agreed as Alex slapped his knapsack down on the picnic table and removed a pile of old magazines and comic books perhaps six inches high. "You want backup?" he asked, handing me the stack.

"Nah," I said. "I got it."

"You sure, Frankie Boy?"

"*I got it.*"

I'd executed this same plan several times and was confident I could get it done again, but if something went wrong I was screwed and didn't want anyone else going down with me.

"All right, all right, don't go all apeshit," Alex said. "Get some fries too."

"Okay." I pulled the twenty from my sock. "Be out in a minute."

Shawn climbed up and sat on the table as Max and Alex took up position on the bench seat. With their eyes on me, I climbed the three steps and opened the door to the Samoset Grill.

The moment I stepped inside the noise hit me first, followed by the smell of fried foods and cigarettes. It was an old and dated building, and a relatively small space where little attention was paid to décor, but between the tables and stools at the lunch counter, there wasn't an empty seat in the house. Behind the counter, an older grizzled guy in a paper hat called Sarge worked a big grill while Marcy, a middle-aged waitress in polyester, hustled between the lunch counter and tables. They'd both been working there for years.

Ignoring the din of conversations and the massive cloud of cigarette smoke drifting through the place, I walked over to the magazine display to the side of the counter. After making sure both Sarge and Marcy had seen me come in with them, I nonchalantly placed my stack of magazines down on a large pile of newspapers in front of the display then approached the counter and waited.

After tending to a few tables, Marcy hurried back behind the counter, grabbed some plates from the side of the grill, served them to the men waiting on them, then rushed over to me. "What do you need, sweetie?" she asked, pulling a pencil from the side of her bouffant and a pad from the pocket of her uniform.

"Can I get four cheeseburgers with everything and an order of fries to go, please?" I held the twenty up so she'd be sure to see it.

Marcy quickly jotted the order down, tore off the slip, and said, "Seven and a quarter, sweetie."

I gave her the money. She ran to the register, got my change, then hurried back. "Be up in about ten, okay?" she said, handing me my change.

"Thank you," I said, throwing in *ma'am* for good measure.

As she hurried off, I noticed two rough-looking guys at the counter a few stools down staring in my direction. I put my change back in my pocket then met their gaze. The key to pulling this off was to go essentially unnoticed, and I couldn't get that done with these guys looking right at me. The one closest held a steaming cup of coffee with both hands and looked vaguely familiar to me. Without taking his eyes from me, he leaned closer to the man next to him, who was shoveling the remains of a fried egg sandwich into his mouth, and mumbled something. Then he called across the counter to me, "You Paul Molinari's kid?"

I noticed one of them had a Samoset Paper Company logo over the breast pocket of his shirt. "Yeah," I answered.

"How's your pop doing?" the other asked, still chewing his eggs.

"Okay," I said.

"Yeah?" the other said, and then looked to his friend. "Is he still crazier than a shithouse rat? How's he like being a housewife?"

They both began to laugh.

A rush of anger surged through me. I wanted to hurt them, to grab the nearest plate and smash it over their heads until they stopped laughing and took those stupid smiles off their cruel faces. Instead, I just glared at them.

They continued chatting and laughing between themselves but paid no further attention to me. Why were they laughing? Did they know things I didn't? Did they know why my father had lost his job? Was it something really bad? Is that why my mother didn't want me to know? Or maybe my father used to be their boss and they didn't like him. Maybe they were glad he didn't work there anymore and were just having a laugh at my expense. I hoped that's all it was as I moved back to the magazine display.

Upset and embarrassed as I was, and as much as I just wanted to leave at that point, I couldn't lose sight of my mission. The guys were depending on me and I didn't want to let them down.

My eyes scanned the rows of offerings until I finally located the latest wrestling and boxing magazines. There were four professional wrestling publications to choose from, and per our rule, I went with the two that had the coolest covers. I first selected one with the current World Wide Wrestling Federation Heavyweight Champion, Superstar Billy Graham—all tie-dye trunks, bleached blond hair, and huge muscles—posing with his belt. His manager, the infamous Grand Wizard, stood next to him with one of those flamboyant turbans he always wore, grinning from ear-to-ear. The second depicted a gruesome bout between a blood-soaked Abdullah the Butcher and an equally gore-covered Bruiser Brody.

I pulled the first from the shelf, and while casually flipping through it, took a quick glance at the counter. Sarge and Marcy were both distracted, and none of the other patrons were looking my way, so rather than return the magazine to the shelf, I put it on top of the newspapers, just inches from the stack of magazines I'd brought with me. Satisfied no one had seen what I did, I repeated the process with the second magazine, then turned my attention to the comic book section.

They didn't have the *Fantastic Four* issue Alex was looking for, but they did have the latest *Captain America, Conan,* and *The Defenders.* After a few subtle looks around, I repeated the process three more times and they joined the wrestling magazines just inches from the stack I'd brought with me.

When I saw Marcy was bagging our order, I started for the counter then acted as if I'd just remembered I left my magazines behind. I went back, grabbed those I'd brought with me, subtly slid them on top of those I'd taken from the shelf, then picked them all up in a single stack and returned to the counter.

"There you go, sweetie," Marcy said, sliding a brown paper bag stained with grease across the counter to me. "Put some napkins in there for you too."

"Thanks a lot," I said, smiling innocently.

As Marcy hurried off, I turned and headed for the exit, the bag in one hand and the stack of magazines tucked under my other arm. It was only about fifteen feet to the door, but as always, it felt like the longest walk of my life.

When I stepped out into the heat, I knew I'd made it.

* * * *

Minutes later we were a mile away and sitting around the base of a giant boulder located at the edge of the property that housed the rectory for Samoset's Catholic Church. The boulder had become an iconic and popular spot for kids to play, meet, or just hang out, but that morning we were the only ones there. We celebrated the swag and devoured our food, and although it wasn't even noon yet, for fourteen-year-old boys it's never too early for cheeseburgers and fries.

I was having fun, but felt bad about stealing. I knew the other guys did too, but we always managed to rationalize it and convince ourselves we weren't really hurting anyone. Besides, I paid for the food. Who knew where magazines came from? Some huge, rich, faceless company somewhere we never saw, knew nothing about, and had never heard of. That's what we told ourselves, and in those days that was enough. It was a simpler time, sure, but also a selfish time, and the only period in one's life where that's not only expected but, to a degree, acceptable, if not outright romanticized.

So as awkwardly as it may have been, we embraced it as best we could. We didn't know anything else. We had the privilege of living in a world that only consisted of our little town and the other nearby places we sometimes went, and that summer, like so many before it, we had each other, our families, and the lives we knew. Those things were far from pristine, but they were all we had.

"You did good, Frankie Boy," Shawn said, chomping on the last of his burger while looking over one of the wrestling mags. "Real good."

Trying to play it cool, I responded with a nod, but it felt good to get that kind of praise from Shawn, even for doing something wrong.

"Works every time," Alex said, stuffing a handful of fries in his mouth.

"And thanks for the food, man," Shawn added.

"Yes," Max said, looking up from his issue of *The Defenders*, "thank you."

Between mouthfuls of fries, Alex thanked me as well.

A while later we decided to go to the beach, and for the next several hours hung out on the sand, reading our comics and magazines, talking, joking around, getting tan, and swimming in the ocean. The beach was packed, and we ran into a lot of people—some we were glad to see and others we weren't—but like usual, we kept mostly to ourselves.

At one point, Ronica showed up with some other high school girls, and although she said hello, she didn't spend any time with us, preferring instead to hang out with kids her own age. We were disappointed, but we understood. She had a public persona to maintain as much as anyone else, and couldn't always be seen hanging out with her little brother and his friends. Of course there were plenty of girls there our age, but they stuck to their little cliques just like we did. Rather than interacting, we mostly conspired amongst ourselves and made awkward attempts at flirting from safe distances, so nothing came of it.

Later, I spent a little more of my birthday money on hot dogs, root beers, and ice cream sandwiches from the snack bar. After we filled our bellies again, we went swimming one last time then decided to take off.

It was late afternoon when we left, tired and sated.

That summer we were just a bunch of kids doing the best we could with the hands we'd been dealt, trying to make sense of a world that demanded our compliance but granted no control, power, or even say. We weren't children anymore, but we weren't adults yet either, so we danced along that razor-thin line separating the two and hoped for the best. And even though it was far from over, that afternoon was the last truly happy memory I have of us that summer.

Later that day, everything changed.

The gypsy moths had invaded Samoset just like Shawn's dad said. But something else had come to town that summer too, something worse.

And it was just as hungry.

CHAPTER SIX

WHEN WE LEFT the beach that afternoon we could've walked straight to my house. I often wonder how things might've been different if we had. The heat was still blistering and the pavement hot as a stovetop, so we decided instead to cut through a patch of forest that, if followed far enough, eventually went past my backyard. We'd gone that way many times over the years, and now and then still hung out in that stretch of woods just for fun. That time, however, it was just an excuse to take advantage of the shade the forest provided, and to prolong what had been a fun and carefree day.

What we hadn't counted on, was Perry Jenkins and Keith Dickinson.

That September they'd begin their senior year of high school, but the duo had been bullying us and a lot of other kids in town for years. They rarely picked on anyone their own age, preferring instead to terrorize those much younger. Both had long histories of assaults, disorderly conducts, acts of vandalism, and numerous school suspensions. It wasn't unusual to run into them around town, though we'd never encountered them in that particular section of forest, so when we came upon them in a small clearing, we were more than a little surprised.

But, as it turned out, not nearly as surprised as they were.

At first I wasn't sure what I was looking at. Through the trees, perhaps thirty yards ahead of us, I saw something on the ground that looked like a shirt. When it moved, I realized it was a person, so I came to an abrupt stop. Because I was in the lead, so did everyone else. Shawn had been cracking jokes about Wendy Dunham, the bustiest girl in our class, and our laughter had apparently startled whoever was up ahead. As Shawn's voice and our laughter died down, I saw we hadn't run into one person, but two.

Both stood and faced us, frantically zipping up their jean shorts.

The moment I recognized them my stomach clenched and I felt a surge of fear fire through me. Like the others, I feigned nonchalance as best I could.

"What are you faggots doing?" Perry said, ambling toward us.

Max's eyes met mine, and although he was as scared as I was, I could tell he was also trying his best not to laugh. I gave him a pleading look, hoping he wouldn't respond. But I knew he would. Max couldn't help it.

"I think the real question is what are *you* faggots doing?"

A tall and wiry kid with long black hair, Perry puffed his chest up and moved toward us. "The fuck you say, you pussy-ass homo?"

Shawn moved slowly to the front of our pack, making sure he stood between Max and them. "Keep moving," he told us quietly.

"Fuck you think you're going?" Perry stepped in front of us. "I'm talking to you assholes. Don't you hear me talking? I can hear me talking."

"Just passing through, all right?" Shawn said. "Come on, guys."

Perry flexed his well-muscled arms. "You leave when *we* say you leave." His sleeveless t-shirt featured a cartoon version of a man riding a dirt bike and a busty blonde girl in a bikini looking on, the words: DO IT IN THE DIRT blazoned across the front of it. "You got it, O'Hara?"

"Yeah, when *we* say," Keith Dickinson added as he moved closer to us. "So until we do, shut your cocksucker, fag."

A chubby kid with bad skin and a wild shock of frizzy red hair, he was the kind of piece of shit that put firecrackers up frog's asses, threw rocks at dogs, liked to kill cats, and took particular glee in terrorizing kids younger than him.

"What are you doing out here sneaking up on us while we were pissing?" Perry asked, giving his partner a quick sideways glance.

A devilish grin crept across Max's face.

Please, Max, I thought, *don't*. But the words were already coming.

"Do you two usually pee lying on top of each other?"

Without warning Perry slapped Max across the face. He hit him so fast and so hard the cracking sound echoed through the forest, and before I even realized what he'd done, Max was on the ground.

"Jesus," Alex said, bending over to help him up. "What the fuck, man?"

Shawn squared his stance, and I saw his hands clench into fists.

"I don't know what you queer boys *thought* you saw," Perry growled, "but you better—"

"We didn't see nothing, all right?" Shawn said. "We just want to take off."

"Then pay the toll."

"We don't have any money," Shawn told him.

"You hear that?" Perry asked Keith without looking at him, his eyes still locked on Shawn. "These pussies got no money."

"Guess they'll have to pay with something else." Keith motioned to Alex's knapsack. "What's in your purse, pussy?"

"Probably tampons." Perry laughed.

"Gimme it."

Alex shook his head no.

"I said, gimme it!"

"No chance," Alex said.

Keith punched him in the mouth, violently snapping Alex's head back.

Alex let out a muffled cry and dropped the knapsack. Bringing his hands to his face, he stumbled back, somehow managing to remain on his feet.

Without really thinking about it, I threw a punch at Keith. He managed to dodge it, then grabbed hold of me and threw me into a tree. My back hit it with such force all the air in my body left me in a single rush. I dropped to my knees, gasping for breath as pain fired up into the back of my neck and fanned out in burning slashes across my shoulder blades.

Shawn responded with a haymaker that landed flush on Keith's jaw. A good shot, it staggered him, but Perry quickly stepped in and hit Shawn with a combination that knocked him onto the seat of his pants. Stunned, he sat there a moment, a trickle of blood leaking from his nose.

"How you like that, faggot?" Perry said, eyes wild.

As breath slowly returned to my lungs, I watched Keith pull a large hunting knife from the back of his belt and brandish it like a madman from a horror movie. "You little puke bags think you got the nuts to swing on us?" he said. "That what you think?"

Shawn scrambled back in a quick crabwalk.

"That's enough!" Max said.

"Shut up, *Mary*." Perry leered at Keith, his chest heaving with excitement. "Teach him a lesson, dude. Teach him fucking good."

I pushed myself to my feet but Perry saw me coming and cracked me in the side of the head so hard it felt like he'd used a cinderblock. I'd been in fights before, and I'd been hit, including numerous times by Perry, but never with such force. A sunburst exploded before my eyes, a stabbing pain ripped through my temple and down into my jaw, and the world tilted and blurred.

Next thing I knew I was kissing the pine needles on the forest floor.

My distraction bought Shawn enough time to get back to his feet and apparently find a large branch somewhere nearby, because suddenly he was holding one like a baseball bat. Though not quite as long as a bat, it was just as thick and looked like it could do serious damage. "Back off!" he snapped, the flow of blood from his nose now ringing his mouth and dripping from his chin. "I mean it, man, back the fuck off!"

Grinning, Perry looked at Keith and gave a quick nod.

Keith crouched and began to circle him, his knife at the ready.

Eyes on him, Shawn moved closer to me. "You okay?"

I'd managed to get to my hands and knees, and everything had stopped spinning, but I felt nauseous and a throbbing pain was still pulsing in my left temple. "Yeah," I said quietly, struggling back to my feet.

"Alex?" Shawn asked.

Having retrieved his knapsack, Alex carefully touched his split lip with his free hand. "I'll live."

"Max?"

"I'm fine," Max told him. "Let's just go."

Shawn cocked his head, indicating he wanted Alex and Max to get behind him and stand over by me. Once they had, he said, "We're gonna take off. You try to stop us and I swear to God I'll split both your fucking heads open."

Keith grinned like the imbecile he was. "Go for it, gay boy."

"Little fucking shit stain thinks he's a badass," Perry said.

"I'm gonna teach you some respect, O'Hara." Keith changed his grip on the knife so the blade faced down. "Gonna give you something to remember."

"Kinda like that fucking I gave your mother last night, huh?"

Perry actually laughed. Keith did not.

"I'm gonna cut you real good, fucker."

"Come and get me, asshole."

"Guys," Max said, raising his hands. "This needs to stop before it gets out of hand and someone's seriously hurt. Let's just—we can—we'll leave, all right? Alex, let them have the knapsack and we'll just go."

"Don't you dare give them that knapsack," Shawn said.

"Wouldn't save you now even if he did, O'Hara," Keith said from his crouch, still circling.

"You guys split," Shawn told us. "I'll catch up to you."

"We're not leaving you here," I said.

"Do what I tell you!"

I stood next to him, fists raised. A second later, Max and Alex took up position on the other side of him and did the same. Even at four against two, we knew we were in for serious beatings, if not worse, but none of us were going anywhere without Shawn.

"Should've left when you had the chance," Perry said.

It was then that something else caught Shawn's attention. He took a step back, his eyes wide and trained on the forest behind Perry and Keith. "What the hell?" he muttered. "What…"

I tried to follow his gaze but all I could see was trees.

"Nice try." Keith chuckled. "Like I'm gonna fall for that lame bullshit."

Perry turned and looked behind them, as if just to be sure, and whatever Shawn had seen, he apparently saw too. He suddenly went pale, his mouth open in shock. "The fuck, dude?"

I quickly looked again. Still nothing.

"Keith," Perry said, his face twisted into a grimace of fear. "Fuck is that?"

"Run!" Shawn screamed.

We all bolted back in the direction from which we'd come, Shawn in the lead and me pulling up the rear. I was still a bit dizzy and not as fast as I normally would've been, but I kept running hard as I could. The sensation that something was closing on me from behind sent a shiver up my back, and at one point I braced myself, certain I was about to be caught and taken down at any moment. But that moment never came.

When we finally reached the street, we pulled up. Out of breath, and trying to figure out what had happened, we all looked to Shawn for some explanation. He still had hold of the branch, and realizing it, threw it aside.

"What was that?" Alex asked. "What'd you see?"

"Nothing, I—I don't know," Shawn said, still watching the woods. "We need to get out of here. Now. Right now."

"I thought they were right behind us," Max said, winded. "Aren't they chasing us?"

"I don't know." Wiping blood from his face, Shawn started off down the street. "Fuck them. Let's go, man, come on."

"*Shawn,*" I said.

He stopped, looked back at us. "What?"

I could tell he was still frightened, and that scared me because I couldn't ever remember Shawn being frightened of anything. "What did you see?"

"Nothing, all right?"

"Bullshit. Whatever it was, Perry saw it too."

"I'm taking off," Shawn said. "You guys want to wait around for those two dipshits to find their way out of there and catch up to us, go ahead, but I'm not sticking around."

As Shawn continued on his way, Alex hurried after him. Max and I exchanged troubled glances, and then did the same.

I wasn't far from home, but that was the last place I wanted to be, so I said nothing more until Shawn had led us a couple miles away to a public playground not far from the town hall and public library. There was no one else around, so we congregated around the swing set, but I could tell Shawn was still jumpy and anxious.

"I'm so sick of those dicks," Alex said. "Asshole split my lip."

Max slid onto one of the canvas seats suspended from chains on the iron swing set and began to slowly glide back and forth. "One of these days those cretins are going to kill someone."

"Yeah," Alex scoffed, "probably one of us."

"If you didn't see anything," I said to Shawn, "why'd you tell us to run?"

"Saw an opening, okay? They were distracted, figured it was our best chance." He looked around, as if to be sure we were still alone. "I'm going home, you guys. I'll see you later."

"What happened back there, Shawn?"

"I just told you."

"What'd you see in the woods?"

"I told you, I—"

"You're full of shit," I said.

"Fuck you, man. I'm going home."

"Why didn't they run too?" I pressed. "They didn't even chase us."

"Go ask them."

"Maybe they ran the other way," Alex suggested.

"Perry saw it too," I said.

"I'm splitting." Shawn headed for the street. "Later."

I grabbed his shoulder. "Hold up a sec, I—"

He spun around, shrugging my hand away. "Get the fuck off me, man!"

"Jesus," I said, stunned. "Take it easy."

Shawn wiped his nose with the back of his hand, but his nostrils were still caked with dried blood. "Sorry, all right? I want to go home, I—just let me go home."

"What happened back there?"

"I don't know."

I turned to the others. "You guys see anything?"

"I didn't see shit except that fucking knife." Alex plopped down on the ground next to the swing set. "Thing was huge."

"Max?"

Uncharacteristically quiet, Max simply shook his head no and continued to slowly sway back and forth on the swing, the chains creaking with each pass.

"Me either," I said, turning to Shawn. "But you did."

"I told you—"

"Come on, man. It's me. It's us."

Shawn fumbled his cigarettes from his pocket, lit one, and took a couple quick drags. "I don't know, I..."

"I saw your face. It scared the shit out of you. You're still scared."

GREG F. GIFUNE

For a moment he looked like he might respond, but then he took another drag on his cigarette, exhaled through his nose, and turned away.

"Maybe you should just let it go, Frankie Boy," Max said.

"Yeah," Shawn mumbled, "listen to Max."

It was still hot, but the sun was low in the sky as late afternoon sauntered toward dusk. Suddenly everything seemed and felt like a dream. Maybe I was just reeling from the blow to the head I'd received. Or maybe the world wasn't what I'd thought it was. Maybe it never had been.

"Fine," I said, exhausted. "Whatever. Fuck it."

Nobody else said anything for a while, and I was sure Shawn would leave. But he didn't. He got as far as the sidewalk then started pacing.

"I don't know what it was, all right?" He shook his head as if that might somehow clear his mind. "I saw a rack. A big one, a..."

"So it was a buck, then?" Alex asked hopefully. "One of those charges you, you're in a world of shit. No wonder you were—"

"No." Shawn flicked his cigarette away, his eyes glistening with terror. "No, I...I mean maybe, but...I don't think that's what it was."

Alex frowned. "Nothing else around here's got antlers like a buck."

"Why don't you think it was a deer?" I asked.

Shawn looked at me with a helplessness I'd never seen in him before. "Because," he said, voice shaking, "it was standing on two legs."

CHAPTER SEVEN
~2017~

JUST BEYOND THE Samoset Town Hall, where a playground once stood, there is now an office building that houses a medical billing establishment of some sort. A drab and unimaginative brick structure with few windows and a peaked roof, the paved lot out front is packed with cars, yet there's no one in sight. It's all so lifeless, sterile and still, so utterly lacking in joy that no amount of memories can resurrect the sounds of laughter and children playing, or the steady creak of those old canvas swings rocking back and forth on rusted lengths of heavy chain.

Despite walking nearly a mile to get here, the fresh air has done little to clear my head. I can still feel the effects of the three drinks I had at Milo's, and the humidity, along with our little stroll through this particular section of town, hasn't helped.

"The playground," Max says sadly. "It's gone. And now there's…"

"This." With a sigh, I run a hand along the back of my neck and give it a squeeze, hoping to loosen the tension collected there.

"Just what the world needs, less playgrounds and more office buildings." Max hikes his satchel up higher on his shoulder, eyes hidden behind his sunglasses. "I suppose it was silly of us to assume it'd be here after all these years. Still, how disappointing. I'm fifty-four years old and was genuinely looking forward to playing on that old swing set. Come to think of it, that may be more disturbing than finding it replaced with such an eyesore."

I laugh lightly, but realize what's really going on inside him because I'm experiencing the same thing. We spent countless hours here over the years, but there's one day in particular we're focused on in this moment. And we both know it. I can almost see Shawn pacing along the sidewalk, his nose bloodied; Alex sitting on the grass with his split lip and knapsack full of stolen magazines and comic books; Max slumped on one of the swings; and me—I'm there too—trying to make sense of things beyond comprehension.

"I don't want to be here."

The words leave me before I can stop them.

"Neither of us is here by choice," Max reminds me. "Truth be told, I never expected to set foot in this town again. But we owe it to Alex...among others."

He's right of course, but that does little to combat the fear slowly tightening its grip on us. "Doesn't seem possible he's gone," I say. "I still see him like the kid he was all those years ago. I can't imagine Alex any other way."

Max nods. He understands. He has no more answers than I do, no cures for what haunts us or remedies to our nightmares, but he understands.

And for now, that'll do.

Max removes his sunglasses. "The first time I held Dana in my arms, she looked up at me with those beautiful eyes and I fell madly in love with her right then and there. From that moment forward, my life—my *existence*—became something very different from what it had been prior. Just like that, it was something better, stronger. I wanted nothing more than to provide for that baby, to protect this pure and precious little girl, and to do everything in my power to make certain her life would be one of safety and laughter and joy."

I already know where he's going with this, but I don't interrupt. He needs to say these things, and he needs me to listen.

"Dana was afraid of the dark when she was little," Max continues. "At bedtime, Dusty always had to reassure her that everything was fine and there was nothing to be afraid of. She always had an incredible imagination, and like most children, she thought a monster might be in her closet, under her bed, or at the window at night, typical stuff. It always upset me, because I'd tried so hard to keep her away from frightening and dark things, influences that might put such horrors in her head in the first place. So I'd say goodnight, tell her how much I loved her, and give her a kiss on the forehead. Then I'd stand in her bedroom doorway and Dusty would say his goodnights and promise her that there was no such thing as monsters and that she was perfectly safe. One night, Dusty asked me why I never told Dana these things myself and why it always fell on him, yet if she had a nightmare, I insisted on being the one to check on her and to make sure she was all right."

I know now that Max's husband doesn't know about the things that happened here, the things Max has seen and experienced. He's never told him, and I don't blame him.

Those of us who know monsters are real never speak of them.

"What could I tell him?" Max says dismally. "*What* could I tell him?"

I don't have an answer. Luckily he isn't really looking for one. Max just needs me to be there. He doesn't want to be alone with his nightmares any more than I do, and with me standing right next to him, he doesn't have to be. It's my turn to understand. And I do.

"I feel so guilty for having left Alex behind," Max says, his eyes brimming with tears.

"He left himself behind."

"Alex was never that good on his own, you know that."

"None of us were," I say, and leave it at that.

"But he could be so goddamn helpless sometimes, I—I just wish I'd spoken to him before he...I should've—"

"You moved on with your life as best you could, and you did well, Max, better than any of us. You made a life that's worth living for you and the people you love."

"Alex was one of the people I loved," he says. "And I abandoned him."

"My heart breaks for him too, Max, but we're grown men now. Christ, we're in our fifties. I'm sorry I wasn't here for him—that *we* weren't here for him—and I wish we could change that, but we were doing our best to survive."

"I sometimes wonder why we fight so hard for it, survival."

"Because we don't know anything else," I tell him. "The rest is belief, faith, maybes, and hope. To survive, to hang on with a death grip to whatever life we have—even when it's awful—beats the alternative of the unknown."

"The Devil you know." Max offers a subtle smile. "But what if that unknown turns out to be better?"

"We'll find out for sure when we get there. Until then, you keep swinging."

Max wipes his eyes then slides his sunglasses back into place. "I swept the past aside, and all of us along with it," he says. "And I'm sorry."

"I am too," I admit. "But Alex didn't die as a child, Max. He was a grown man, just like the rest of us. Hell, I'd give almost anything to have him standing here with us right now, but he made his decisions, same as we did."

"You're right, of course. All we can do now is keep on loving him." Max returns his attention to the building before us. "And remember."

I turn, look to the corner and street beyond. Max and I know all too well where it leads, and yet somehow, we've managed to avoid speaking of it until now. "Do you think we should...I mean..."

"I assumed you'd either already done it or preferred to do it alone."

"Drove by twice when I first got to town, just couldn't seem to get myself to pull in. I figured we'd be there for Alex tomorrow anyway, thought maybe I'd just do it then."

Max gently places his hand on my arm, as if mistakenly. "Whatever you need to do," he says, "I'm here."

"Let's go back and get one of the cars," I say. "Then we'll go."

"Sure, a little more walking will do us good."

I don't know why, or maybe I do, but we embrace again, suddenly. This time it feels different, more familiar and comfortable, as if all those things from so very long ago have flooded back to us in a single surging wave. Grown men, yes, but also frightened boys finding refuge in each other from a storm the likes of which few can ever know or even begin to understand.

After a moment, we let go.

Nothing more is said. There's no need, not yet.

Instead, together in our self-imposed silence, we leave that dismal brick building behind, and walk back in the direction from which we came.

CHAPTER EIGHT
~1977~

NOTHING MOVED. EVERYTHING was oddly still, suspiciously quiet. Night was a couple hours off, but on its way. The sun was lower in the sky now, nearly touching the horizon, though the heat remained oppressive as ever. In that strange and uncertain moment, I feared it might suffocate and strangle us all.

Alex stood up, breaking the spell. "Sometimes deer stand up on their hind legs," he said, retrieving his knapsack from the ground. "You know, like when they can't reach something? They put their front legs up against trees and sort of stand up. That kind of shit happens. It's not a big deal."

"I don't know, man." Shawn drew a deep breath, let it out slowly. "This was different."

"You guys, there aren't any other animals around here with racks," Alex insisted. "It had to be a deer. You probably didn't get a good look at it and freaked out because you figured it was walking on two legs is all."

"I didn't freak out, asshole," Shawn growled.

"I'm just saying—"

"I don't know what the hell it was, all right? There was nothing there and then there was, and whatever it was, it didn't look...I don't know...right."

I knew Shawn was holding something back, and while I didn't know why just yet, I could tell Max was too. "It wasn't any goddamn deer," I said.

"How the fuck would you know?" Shawn turned away and hocked a huge loogie into the street. "You didn't even see it."

"Frankie Boy," Alex said, "it couldn't be anything else, it had to be a deer. Why are you so sure it wasn't?"

"Because he thinks it's the same thing his father saw."

The words hit me like a sledgehammer to the chest. I looked over at Max, who was still sitting on the swing and staring down into the dirt at his feet. I watched him a moment, wanting to be certain I'd heard him correctly. "How do you know about that?" I asked.

"Go home and ask your father," he said softly.

"I'm asking you, Max."

His eyes lifted, found me. "Samoset's a small town. People talk."

"Oh yeah, do they? And what do they say, Max?" Embarrassment and confusion rose in me, roiling into a boil of frustration and rage. "What do they say about my *father*?"

Max slipped out of the swing and stood there like he didn't know what to do next. "That one night when he was at work, on a break out in the parking lot, he saw something in the woods. It scared him so bad he had a breakdown and they had to call an ambulance and take him to the ER. No one else saw it, but a lot of people he worked with were there when he lost it. Some of those people go to the same church my parents do. I heard my mother talking to my father about it one night."

Alex knit his brow, staring at me with such shock and concern I knew this was as much of a surprise to him as it was to me. As for Shawn, I couldn't be so sure. All I knew was that my father's gibberish and insistence that something was watching and waiting and stalking us suddenly made sense, and that was terrifying, maybe even more terrifying than him losing his mind.

Still trembling with fear and anger, I turned back to Shawn. "Did you know anything about this?"

"My old man heard something about it. He asked me if your dad was all right and if you were going to be okay. I told him I didn't know if you even knew anything. I mean, I knew you knew he lost his job, but I didn't know if you knew why. So I didn't say anything."

"I can't believe in all this time neither one of you fucking told me."

"I figured if you wanted to talk to me about it you would," Shawn said.

"We didn't know what you did or didn't know," Max told me, "and we didn't want to make things worse. All we knew—all we *know*—is that your father was having problems because of what he said he saw."

I ran a hand through my hair. It came back damp and sticky with sweat and a few grains of sand from the beach. "And now Shawn saw this thing too."

"I didn't fucking say that!" Shawn snapped. "Whatever it was, I told you I didn't get a good look. But I...I don't think it was a deer, okay?"

"You guys aren't getting it," Alex said again. "It couldn't be anything else."

"You think a deer would've scared my dad that bad? You think his whole life would go to shit over a fucking deer?"

Alex slung his knapsack over his shoulder and moved back a bit. "I don't know what your father saw, Frankie Boy. I'm just saying if what Shawn saw had a rack, then it couldn't be anything but a deer."

"Yeah, I know what you're saying, Alex. You know how I know? Because you keep saying the same fucking thing over and over again like we're morons."

Alex blanched. "I didn't—I don't mean it like that, I—why you mad at me?"

"Everyone calm down," Max said through a sigh. "Alex is right. It must've been a deer. What else could it be?"

"The same thing my dad saw, obviously."

"And what was that?"

"I don't know. But it scared him enough to ruin his life, and back there in the woods, I've never seen Shawn so scared."

"I wasn't scared," Shawn said. "I was…"

I waited for him to finish even though I knew he never would.

"Fuck it," he said instead. "I'll catch you guys later. I'm going home."

"Are you all right?" Max asked.

"Yeah, don't worry about it. I just want to go home."

This time when he tried to leave no one stopped him. We all stood there and watched until he reached the end of the street and disappeared around the corner with a quick wave.

"Think I'll head home too," Max finally said.

On his way by, he dropped a hand on my shoulder. Then he was gone, and it was just Alex and me on that old playground.

"You better get going too," I told him.

"You mad at me, Frankie Boy?"

He looked so helpless standing there, like a much younger kid left on his own to negotiate wholly foreign territory. "Nah, it's cool. Sorry I got pissed."

"No problem." He cocked his head, indicating the knapsack on his shoulder. "Want me to hang onto the swag for now?"

"Yeah," I said. "I'll grab the *Conan* off you tomorrow, cool?"

"Cool."

I gave him a playful punch in the shoulder. "Later, man."

Alex started toward the street then stopped and looked back at me. "You really think there's something out there, some kind of *monster* or something?"

I remembered the message from the Ouija board.

I AM WATCHING

I looked around at the trees and the grass and the dirt. I had no doubt the gypsy moth invasion Mr. O'Hara warned me about was real, but the creatures he'd described were nowhere in sight. Maybe they were hiding, waiting for the right time to strike. Maybe they were slowly devouring our town along with everything and everyone in it right under our noses, only we couldn't see them. Or maybe you could only see them if they let you.

It doesn't want you to see it, not yet...

Regardless, the answer to Alex's question was *yes*. I *did* think there was a monster out there. And if there really was, then maybe my father wasn't losing his mind after all.

He'd been right all along.

* * * *

The walk home was more harrowing than I'd hoped. Like I'd been fitted with blinders, I looked straight ahead and tried not to let anything distract me. But my fear only intensified, turning the town and streets I knew so well into unfamiliar and dangerous terrain. Despite my best efforts to prevent it, my mind continued to conjure visions of whatever was in the woods watching me from the shadows. I could feel its eyes on me. *Inside* me, like it knew things about me, my secrets and most private thoughts. When my house was finally in sight, and I saw both cars in the driveway, I broke into a full run until I reached the front door.

Once inside I closed the door behind me and listened to the silence of the house a moment, my chest heaving. I had no idea what I expected to see, but I peeked out the front window. Nothing seemed out of the ordinary, and there was no one there, nothing watching.

As my fear settled and began to recede, I moved through the living room and into the kitchen. No one was around, so I checked the rest of the house but didn't find anyone until I followed the hallway to the den. There was no sign of my mother, but my father was slumped in a recliner in the corner. The Ouija board was still sitting on the coffee table, and the couch across from it was littered with crumpled pieces of paper, two empty Coke cans, and a plate with the remains of a ham sandwich and potato chip crumbs on it.

Still dressed in his robe, my father was awake but looked like he'd been sleeping. "You all right?" he asked groggily. "You just get home?"

"Yeah," I said. "Jesus, Dad, have you been in here all day?"

He stared at me like I'd presented him with a question so profoundly complex he couldn't even begin to comprehend it, much less provide an answer. "I think I fell asleep, but it's hard to say for sure."

"That's good. You need to sleep. Where's Mom at?"

"She went out."

"Her car's still here," I told him.

"She must be back then."

"I checked the whole house. She's not here."

"Huh," he said, perplexed.

"Where'd she go?"

"She didn't say." He absently scratched at his armpit. A wave of pungent body odor drifted free of him. "She just said she'd be back in a while."

It was very unusual for my mother to leave the house on weekends unless it was to run errands or to do the grocery shopping, and she always did those things in the morning. Even if for some reason she'd decided to do them later than usual, she certainly wouldn't do it on foot.

"When did she leave?" I asked.

He stared at his wrist but he wasn't wearing a watch. "Earlier, I guess. Time's a funny thing, son. I can't seem to keep track of it worth a damn lately."

"Did she get a ride?"

"I don't know. I'm sure she's fine. She'll be home soon." My father struggled up out of his slumped posture but remained seated. "Been trying all day to get that board to tell me more about—"

"Dad," I interrupted, raising my voice in the hopes that it might help hold his attention. "I have to ask you something. It's important, so you got to listen, okay?

"Sure, Frankie Boy, okay." He clenched shut his bloodshot eyes, holding them closed for a moment before opening them and squinting at me like he was trying his best to focus. "What is it?"

I took a moment to try and put together a question that made sense, but none of this made anything even close to sense. With my frustration rising, I blurted, "The thing out there that's watching you keep telling me about, does it have antlers like a deer?"

He thought it over a while before answering. "It depends."

"*Depends*? On what?"

"Who it's showing itself to."

My fear returned, if it had ever really left, pulsed along the back of my neck like an exhale of grave-cold breath then curled up at the base of my spine. Before I could ask my father anything else, I heard a car door slam. He heard it too, though he pretended he hadn't. He just sat there looking into his lap like something there had drawn his attention.

I hurried back through the house to the living room.

At the window I saw my mother approaching the house as a big Lincoln Continental, shiny and new, slowly backed out of the driveway.

Behind the wheel of the gold car was an older heavyset man I didn't recognize. Sporting only a thin horseshoe of gray hair, he was otherwise bald and wore aviator sunglasses, his shirt open at the collar.

As I moved from the window, the front door swung open and my mother stepped inside. Startled, she jumped then closed the door and flashed me a disapproving sideways glance. "What are you doing lurching out at me like something from a funhouse?" she said. Her speech was slurred and she smelled like cigarettes and liquor. "Are you trying to give me a heart attack?"

"I didn't lurch out, Mom," I said flatly. "I'm just standing here."

"Well stop *just standing here*." She removed her sunglasses and hooked them on the front of her top, which was very tight and low-cut. It was obvious she wasn't wearing a bra, and her denim shorts looked new and were much shorter than any I'd seen her in before. She held a pair of sandals in one hand, dangling them from her fingers by the straps. Except for occasionally in the backyard or at the beach, I'd never known her to go barefoot. "It's unsettling to walk into the house and find someone right in my face like that."

"Who was that guy?" I asked, cocking my head toward the window.

"Someone to do with my job," she said, and headed for the kitchen.

I followed close behind her. "It's Saturday."

"All day, in fact, what's your point?"

"You don't work on Saturdays."

In the doorway to the kitchen my mother stopped and turned back, facing me. "I didn't say I was working," she said with forced pleasantness, and though she smiled I could tell she was upset with me. "You asked who that was and I told you. If you'd like further clarification for some reason, his name is Mr. Harry Ralston, and he's the regional vice president of our company. He's visiting from Connecticut—Hartford, actually—and only in town for a few days for some very important meetings with our office. He asked if I'd like to get some lunch with him so we could discuss things pertaining to my job and future at the company."

Her outfit, coupled with the venom in her eyes, left me unsure of where to look. It was as if someone had kidnapped my mother and replaced her with the woman standing before me. "You're not even wearing shoes," I said, heart racing. "Why are you dressed like that?"

She let out something between a sigh and a quiet laugh. "Like what?"

Head bowed, I shrugged. I didn't know what else to do.

"If you think I'm going to allow myself to be subjected to an interrogation from my teenage son," she said evenly, "I'm afraid you're sorely mistaken."

I was still looking at the carpet when she walked away. As it blurred through the tears filling my eyes, part of me wanted to go right out the door and as far away from all this as possible. But after everything that had happened today, I wasn't exactly in a hurry to run headlong into the coming darkness. Still, could I be certain anymore if *in here* was any less horrifying than *out there*?

There wasn't anywhere safe anymore. Not for me. Not for any of us.

CHAPTER NINE

SAMOSET DIDN'T HAVE much in the way of gathering spots for young people, unless it was one of the sports fields or something promoted by the churches in town. There was a Boys and Girls Club, but none of my friends ever went there. It was mostly used to host a local elementary-school-age basketball league and served as a kind of after school daycare for kids a lot younger than me. As a result, teenagers tended to congregate at various spots outdoors. The boulder over by the rectory, the beach, on the lawn of a bandstand where music ensembles sometimes performed in the warmer months, or downtown in front of the general store.

A few weeks ago, Shawn and I had been hanging out on the bandstand lawn, just sitting around and debating which recent album was better, *Rock and Roll Over* by KISS or *Jailbreak* from Thin Lizzy. I liked both but was more in the Thin Lizzy camp, while Shawn favored the KISS release. We'd been there maybe half an hour, just killing time and trying to figure out what else we could get into, when Ronica and four of her friends showed up and joined us on the lawn. One of her friends, a pretty redhead whose name I couldn't remember, brought a blanket, so we all sat on that. Nothing much transpired for a good long while, and though Shawn had the ability to seamlessly interject himself into their conversation now and then, I felt less confident in attempting that, so I mostly stayed quiet, pretending to listen to whatever these older girls were talking about while all I was really doing was taking in Ronica and trying to keep my lust for her under control. I remember she wore jeans and knee-high suede boots, along with a peasant blouse and a pair of dangle earrings in the shape of peace signs. With her long hair pulled back into a ponytail and a flower tucked above her right ear, she was more beautiful than ever. She'd taken up position right next to me from the start, and smelled so good it made me dizzy. I couldn't take my eyes off her. In those strange moments, with one of my best friends right there and both of us surrounded by these cool older girls, oddly, I'd never felt more alone in my life. Shawn was able to feel part of it all—or was at least good enough to fake it effectively—but I lacked those skills. I was just sort of *there*, and certain I could get up and walk away without anyone even noticing. So when the conversation died down and Ronica focused on me, I was both surprised and flattered. She'd just lit a cigarette and was taking deep drags before throwing her head back and exhaling streams of smoke up at the sky like some sort of movie queen.

"There's a dance this Friday night at the VFW," she said, looking right at me. "Are you going?"

I'd been to some dances at school but that was it. The ones held at the VFW were generally for older kids. "Not sure," I said, trying my best to come off nonchalant as possible. "Depends if I got anything else going on, I guess."

"I don't know if I'm going either," she said. "I mean, I keep waiting to see if someone worth going with asks me, you know?"

I of course had no idea what that was like at all, but I nodded knowingly anyway. Suddenly cognizant and more than a little nervous that everyone else had gone quiet and was now zeroed in on our conversation, I tried desperately to think of some other topic.

"It's like, I'm sure some guys will ask me or whatever," Ronica said, "but I'm holding out for someone that's actually nice and just wants to have fun and maybe actually *dance*."

"Yeah, definitely," I said. "Cool."

"I could go without a date, but I'm thinking if nobody worth going with asks I'll just stay home, you know?"

"I don't blame you."

"So many guys in this town," she said. "Hardly any decent ones, though."

As her girlfriends all agreed with this assessment, Ronica smoked her cigarette and gazed at me in a way I hoped was flirtatious but might have simply been amusement. I couldn't tell for sure, so I glanced at Shawn. When he subtly raised an eyebrow I knew he was picking up on it too.

We'd known Ronica for years, and though she was often kind of flirty with us we all knew better than to take it too seriously. This time seemed different though, and she wouldn't let it go.

"You know what I need?" she asked suddenly. "A gentleman, that's what. Just once that might be nice. Not many in these parts, you ask me."

"Yup," Shawn said with a smirk, "we're a dying breed."

The other girls laughed, but Ronica kept looking at me as if she hadn't heard him. "Like you, Frankie Boy," she said. "You're always so polite and such a gentleman."

I felt heat flush across my cheeks. "Thanks."

She took a drag on her cigarette, exhaled through her nose, then smiled. "Now if someone like you asked me, for example, I would definitely say yes."

I couldn't believe my ears. Smiling nervously, I glanced at the other girls sitting on the blanket. They were all looking at me. When my eyes made it back around to Ronica, she was still gazing at me and smiling too.

Do it, I told myself. *You might never get another chance.*

"Well," I said, clearing my throat, "I guess if you really wanted to go, I could...I mean if you want, I could take you or... Do you want to go with me?"

Ronica blinked, as if I'd broken her out of some sort of trance. "Huh?"

"The dance," I said, my heart sinking. "Did you want to go with me?"

"Oh my God that is *so* sweet." She took another drag on her cigarette then crushed it in the grass just beyond the blanket. "You're adorable, and thank you, seriously, but I can't go with you, Frankie Boy. You're only fourteen."

I wanted to quietly slink away and die somewhere, but I was trapped on that blanket. "I thought, I mean, I—Okay—I just—I thought that's what you were saying. Sorry."

"Well, that's why I said someone *like* you." Ronica put a hand to her mouth. "I'm sorry I gave you the wrong impression, really I am."

"Don't worry about it," I said, certain I was dying. "No problem."

Her girlfriends all laughed quietly while Ronica sat there looking like I was the cutest little puppy she'd ever seen.

I grinned helplessly, completely humiliated.

"Come on, man." Shawn was suddenly on his feet. "Let's go. The guys are waiting on us, remember? We don't want to be late."

He was doing his best to rescue me, and at that point I wasn't about to pass up the chance. "Yeah," I said. "We better get going."

"Frankie Boy," Ronica said, "I'm sorry."

"It's okay," I replied in the most unaffected tone I could muster. "No biggie."

"Later," Shawn said, and taking hold of my arm, led me away.

When we'd made it to the street, I pulled free and said, "Jesus Christ, I'm *such* a fucking idiot!"

"No, you're not, man. Ronica just loves the attention."

I was so embarrassed I didn't even know where to begin. "I thought she wanted me to ask her, I—"

"She did. So she could say no. She was fucking with you, dude."

"Why would she do that?"

"I don't know, because she can?"

"That's fucked up."

"Yeah, it is, but she knows we all follow her around like dogs in heat, kissing her ass and drooling all over her. And she loves it. So she let you hump her leg for a minute then shook you off. Look at it that way."

"Is that supposed to make me feel better? They were all laughing at me."

"Fuck them, who cares? Besides, Ronica's like that with every guy in this town, why you think we'd be any different?"

"I guess I thought we were friends too."

"In a way we are."

"Yeah, but—"

Shawn slapped my chest with the back of his hand hard enough to get my attention. "You, me, Max, and Alex, *we're* friends. Ronica's cool, she's Alex's big sister, and I try to respect that as much as the next guy, okay? But she drives me crazy too. End of the day, man, she's just a fine chick we want to fuck that hangs out with us sometimes because the attention turns her on."

"I made a complete ass of myself."

"So what else is new?"

I called him a dick but couldn't prevent a smile.

"Come on," Shawn said, slinging an arm around my shoulder as we continued down the street. "Who needs chicks anyway? You want to go to the dance, you sex machine? Take me, I'll go with you."

Laughing, I pushed him away. "Get off me, you fucking clown."

Weeks later, lying on my bed, staring at the ceiling with *Frampton Comes Alive* on my record player and blaring through my headphones, our laughter from that day echoed in my mind. I remembered how Shawn had been there for me, and how badly Ronica's bullshit had embarrassed and hurt me. I forgave her, of course—the next time I saw her, in fact—as she made it a point of throwing her arms around me, crushing her tits against me, and whispering in my ear how I was the cutest thing she'd ever seen. I knew she was just saying that because she felt bad, and part of me wanted to tell her to go fuck herself, but I couldn't. Hell, I didn't even really want to. I couldn't help myself.

None of us could.

As for Shawn, his heroics were nothing new. He'd always been our leader and had always looked out for us, even when sometimes he had a hard enough time looking out for himself. All the instances when he'd saved my ass over the years came to me in a steady stream, running through my mind before my thoughts returned to that day at the bandstand. Shawn spent the next several hours taking care of me as best he could, distracting me with one-on-one basketball games at the courts down by the beach, or later, listening to records in my room and talking comics and horror movies and wrestling—all the things we were into—and all the while making sure I was thinking about something—anything—other than what had happened with Ronica. Truth was, I owed him better than I'd given earlier. I let my own fears about my father's condition get the best of me, and I'd taken it out on Shawn. Now, with Frampton rocking "Do You Feel Like We Do" in my ears, I decided in the morning I'd go smooth things over and make them right. Until then, I had to survive in this madhouse the best I could, and hiding out in my room listening to tunes seemed as good an escape as any.

Although it worked for a little over an hour, unfortunately it came to an end when my bedroom door opened to reveal my mother standing before me. She'd changed into Capri pants, slippers, and a t-shirt, and looked more like herself.

I pulled one headphone away from my ear. "What?"

Nibbling her bottom lip, she watched me a moment. I could tell she was deciding whether to go on the offensive or grant my attitude a pass. "Dinner," she said at last. "It's ready."

"I'm not hungry."

"Come have dinner anyway."

"No thanks."

"I'm not asking."

"Yeah, well like I said, I'm not hungry."

"I went to the trouble of making us a meal." She took a step into my room. "The least you can do is come and eat some of it. Besides, it might do us good to sit down and have a meal together like a real family for a change."

It took everything I had not to laugh, though there was no humor or joy in it. The only laughter I was suppressing was one of irony and anger. I loved my mother desperately, but I was so confused and upset with her behavior of late I no longer knew what to do with that love.

"Fine," I said, making sure she saw me roll my eyes. "I'll be right there."

She nodded and left without another word.

My door closed behind her, and as Frampton started to make his guitar talk, I shut my eyes, did my best to block out the rest of the world, and fell away to darkness.

* * * *

A silver bowl of freshly cut flowers sat in the center of the kitchen table, bookended by two lit candles in matching silver holders. I didn't want to know where the flowers came from, so I focused on the three place settings instead. My mother had used fancy cloth napkins and placemats that usually only appeared during the holidays or on special occasions, and she'd already set out a big bowl of salad, scalloped potatoes in a casserole dish, and a platter of sizzling pork chops. My father hadn't taken a meal anywhere other than the den in quite a while, so I was surprised to find him sitting at the table.

As I unceremoniously plopped myself onto the chair across from him, he gave me one of his sad and awkward little smiles. He looked exhausted and crazed as ever, but I noticed something else in him as well. Pain.

My mother placed three fancy glass goblets of water at each of our places then stood back and admired the table. "Well," she said softly, "doesn't look half bad, does it?"

"Very nice, Kelly," my father said. "Everything looks delicious."

He was trying, which was more than I was willing to do. "What's with the candles and the holiday napkins?" I asked.

"I just thought it might be nice for a change."

"And I hate these goblet things. Can I just have a regular glass?"

She tried to mask her anger, but as they so often did, her eyes gave her away. "You're well aware of where we keep the glasses," she said, and sat down. "Feel free to go get yourself one."

"Whatever," I said, sighing dramatically.

"Would you like to say grace?"

I didn't want to but did it anyway. "Bless us oh Lord, and these thy gifts, which we are about to receive, from thy bounty, through Christ our Lord. Amen."

"Amen," my mother said, smiling sweetly.

My father nodded. "Yes. Amen."

We all helped ourselves to the food. I took one pork chop, a small scoop of potatoes and passed on the salad, while my dad took one chop and paltry amounts of the rest.

"Is that all you're having?" my mother asked.

My father reached over to the platter, stabbed another pork chop with his fork and dropped it on his plate. "I can eat two," he muttered. "Two's good."

"Frankie Boy?"

"I told you I wasn't hungry," I said.

She nodded and began to eat. "Suit yourself."

No one said anything more for a while. The three of us ate in our little candlelit kitchen, using our cloth napkins and drinking from our goblets and pretending all was right with us and the world.

When I'd finished I started to get up but my mother stopped me.

"You are *not* excused from the table."

With another dramatic sigh I said, "May I please be excused?"

"No, you may not." She pointed to my chair with her fork. "Sit."

I sank back down, angry and feeling caged. "I'm done eating."

"Be that as it may, your father and I haven't finished our dinner yet."

"So I have to sit here and watch you two eat?"

My mother took a sip of water. "Frankie Boy, what, *exactly*, has gotten into you tonight?"

I didn't want to fight, I only wanted to leave. "Can I just go, please?"

"No, you may not."

My father kept eating, his head down.

"My God, is it really so difficult for us to enjoy a nice meal together?"

I turned to my father. "Dad, why did you lose your job?"

He looked up from his plate.

I don't know why, maybe it was wishful thinking, but I figured my mother would save him. She didn't. Instead, with an expression bright with anticipation, she popped a bite of salad in her mouth.

"Seems like everybody else in town knows," I said. "Why can't I?"

I could tell he didn't want to discuss it in front of my mother, so rather than answer he resumed chewing, slowly and deliberately.

"Is it true what people say?" I asked. "That you saw it at work? The thing you've been telling me and warning me about? And it scared you so bad you had a breakdown and couldn't work anymore?"

He put his fork down but still didn't answer.

"I want to know what happened," I pressed. "I have a right to know."

"You're right, son," he said in a quietly defeated voice. "You do."

Then my father rose to his feet and slowly left the room.

I hadn't set out to hurt him, but I'd done it anyway, and hated myself for it.

"I know you're trying to make sense of what happened," my mother said in a quiet, conspiratorial tone. "And you're hearing things around town. I hear them too. I see the looks from people. I hear the whispers and the laughing behind my back. It wasn't right of us to keep you in the dark on this. I should've sat you down and better explained what had happened, but I wasn't entirely sure myself at first. And there are other, underlying things going on, complicated and adult things that are difficult to explain or even understand. Still, you do have a right to know. You're right about that."

"Am I right about what happened too?"

She stood up, carried her plate to the sink, then grabbed her cigarettes and lighter from the counter. "I think you should go apologize for embarrassing him. Then you two need to have a discussion, as best as he's able to at this point anyway. When you're done, you and I can talk, all right? Just do your best to remember that your father is in a very fragile state right now. Try to be a bit gentler, and use some tact, understand?"

This time I wanted my words to hurt. "You mean like coming home drunk after being out all day with some guy?"

I'd wounded her, and I could tell her instinct was to fight back. Carefully selecting a cigarette from the pack and pulling it free, she rolled it into the corner of her mouth, lit it, and feigned subtle amusement instead. "I don't know who it is you *think* you're talking to," she said, drawing in the smoke and exhaling through her nostrils. "But don't you ever speak to me that way again. Not ever."

I stood up and tossed my napkin on the table.

"I don't recall excusing you from dinner."

"You just told me to go apologize and talk to Dad," I reminded her. "Am I supposed to yell to him from here?"

My mother cocked her elbow and looked at her cigarette as if she'd never seen one before. "I know things are difficult," she said, her eyes following the smoke as it rose and slowly spiraled toward the ceiling. "You're confused and scared—obviously angry—and striking out because you think I'm an easy target and will take it. I'm not, and I won't. Do you understand me?"

"Yeah, been speaking English all my life."

I expected a look that should've maimed if not killed, but instead she leaned back against the counter, as if it was the only thing keeping her upright. "My God," she said. "How did we become these people so quickly, so easily? We've always been close, you and I. Haven't we? *Haven't* we?"

I nodded. We had been. She'd always been there for me, and I adored her. But the truth of the matter was I'd never really known my mother as well as I'd have liked. No matter how close we became, she remained somewhat aloof, concealing a part of her I could never quite get to. Over the years I'd grown to believe and accept that she kept it for herself because she needed it more than anyone else did, even me. Now, I wasn't so sure.

"You've never behaved this way before," she said.

"None of us have."

"No," she said, "we haven't."

I stood there like a moron, unsure of what to do or say next.

"Truth is I'm just as scared and confused as you are." My mother brought the cigarette to her lips then reconsidered. "And trust me, just as angry."

I had some anger, but that's not what was driving this. It was just coming out as anger because I didn't want to admit how scared I really was, and that more than anything, I was sad. Horribly, deeply, desperately sad, and to degrees I'd never been before and didn't realize were even possible.

Arguing, yelling and screaming, or breaking things was the last thing I wanted to do.

I just felt like crying.

"But I won't have your disrespect and ugliness," she continued. "I don't deserve them and I won't have it. Do I make myself clear?"

"Yes," I said without looking at her.

She let her forehead rest against the base of her palm, her cigarette between her index and middle fingers. A long gray ash had formed and fell free, but she didn't notice. "The things you've heard about your father are true," she said through a heavy sigh. "He was working a nightshift, covering for another supervisor who was on vacation, and apparently he went outside to get some fresh air. He saw...*something*. He couldn't explain what it was, but it frightened him so badly he lost control of himself. He caused quite a scene and a lot of people saw it. Of course they thought he'd lost his mind."

"Has he?" I asked.

"I kept thinking it would get better," she said. "It had to. No one as solid and reliable as your father could completely fall apart over something like that."

"It must've been awful bad," I said. "Whatever he saw, it must've—"

"Whatever he saw was explainable, I'm sure. But there was no talking to him. You remember how he behaved from the moment he lost his job. He's only gotten worse. Not working, running around the house without shaving or bathing, scribbling in those notebooks. And now he's playing with that asinine Ouija board." She took another pull on her cigarette then put it out in a small glass ashtray on the counter. "We didn't want you to be afraid or think less of him, so we tried to keep it from you at first. When his behavior became so bad there was no way to hide what was happening, I tried to assure you he was all right, that he was just going through some things he needed to—and would—work out."

"Did you really think he'd be all right?" I asked.

"I did. But he refused to go back to the doctor."

"I didn't know he ever went."

"He didn't want you to know. He was ashamed."

"What did the doctor say?"

"Your father had a nervous breakdown." My mother folded her arms across her chest. "The doctor recommended he go into the hospital for treatment, but he refused. Because he isn't a danger to himself or anyone else—you know your father, he wouldn't hurt a fly—there are no legal means to force him into the hospital. So he came home. And now, here we are."

Despite the growing lump in my throat, I forced a swallow. "Will he ever get better, Mom?"

"I don't know."

"But it's possible, right?"

"The doctor thinks there's a good chance he'll eventually come out of it, and if he seeks help, with the correct care and medication, he could get himself back on track. But I don't need to tell you that so far that's not what's happened."

"What if he's telling the truth?" Through the small windows over the sink behind her, I saw that night had fallen. "What if he really saw something he couldn't explain that scared him so bad it—"

"Look, I believe he saw something, all right? But he misidentified it, took it for something it wasn't. The only monsters your father sees are in his head."

"How can you be so sure?"

"Because there's no such thing as monsters," she said. "At least not outside the human kind anyway."

I nodded, but wasn't sure I agreed.

"Go apologize," she said. "He's struggling, but he loves you more than anything in the world. He always has. And despite what you may think of me at the moment, so have I. If you want to help, just love us back."

"Don't you know that I do?" I asked, fighting tears.

She pushed away from the counter and came to me quickly. I thought she was going to hug me, but instead she kissed my forehead, and with teary eyes of her own said, "Of course."

And then she was gone and I was alone in the kitchen.

I wiped my eyes, tried to forget about what I'd seen when she'd come home, and focused instead on what to say to my father.

Eventually I found my way to the den.

He was sitting up but had fallen asleep on the couch. Rather than wake him, I sat down and gently rested my head on his shoulder. In a way, I was glad he was finally sleeping again. We didn't need to talk any more about it, not tonight, so I stayed there and did what my mother had suggested.

I loved him back.

For a while, at least, that seemed good.

Until three days later, when word spread through town that Perry Jenkins and Keith Dickinson had been reported missing by their families.

CHAPTER TEN

IN THE NIGHTMARE, I'm running through a dark forest carpeted in roiling fog. Everything has the look of the old monster movies from Universal Pictures the Boston UHF channel often shows during their Saturday afternoon Creature Feature lineup. I love those old flicks, but this is something different.

This is all too real.

As I stumble through the forest, moving fast as I can along the uneven terrain, I see a silhouette of a boy kneeling in a clearing up ahead. I pull up just short of him, doubled over and trying to catch my breath. Even before he looks up and sees me there, I know who it is.

"Shawn," I say. "Are you all right?"

He leans into the sparse moonlight, and I see his face. Blood runs from his eyes in two long swaths, and as he cocks his head, as if to hear me better, I realize his eyes are gone, torn from the now empty, black and bloody sockets.

"Do you see it, Frankie Boy?" he says, the words slow and drawn out, his voice horribly deep and guttural and sounding as if it belongs to someone else...someone who's been gargling crushed glass. "Do you see it?"

Recoiling in horror, I stagger back.

It's then that I see Max and Alex floating impossibly in midair above the clearing, arms stretched out like victims of crucifixion, their feet dangling in the darkness and their chests ripped open, hearts gone. Taken...

"Run," Shawn says, vomiting blood.

And I do.

Something chases after me. I look back, can't see what it is.

But I can hear it. Like the hissing of snakes, it is accompanied by an ominous rumbling sound that shakes the ground and echoes through the dark forest, pulsing in time with a terrible pounding in my head.

I snapped awake, and within seconds realized I'd been dreaming. As I lay there trembling with fear and watching the shadows along my bedroom ceiling, I realized I could still hear that awful noise. This was no lingering remnant from my nightmare. It was real. And it was coming from just outside my window.

The alarm clock on my nightstand read: 5:18. I rubbed my eyes and gave Farrah a quick glance. As usual, she was all dazzling smiles and excited nipples, but wasn't talking, so I made my way to the window, lifted the shade, and peeked out.

There was just enough light to reveal an old town pickup truck slowly rolling by our house. In the flatbed, a machine that looked even older than the truck sprayed a steady cloud of pesticide into the air. A grizzled man that had been employed by the town for as long as I could remember sat behind the wheel. Although a longtime resident, I didn't know his name, just that he worked with Shawn's father at the DPW. He wore a ratty Red Sox cap, and a cigarette hung from his mouth as he drove, one beefy arm slung casually over the wheel, the other dangling out the window. He appeared bored beyond measure.

I let out a sigh of relief and tried to force the horrible mutilated images of my friends from my mind as my body gradually began to relax.

Mr. O'Hara told me they'd be spraying due to the gypsy moths, so I assumed that's likely all this was. But there was still something unsettling about that old truck skulking along our street—the machine in back shaking and growling as if alive—particularly in the early morning hours when the world was stuck in that eerie chasm between darkness and light. The entire episode had the sinister feel of a covert government operation purposely taking place when most people were asleep and unaware of what was happening.

My father's paranoia was rubbing off on me, it seemed. Or maybe it wasn't paranoia at all. I could no longer be sure, but as the truck vanished around the corner at the top of the street in a cloud of smoke, it occurred to me that I'd still yet to see a single one of these moths that were supposedly such a menace. Were they hiding somewhere nearby? Were they already dying?

Rattled by my nightmare, the idea of dead moths falling from the trees, and that truck creeping through the neighborhood, I turned from the window. My eyes settled on a Wolf Man action figure standing atop a bookcase on the opposite wall. He was bookended by a robot toy, a 12-inch plastic Godzilla, and another action figure from the *Planet of the Apes* films. I'd had them since I was little, and although I stopped playing with them a few years before, unlike most of my other toys, I still kept them around. I didn't know why, exactly, but in that disquieting moment there was something comforting about these things. Even the sneering Wolf Man gave me a sense of safety. A link to an earlier time when I wasn't afraid and believed everything was right with the world and always would be, now I feared that whatever was waiting for me in the woods planned to drag me farther and farther away from ever knowing such things again.

I wondered if Perry and Keith were afraid too, wherever they were. Even though I couldn't stand them, I found myself hoping they'd simply stolen a car and left town. The alternative was that whatever had been out there with us a few days ago was responsible for their disappearance, and that was something I didn't even want to begin to broach, especially without the guys. But there it was, gnawing its way into my head anyway.

Going back to bed was no longer an option. I'd no longer be able to sleep, so I had no choice but to ride it out until sunrise. Here, in this house, where my parents had both gone mad, and where maybe I had too. As I sat down at my desk, a small framed photograph of my cat Fred caught my attention. Although I got him when I was just a toddler, and never remembered a time when he wasn't in my life, Fred had died a year ago, and I missed him terribly. Whenever I was upset, he sat with me and made me focus on him. In time, whatever was bothering me didn't seem quite so bad. Had he still been alive, he would've been right here with me, sitting in my lap or snuggled up with me in bed, purring away.

"Wish you were here with me now," I whispered, struggling to hold my emotions in check. "I miss you, buddy."

Wherever Fred was, I bet he missed me too.

The day my father and I buried Fred in the backyard, he'd insisted on digging the grave. He'd come home with Fred as a kitten, and loved him as much as I did. I remembered my mother stood at the back sliders, smoking a cigarette and watching us, a single tear rolling the length of her cheek. Unlike my father, she remained at a distance from the situation, and from us. I knew she was upset, but all she ever said to me about it was, "Fred was very old. He's at peace now." She mourned him sincerely, but efficiently, and then moved on.

My father could not have been more different in that regard.

"I know we can never replace Freddy," he'd told me, sobbing quietly as he slammed the shovel into the ground. "You've had him your entire life. But we'll get another cat, okay? Maybe a dog or—or maybe even both. Would you like that, son? We'll get a dog *and* a cat."

The loss of Fred had been so devastating I passed on getting either one. My father was right, we could never replace Fred, but I also never wanted to feel what I was experiencing in that moment again. Naively, I'd imagined that might actually be possible by simply avoiding getting another cat or dog.

Now I wished I'd made a different decision.

I switched on my desk lamp, thinking maybe the light would make me feel better. It didn't, so I went to my bookcase and selected a dog-eared paperback copy of *That Was Then, This Is Now* by S.E. Hinton. I'd read it a few months ago, and like most of Hinton's novels, I not only enjoyed it, but felt a connection to it I knew was genuine but couldn't quite define.

I flipped to the end of the book, and read the novel's final line.

I wish I was a kid again, when I had all the answers.

Before I could fully process those words, there was a gentle knock on the door. Rather than answer, I waited a moment, hoping maybe that would be the end of it, but a few seconds later the knob turned and the door opened a crack.

My father peered in at me, and once he saw the lamp was on and I was sitting at my desk, he stepped into the room and closed the door behind him. In his robe and wrinkled pajamas, he looked as crazed and exhausted as ever. I was sure he'd been up all night, huddled over the Ouija board while maniacally smoking cigarettes and trying to understand what was happening. In a loud, conspiratorial whisper he said, "Glad you're awake, Frankie Boy, I—I was hoping you'd be awake."

"It's early." I tossed the paperback onto my desk. "What's up?"

"Did that truck wake you?"

"Yeah, I was having a nightmare."

"Did you see it, the truck?"

"I saw it go by."

"I did too, saw the whole thing."

"They're spraying for gypsy moths."

"Who told you that?"

"Shawn's dad," I said.

He quickly scratched the side of his head and muttered, "A *swarm*. A swarm of gypsy moths, I—it told me there was a swarm coming, remember?"

"I remember."

"That must've been what it meant. And now they're spraying *against* the swarm…in secret."

"Wasn't really secret, Dad, just kind of early."

"Maybe they know more than they're telling us."

"I don't think Mr. O'Hara would lie to me. He's a really good guy."

"I know he is, son." His eyes darted back and forth, taking in my room as if he'd never seen it before. "Of course, they could be lying to him too. They could be spraying damn near anything."

"*They?*"

"He and others like him may think that's what they're spraying because that's what they've been told and they believe it," he said. "Why wouldn't they? They'd have no reason to question it. Could be simple as that, see? Sometimes people are a part of conspiracies without even realizing it."

I knew where he was going with this. There was no point in dancing around until he leveled with me. "You think it has something to do with the thing you saw, don't you?"

My father shook his head, like it was all too much for him. "Frankie Boy, remember the other night when your mother made us that nice meal? You asked me about what I saw. You asked what it looks like, do you remember?"

I nodded.

"Why did you ask if it had antlers like a deer?"

Part of me didn't want to tell him, but at that point I didn't have much choice. I needed answers same as he did. "I think Shawn saw it too."

His eyes narrowed. "When?"

"A couple days ago, in the woods behind the house, quite a ways back."

"Were you with him?"

"Yes."

He ran a hand across his mouth. "Did you see it too?"

I shook my head no.

"Good, that—that's good."

"I will though, won't I?"

"Yes, son, eventually you will."

"And then what?"

"In some ways you'll understand...in others...you'll understand even less."

"Is it still waiting for me?" I asked. "Like you said?"

My father looked away, anywhere but at me.

"Do you know what it wants?" I pressed.

"No, but it is talking to me, telling me things through the Ouija board," he said, his face twisted with fear. "That's how it's communicating with me. I just don't know why."

"I thought it was a flesh and blood kind of thing. Like...an animal."

"It's more than that."

"Dad—"

"I don't know what it is!" he snapped, and then, realizing he'd raised his voice, sheepishly added, "I have to figure that out. It's the only way to stop it."

"Stop it from doing what?"

He clenched shut his eyes, his lips moving silently in what could only be frenzied prayer. A moment later he said, "I just need more time."

Time, it seemed to me, was about the only thing my father didn't have. If he didn't come back from this precipice soon, he never would. And now I was right there with him. If he was going off that ledge, he wouldn't be going alone.

Just love us back.

I was doing my best. I just wasn't sure that was enough.

"Everything's changing," I said sadly. "Nothing seems right anymore."

"That's because it isn't."

Visions flashed across my mind's eye. Max and Alex floating in darkness, their eyes torn from their skulls as Shawn knelt in the clearing, blinded too, gore spewing from his mouth, choking his screams.

Run...

The nightmare faded, replaced with my mother in her black dress, sitting at the kitchen table in her stocking feet, smoking a cigarette and staring off into the darkness.

Then it all spiraled off and fell away to the blackest corners of my psyche, and all that was left was my father and me...and the horrible feelings of dread and hopelessness throttling us both.

"Why is this happening to us?"

"I don't know, son. But I'm going to find out if it kills me."

If it hasn't already, I thought.

My father opened the door, stepped into the hallway, then looked back at me as if he'd forgotten something. "And the answer to your question is yes. When I saw that thing...it had antlers like a deer."

CHAPTER ELEVEN

ON SATURDAYS, THE Samoset Public Library opened at 10:00am. Originally the home of one of the town's founders, the two-story Victorian was converted to a public library back in the 1920s. Although it had been renovated a few times over the years, it retained much of its original look, and remained one of the oldest and most historically significant buildings in Samoset.

The only patron there when the doors were unlocked, I was welcomed in by the librarian, Margaret O'Doul. An elderly woman, she began working there in the 1930s, though people often joked she'd really been hired at the conclusion of the Revolutionary War. As a stern New England spinster straight out of Central Casting, in her dated dresses and long gray hair piled up in a tight bun atop her head, there were days when that didn't seem terribly far-fetched. Never married, she still lived in the same home she'd been born and raised in, and when not at the library, spent most of her time volunteering at functions for the historical society or Congregational church. She'd been old as long as I'd known her, and while some found Miss O'Doul to be cold and officious, I got along with her rather well, probably because I was at the library a lot, and never gave her a hard time.

After a brief exchange of polite pleasantries, Miss O'Doul wandered off to resume her duties while I went in search of reference books dealing with myths and monsters. I was sure there must be at least some information on something that looked like whatever my father and Shawn had seen, but after nearly an hour of scouring several books, all I came up with was stories about encounters with ghosts, aliens, Bigfoot, the Loch Ness Monster and other sea creatures, and some sort of lizard man that attacked a guy somewhere down south in the 1950s. None of the descriptions sounded anything like a deer or antlered animal.

"*Monsters*, Mr. Molinari?"

Startled, I looked up from the pile of books scattered across the table to see Miss O'Doul scowling at me, an eyebrow arched.

"Yes, ma'am," I said with a soft exhale of self-conscious, nervous laughter.

She raised a pair of eyeglasses attached to a chain around her neck and slid them onto the bridge of her tiny nose. "Do tell, Mr. Molinari. Why are so many young men your age fascinated with such things?"

"I'm just doing some research is all," I said sheepishly.

"I know you to be an exemplary student. You can't possibly be in summer school, so enlighten me, won't you? What is the purpose of this *research*?"

I tried to think fast, but with her laser stare burning down on me I couldn't come up with anything other than a version of the truth. "It's just for me, I guess."

Her expression shifted, as if she'd suddenly remembered something, and I realized she'd put it together. Samoset was such a small town even Miss O'Doul apparently knew about what had happened with my father.

Rather than make an issue of it, she played along. "I see, strictly for your own edification then?" She no longer looked inquisitive, just like she felt sorry for me. "Well now, isn't that refreshing?"

I nodded despite having only a vague idea of what *edification* meant.

"And have you found what you were looking for?"

"No, ma'am," I answered. "Not yet."

Miss O'Doul glanced at the books on the table before me. "You appear to have exhausted every book we have on the subject. Is there something specific you were hoping to find?"

"I was sort of looking for things more local."

"Well, we've certainly no shortage of local lore." She put a hand to her chin. "This is New England, after all."

"Are there any books about monsters that live in the woods?" I asked.

"The indigenous peoples certainly have a rich history of fascinating lore and mythology," she explained. "Much of it has to do with forest creatures and the like. Perhaps you can find what you're looking for in some of their stories and traditions."

I could only hope I didn't look nearly as moronic as I felt.

"*Indians*, Mr. Molinari," she said, clearly disappointed in me.

"Oh, I—yeah, right—sure, that sounds good."

"All right then, you get to work putting all this away and I'll locate some appropriate selections for you. Yes?"

"Yes, ma'am," I said, gathering the books from the table. "Thank you."

Five minutes later Miss O'Doul was back with two thick and heavy books on Native American legends and myths. Both volumes were hardbacks and appeared to be quite old, but they not only contained a great deal of information, they were full of illustrations as well. I set to work, and spent the next hour or so carefully searching the first book, and then the second. After coming up empty, I was close to giving up, when I flipped another page and settled on illustration that stopped me cold. On the opposite page, a single word leapt off the page at me: *WENDIGO.*

I quickly read the description.

A mythological man-eating creature, sometimes an evil spirit, spoken of by the First Nations Algonquian tribes of Nova Scotia, Canada, upstate New York, and the north and southeast coast of the United States, among others. Gigantic and emaciated, it is often without lips, as it is said to gnaw them off in frenzied rage and hunger. Their horrifying screams have the ability to incapacitate or even kill those who hear them. A malevolent and sometimes cannibalistic supernatural being, the Wendigo gains its power and size from the flesh of the living, and its life from a human-shaped lump of ice that has replaced its heart. Although strongly associated with winter and starvation, the Wendigo can appear at any time, under any conditions, and in any locale it chooses. Often looking gaunt, it gives off a horrible stench of death and decay. Although different tribes have various names for it, in what is now known as the Commonwealth of Massachusetts, the Wampanoag Nation referred to the beast as a Chenoo, and believed it to be an evil spirit that in some cases had once been human but became possessed.

Seeing or encountering a Wendigo is sometimes interpreted as an omen, a warning of horrible or tragic things to come. It can also mean the person will soon become possessed by evil and gradually become a Wendigo themselves. Although some tribes had ceremonial rituals they believed could save a person being stalked or even possessed by a Wendigo, in most cases, once a person is overtaken, the only escape is death.

My eyes returned to the illustration of the creature.

Tall, thin, and gangly, its bones pushing out against gray skin partially covered in hair, it stood on two spindly but powerful-looking legs, possessed hoof-like feet and long arms with razor-like talons at the end of its hands. Its eyes were black and sunken into its skeletal, bizarre skull, which resembled a cross between a human being's and one belonging to some sort of long-snouted animal. Worse, jutting from its skull were large, bloody antlers.

I closed the book, my hands shaking. Could this really be true? Is this what my father and Shawn had seen, some crazy monster from ancient Indian legends, an evil spirit roaming the woods in search of human flesh to devour or souls to possess? It didn't seem possible, any of it. But I wasn't so sure that mattered now.

Scooping up the books, I carried them over to the front desk, where Miss O'Doul had taken up position, and returned them to her. I wanted to get out of there and get some fresh air and try to think. "Thanks again," I said.

"Any luck?"

"I'm not sure, but they were really interesting. Thanks."

"You're most welcome." She held an expression of deep concern I'd never seen in her before. "Are you all right, Francis? I hope the books didn't upset you."

"No, ma'am, they didn't." I forced a quick smile. "I just have to go. I got some stuff I got to do."

Miss O'Doul looked me over without subtlety. "Given the *circumstances* you've been through with your family of late, forgive me for saying so, but you look as if you've seen a ghost."

"Yeah," I said softly, heading for the exit. "I think maybe I have."

* * * *

As I pushed out through the heavy double front doors and down the cement steps to the walkway leading back to the street, I was greeted with a burst of heat. The sun was higher in the sky now, and the temperature had risen significantly. But that's not what stopped me in my tracks. It was something more. I looked back at the old building a moment. From a very young age I'd loved to read, and not just comics and magazines, but novels too. My parents were voracious readers and encouraged it in me, so by the 6th grade I'd started reading young adult novels, and by seventh I'd started in on adult novels too. J.R.R. Tolkien, Alistair MacLean, Hammond Innes, Ian Fleming, Ray Bradbury, I devoured them all. And when I came across an old edition of *I Am Legend* by Richard Matheson on one of the library paperback racks, brought it home and read it under the covers for three straight nights, it changed everything and helped me to understand that through these stories, anything was possible. Books allowed me to escape, but they also taught me things about myself and the world and those around me. By the time I'd finished *I Am Legend* I was so excited I showed it to the guys and they all read it too, even Shawn, who wasn't much of a novel reader. Books changed my life, and the library had always been something of a sanctuary for me, a place where all the answers were, all the knowledge, all the adventures, a place of endless possibilities. Everything was there, within those walls, sitting on those shelves, hidden between the covers of all those books. One only had to go and find them. And I had, as best as I knew how. But now, even this wonderful old place that had brought me such solace was suspect, as if whatever was between the covers of those old books had been waiting just for me this time, ready to jump out and burrow into my brain like a bad dream that wouldn't let go.

Maybe knowledge wasn't always a good thing after all.

"Figured this is where I'd find you."

Shawn, hands in his jean pockets, stood at the end of the walkway.

"What's up?" I said.

"Went by your house this morning," he told me. "Your dad answered the door like he was expecting the fucking Gestapo, wouldn't open it more than a crack. He looks rough, dude."

"Yeah," I said. "He hasn't been sleeping a lot lately."

"Me either." Shawn gave a little shrug. "I guess maybe I kinda know how he feels now, huh?"

I could only hope not.

"Anyway, he said you were out but he didn't know where, so I went looking for you. Thought this was as good a place to start as any."

There was a lot weighing on him. I felt it too. "Are you all right?" I asked.

He thought about it a while before he gave me an answer. "I don't know."

In all the years I'd known Shawn, I'd never heard his voice waver like that, never seen such indecision in him, such profound uncertainty, the kind that went right down to the bone.

I closed the gap between us and joined him on the sidewalk. "Shawn, the other day, I—"

"Don't worry about it."

"I'm sorry, man. I should've had your back, I—"

"I was being a dick."

"Me too," I said, offering my hand.

He slapped it and we stood there a while, draped in an awkward silence.

"You heard about Perry and Keith?" he finally asked.

I nodded.

Shawn motioned to the library with his chin. "You come here looking for an answer?"

"That was the plan," I said.

"You find one?"

"I don't know yet."

I noticed a police cruiser rolling down the street. As it drove past the library, I saw Officer Daniels behind the wheel. All stiff-brim hat, square jaw, and mirrored sunglasses, face as expressionless as always, like a mannequin, he slowly panned his head and looked in our direction.

"Oh, come on," I muttered. "Not this fucking asshole."

"Be cool," Shawn said as he struck a casual pose I'm sure he thought was inconspicuous. "We're not doing anything."

Thankfully, although it slowed, the police car never stopped. As it turned the corner and was gone, I let out a sigh of relief. Most of the police in town were okay and didn't bother with us unless we were truly in trouble. Officer Daniels was the exception. The least popular cop in town, he had a reputation for being wildly officious. He also liked hassling kids for no reason, including us, so I was glad he'd left us alone this time. Had we been anywhere other than in front of the library, we likely wouldn't have been so lucky.

But as soon as one fear receded, another took its place.

"Come on," Shawn said. "Let's get the hell out of here."

"Hold up."

He stopped, unsure of me again.

"Did you talk to the guys about Perry and Keith yet?" I asked.

"Nah, wanted to wait until we were all together."

"I think we should."

Shawn produced one of his bandanas from his back pocket and tied it around his head. "Want to do it now?"

"Yeah, I got an idea."

Somewhere deep in Shawn's eyes, the fondness he felt for me did its best to escape. "I was hoping you might."

CHAPTER TWELVE

EVERY SUMMER, THE Catholic church in town hosted bi-monthly dances as fundraisers. Aimed at teenagers, only kids 13 to 18 were allowed to attend. Generally hideous affairs, they were held in the rectory, an unimaginative and perpetually dusty building littered with religious statues. Normally crowded with banquet tables and chairs for bingo and other activities, they were cleared away to form a makeshift dancefloor ringed with metal folding chairs. On a riser along the back wall, a big bowl of fruit punch and homemade baked goods no one ever ate were displayed, and a morbidly obese middle-aged DJ with no concept of what kids our age were listening to spun old records from an antiquated sound system. Meanwhile, the parish priest, Father Dennis, along with a couple nuns, hovered over everyone to make sure none of those brave enough to actually do any dancing engaged in "inappropriate touching." If you could avoid getting your ass kicked or ridiculed by the older kids and maybe get a dance or two in with a girl that didn't find you too repellant, it was considered a win. And, of course, if you could get ahold of liquor, beer, or pot, it was best to show up stoned or drunk, both if at all possible. That's how awful these things were. But in 1977, in a town like Samoset, there wasn't a hell of a lot for kids to do, so most went to the dances anyway and, oddly, even looked forward to them.

One such funfest extravaganza was scheduled for that coming Friday night. Normally that would've been on our minds, as we were hormone-crazed virgins, and the dances provided one of the few opportunities we had to interact with girls in an environment where they might actually want to have something to do with us too. Shawn and I had both kissed girls by then, and even fooled around a little once or twice. Alex had done neither, and Max had his own deal, which in a sense freed him to be comfortable and better around girls. As a result, he was also far more popular with them than the rest of us were, so if he could avoid getting bullied—because crotches touching or brushing against a boob was unacceptable and sinful, but being beaten to a pulp outside by older kids for being gay was no problem whatsoever—he usually had a good time just dancing and having fun.

Same as a lot of other spots in town, a mimeographed handmade sign advertising the dance had been stapled to a telephone pole out in front of the local VFW building. It's what had set my mind to thinking about it in the first place, and it was then that I realized none of us had even mentioned the upcoming dance. It also reminded me what we should've been preoccupied with, and what we were burdened with instead.

Set back from the road and nestled in a horseshoe of forest, the VFW building was closed and quiet. It was a good place to talk, where we wouldn't have to worry about other people being around. We met out front and then walked around to the rear of the building where there were picnic tables and we could sit and talk and have some privacy. Since the things we needed to discuss were already weighing on us, our procession was quiet and solemn. As we made our way to the tables, I kept a close eye on the trees, worried a Wendigo really *was* out there, starving for human flesh and watching our every move.

Shawn climbed onto one of the tables and plunked himself down. "Okay, so, what do we do?"

He was looking at me, but it was Max that answered him.

"I think we need to tell the police."

"Fuck the pigs."

Max sighed. "Well, we need to tell someone."

"Tell them what?" Shawn asked.

"That we saw Perry and Keith in the woods and—"

"Why the fuck would we tell anyone that?"

Max sat on the bench. "Because it might be important, that's why."

"What do you think?" Shawn said, looking to Alex.

His expression revealed the level of his surprise at having been asked. "We tell people we saw those guys out there, it could get us in trouble, and—"

"Why would we get in trouble for trying to help?" Max asked.

"You need to think about something," Shawn said. "What if we were the last ones to see them?"

"What if we were?"

"Then we'll be right in the middle of this."

"But we didn't do anything wrong."

"Yeah, *we* know that, but you gonna trust the cops to believe it?"

"Perry and Keith are missing," Max said. "Maybe if the police knew where they'd last been seen it might help."

"Like I give two shits about helping the pigs or them." Shawn lit a cigarette. "Getting involved is a mistake, a big one."

"We're already involved," Max said. "We were there."

Sunlight bled through the trees, but the shade here was more than enough to protect us. Nearby, the sounds of passing cars along the road reached us, and then everything went quiet again. Unable to shake the sensation we were being observed, I tried to watch the forest without being too obvious about it.

"Shawn's right," I said. "Going to the cops is a bad idea, at least for now."

They all looked to me, as I'd been quiet since we got there.

"Why is it a bad idea?" Max pressed.

"What if they're still out there?"

"What do you mean by that?" Alex asked, edging closer to panic.

Before I could tell him, Shawn did it for me. "He means what if they're still out there, and they're not alive no more?"

"Jesus Christ, you—you think they're—you think they're fucking *dead*?"

"I don't know," I said. "But if they are and we were the last ones to see them alive then this could all come down on our heads."

Shawn exhaled a stream of smoke in Max's direction. "Get it now?"

"Yeah, I got it." Max rolled his eyes. "Thanks for checking in, Shawn."

"They probably just took off," Alex said. "Did I miss something? Why would you think they were dead?"

Max held his hands up. "Here's all I'm saying. Even if something did happen to them, why would it come down on our heads? We're not killers. We're a bunch of kids."

"A bunch of kids who've been bullied by those two assholes for years," Shawn reminded him.

"Along with almost everyone else in town," Max said.

"Yeah, well maybe we had enough, or maybe it was an accident. That's how the fucking pigs think."

"Oh, you're an expert on the police now?"

"I know enough to know I don't fucking trust them."

"This is crazy."

You have no idea, I thought. But that was about to change.

"I think there's more to what's going on in this town," I announced, letting the words hang in the air a while. No one responded, they all just looked at me and waited. "I think I might know what Shawn saw in the woods that day."

"Man, come on, not this bullshit again." Alex dismissively waved a hand in the air. "He saw a fucking deer."

"No he didn't."

Shawn took a couple pulls on his cigarette. "I didn't get a close enough look to know for sure what it was. But Frankie Boy's right. It wasn't a deer."

"You guys ever heard of something called a Wendigo?" I asked.

"Yeah," Alex said.

He answered me so quickly I was stunned.

"You have?"

"Yeah," he looked at each of us in turn like we'd lost our minds. "Couple years ago Hulk fought a Wendigo. I don't remember the issue, but I got it at home."

"I don't know what it is," Max said, "but are you seriously standing there telling us you think Shawn saw something from a Hulk comic?"

"It's a real thing," Alex said. "Well, I mean, it's like—what do you call it—*based*—it's based on a real thing. Like a legend or whatever. It's kinda like a Bigfoot sorta, or at least that's what it was like in the comic. Like a Adombidle Snowman, or something."

"*Abominable*," Max said.

"Whatever, you know what I mean."

"It's an Indian legend," I said. "And the real thing, if there is a real thing, isn't like that at all. It's something else. It's something a whole lot worse."

"This is stupid." Max stood up, looking like he intended to leave. "I mean *really* stupid. It's so stupid it's actually too stupid to even talk about."

"Right on," Alex said. "It was cool when Hulk fought him, but it's not real, Frankie Boy. It's just stories, man, it's a fucking monster."

"So what?"

"No such thing."

"You sure? Because I'm not, and I...*we*...need to find out."

"I know garden gnomes aren't real," Max said. "I don't need to find evidence that they're not real. I just know they're not, because I'm not a moron and I'm not six fucking years old."

"You think I'm either of those things, Max?" I asked. "Do you think Shawn is, or how about my father?"

"Of course not, I just..."

Shawn slid down off the table. "I know I saw something. I don't know what, but I know what it wasn't too. You say we need to find out if this thing's real. This..."

"Wendigo. The Indians around here called it a Chenoo. That's what I was researching at the library this morning."

"Fine, whatever the fuck it's called." Shawn dropped his cigarette to the ground and squished it with his sneaker. "How do we find out?"

"Been thinking about that," I said. "And the way I figure it, we've got a couple things we can do. One, we talk to somebody who might know."

"Like who?"

"A real Indian."

"Shit," Alex chuckled. "Only Indian I know is Mean Earl."

I nodded. "Yeah."

"You really have lost your mind," Max said through another sigh.

Shawn slid his sunglasses on. "What's the other thing?"

"We go back to the woods and see for ourselves if there's any trace of the Wendigo or Perry and Keith," I said. "Or any clue about what happened to them."

"That one sounds safer than going anywhere near Mean Earl," Alex said.

I was about to tell them I'd do it alone if need be, when the sound of tires on dirt distracted us all, turning our attention toward the road.

A police cruiser slowly rolled around to the back of the building.

"Great, it's that piece of shit Daniels again," Shawn said.

Alex was already jittery, and I couldn't blame him. "Again?"

"We saw him before over by the library. He must've followed us, saw us meet up with you guys and come back here."

"Oh, man," Alex said. "Fuck off."

I looked to Max. "Don't be a wiseass."

Max placed a hand flat against his chest and feigned shock. "*Moi?*"

"I'm serious."

He gave me a look that said he'd try, but there were never any promises from Max when it came to such things. "This day just keeps getting better."

We watched as the police car came to a stop, dust from the dirt road kicking up, swirling and dancing around like ghosts. The sun reflecting off the windshield made it difficult to see the officer behind the wheel, but as was his custom, Daniels remained there for what seemed an inordinate amount of time before finally stepping from his vehicle.

He stood watching us, silent and expressionless, our images reflected in the mirrored lenses of his sunglasses. I became aware of Officer Daniels when I was nine years old, and had literally never seen him without them. He wore them year round, and if he ever worked nights he probably had them on then too.

"Line up right there," he finally said, motioning to the closest picnic table. "Keep your hands out of your pockets and where I can see them."

"Is there a problem, officer?" Max asked.

Daniels' expression remained blank. "I'll say it one more time. Line up right there. Keep your hands out of your pockets and where I can see them."

We all grudgingly shuffled into a line, hands at our sides.

With one hand resting on the butt of his holstered revolver, he took a step closer and placed his other hand on his waist. "What are you doing back here?"

"Just talking," Shawn said. "You know, hanging out."

He moved down the line, stopped in front of me. "That right?"

"Yes, sir," I said.

"Who gave you permission to be here?"

None of us answered, but my heart was pounding my chest so hard it was starting to hurt. Usually our interactions with Daniels consisted of him telling us to move along or enduring a quick hassle and it was over and done with. He'd threaten us but never actually do anything. But we'd never encountered him in a situation like this, away from the road and any potential witnesses.

"I asked you punks a question."

"Nobody," Shawn said.

Daniels slid back down the line so he could stand in front of Shawn. "This is private property," he said evenly. "State your business here."

"Are you serious?" Max said. "We were just sitting at the tables getting some shade and talking, all right? We didn't do anything wrong."

"Trespassing is illegal." Daniels' upper lip quivered a bit. It reminded me of a dog right before it bites. "It's a crime. A crime you're all committing by being here without permission."

"We can just take off," I said. "We didn't mean to do anything wrong."

Daniels stood staring at Max for what seemed an eternity. At least I think he was staring at him. His eyes were hidden but he took up position directly in front of him and hadn't moved.

"So?" Max asked after a moment. "Can we go?"

"Negative."

"What do you want us to say? We're sorry? Fine, we're sorry."

"Shut your mouth," Daniels said, but his voice was still even and eerily calm. "And keep it shut, Sally."

Max's face flushed. "My name's not Sally. It's Max, and this is—"

"Speak when spoken to." One hand still on his gun, his other slowly slid the nightstick from his belt. "Understood, Sally?"

Daniels stood before him, subtly tapping the nightstick down against his leg. When Max didn't answer, he brought it up quickly, placing it under Max's chin and using it to raise his head so that he was looking at him.

"Yes, all right?" Max said. "I understand. Jesus."

"You got one hell of an attitude on you, faggot. Now either you adjust it," he said, leaning so close to Max that the brim of his hat made contact with his forehead. "Or I'll do it for you. Do you read me?"

"Yes," Max said softly.

Daniels stepped back and seemed to notice Alex for the first time. The smallest of us and clearly the most frightened, he was too easy of a mark to miss. "You boys come back here to break in and rob the place?"

"No, sir," Alex said, staring straight ahead.

"Who robs a VFW?" Shawn said.

He didn't need to speak just then, and I wished he'd just be quiet and let this be over, but I knew what he was doing. He was saving us like always, trying to take a bullet so we wouldn't have to.

Daniels moved in front of him again. "Unless I ask you a question, keep your mouth shut."

Shawn gave a defiant smirk. "What do you think we're gonna steal, banquet chairs?"

Daniels placed the end of the nightstick against Shawn's chest. "You're a tough guy, is that it, O'Hara?"

"Tough enough."

"You're just a punk."

"And you're an idiot."

In a flash, the nightstick lunged into Shawn's abdomen. With a grunt, he collapsed to his knees, clutching his midsection.

"What do think you're doing?" Max dropped next to Shawn and put his arms around him. "Are you okay?"

Rather than answer, Shawn vomited.

"Back in line," Daniels said.

"Are you out of your mind?" Max stood up. "You just assaulted a fourteen-year-old kid."

"Who says?"

"We're all witnesses."

"O'Hara got sick, threw up all over the place. Probably nerves, I'm sure he'll be just fine." Using the stick, Daniels moved Max back into line. "It's the word of a police officer with an impeccable record against a bunch of little punks. Now unless you want to join badass down there holding your guts, shut your queer-boy mouth. Fucking faggot, you make me sick."

"Look, what do you want us to do?" I asked. Last thing I wanted to do was make things worse, but I couldn't take much more of this. From the looks of Alex and Max, they couldn't either. "You know us, Officer Daniels. You know we're not bad kids. We just came back here to talk and get some shade. That's all, I swear. We won't say anything about any of this and we won't come back here again. We just want to leave, okay?"

Daniels moved back toward me, his movements reminiscent of a drill sergeant walking back and forth in front of a line of recruits. "There doesn't seem to be any damage to the building or surrounding area," he said. "So

I'm willing to consider that, Molinari. Are any of you holding anything I need to be aware of?"

"No, sir," I said.

"You sure about that, boy?"

"Yes, sir."

He nodded. "Then we can resolve this situation with some apologies."

Shawn had gotten back to his feet, but he was fuming. "What do you want us to apologize for?"

"Wasting my time with this nonsense when I could be doing important police business," Daniels said. "Running that wise mouth of yours, and hell, O'Hara, you almost got vomit on my shoes. Next time might be blood."

"We're all sorry," I said.

Daniels pointed at Alex with his nightstick.

"I'm sorry."

When Daniels next pointed to Max, he mumbled an apology.

I did the same, and then glanced at Shawn. Our eyes met and I quickly mouthed the words: *Do it.*

"What about you, vomit boy? Are you sorry too?"

Shawn drew a deep breath. "Yeah."

"Yeah what?"

"Yeah," he said, nibbling his lower lip, "I'm sorry."

Daniels slid the nightstick into his belt and started back toward his car. He'd only gotten a few steps when he stopped, looked back at us, and made a sweeping gesture in the direction of the road. "You're free to go, gentlemen."

We filed out. No one said anything or looked back, but we could hear the cruiser slowly coming up behind us. When we reached the road and started down the sidewalk, Daniels pulled out and sped off.

Max put a hand on Shawn's shoulder. "Are you all right?"

"Yeah, don't worry about it. Thanks."

"That guy's such an asshole," Alex said. "Jesus, I thought I was gonna piss my fucking pants, fellas, no lie."

"He's fucking crazy, that's what he is." Max ran a hand through his hair and watched the street as if he expected Daniels to hear him and return at any moment. "Bastard gets his jollies fucking with us."

Shawn lit a cigarette. His hands were shaking. "So what do you guys think now, huh? Still want to go to the pigs?"

"He's one cop," Max said. "There are other good officers that—"

"Aw, horseshit, this is—"

"We handle it ourselves," I said, stretching a little in an attempt to lessen the tension in my body. "Period, that's it."

Max frowned. "Can't we talk about this?"

"We're done talking. We go back to the woods and see what we can see. If I have to, I'll even talk to Mean Earl, but we're handling this shit ourselves." I looked at each of them in turn. No one argued. "There's no other way."

There never really had been. Deep down I'd known that for quite a while.

Now, they did too.

CHAPTER THIRTEEN
~2017~

WE STAND AT the gates to this sea of tombstones, this place of death and loss, a couple old ghosts ourselves. Haunted by those boys we'd once been, and the forty years since we've spent trying to forget, we scan the grounds and realize that now, we are three.

"My God," Max says. "It's him."

Several rows in, a large Harley Davidson motorcycle is parked, a man dressed in a black leather jacket, black jeans, and black boots leaned against it. Smoking a cigarette, he stares at the headstone before him. His hair, once dirty blond, is now gone, his head completely shaved.

We start toward him, moving carefully amidst the graves. The same as it's always been, this is a place where time stands still. We're outsiders, intruders in this land of the departed, but only for now. I can feel the objections of the dead swirling around us like dust devils—not anger, only sorrow—and the deeper we go the more unsettling it becomes.

This is no place for the living.

Even as I get within a few feet of him, I still can't believe it. Yet when he turns and looks at me with those ice-blue eyes, there is no mistaking who it is. They no longer hold the fire they once did—time and trauma has dulled them—and he's significantly older, with gray stubble dotting his face, the lines there pronounced against skin leathery and darkened from years spent in the sun.

Slowly, he turns in our direction and squints at us through a cloud of smoke. The life he's led these years is burned into him like a brand, his scars obvious, both figurative and literal. He couldn't hide them if he wanted to, and I suspect it's been a very long time since he's even tried.

"Shawn," I say with a cautious smile.

At first he doesn't say anything, and for a moment I fear he never will. But then he takes another drag on his cigarette, drops it to the ground, grinds it out with the toe of his scuffed boot, and pushes away from his bike.

"It's really you," I say.

"Live in person." He extends a hand. "What do you say, Frankie Boy?"

I shake his hand. Years of manual labor has left his skin cracked and rough with calluses, and his grip is powerful to the point of being painful, like maybe he's still trying to prove something even all these years later.

"It's good to see you," I say, as he releases my hand.

"You too, man." He turns to Max. "Get a load of this guy. Hiya, Max."

Ignoring his offer to shake hands, Max goes in for a hug instead.

At first Shawn remains perfectly still, but eventually he hugs back, pulling him in close. After a moment, he motions for me to join them, and I do.

Once our embrace ends, Shawn wanders back to his motorcycle and motions halfheartedly at the headstone before us. It belongs to his parents. According to the dates, his father died in 1999, at only sixty-one, and his mother followed in 2008, not long after her seventieth birthday. "First time I've ever seen their graves," he says with a sigh. "Ain't that a bitch?"

"I'm sorry," I say, remembering how cool his father was, and how he always called me *youngblood*. Memories of his mother hit me next, of what a kind and sweet person she was, and how she'd pranced around like something conjured straight out of our adolescent fantasies. "I didn't know they were gone."

"The old man dropped dead of a heart attack." He states this matter-of-factly and with a troubling lack of emotion, as if he's explaining something terribly mundane. "Mom got colon cancer, wasted away a while before it took her."

"I'm sorry, Shawn," Max says. "I had no idea they'd passed either. You didn't come back for their funerals?"

"Couldn't," he says. "Turns out I had a previous engagement as a guest of the state of New Mexico at the time. Armed robbery, hit a bank with a couple other idiots. I'd been in jail here and there a few times over the years, but nothing major. Outdid myself on that one though. Prison ain't jail, learned that real quick."

"How long were you incarcerated?" Max asks.

"Ten years."

His words hang there between us. I try to imagine Shawn locked in a cage for a decade, but it's too horrific.

"One stretch in the big leagues was enough for me," he says. "I've been working construction ever since. I don't much like talking about all that, but I figured I'd get it out of the way right off the bat with you guys."

"I'm just glad you straightened out." Max awkwardly clears his throat.

"Yeah," I add. "Good to hear that's over with."

Shawn eyes us a moment, as if to be sure we're serious. "Anyway, my old man died a few months after I went in, my mom a year before I got out. I've been free and clear for nine years now, just never saw any reason to come back. Not like they know I'm here. Shit, they're not even here, not really."

I'm not so certain.

"To be honest," Max says, "I wasn't sure you'd come back this time either."

"That makes two of us." Shawn gazes out at a newer section of cemetery a few rows away. On the backside of the headstone marking the graves of both Alex's mother and her boyfriend Rafe, a third plot is open but covered with a blue tarp, awaiting the body. "I always hoped I'd never have to come back to this fucking town. But I couldn't avoid it. Not this time. I just didn't expect to see you guys here. Figured I'd see you tomorrow, but…"

"We didn't mean to ambush you," I explain. "We didn't even know you were in town yet. We just came to visit my dad's grave."

The respect Shawn feels for my father is evident in his expression, as I knew it would be. We're forever tied to him, all of us. "That was my next stop."

"My mother's gone too. She died in California. She was cremated out there and her ashes were scattered over the Pacific."

"So we're both orphans then." Shawn flashes the same wiseass smirk I remember. "How about you Max? You in the club too?"

"Afraid not, somehow my parents are both still kicking."

I expect a darkly humorous retort. Instead, we fall awkwardly silent, alone with the dead. None of this seems possible. But then, it never much has.

With a casual look of menace I assume has become second nature for him, Shawn slips out of his leather jacket and throws it across the seat of his motorcycle. He's wearing nothing under it, and as he grabs a t-shirt from a roll of clothes fastened to the rear of the bike, I'm envious of the shape he's stayed in over the years. Slim but thickly muscled, there isn't an ounce of fat on him. Both ears are pierced, and tattoos adorn his arms as well as his chest and stomach and back—mostly devils, demons, skulls and the like, along with black vines and barbed wire that curls around his biceps and forearms—his fears literally written and drawn across his flesh. If I didn't know him—and I hope I still do—I'd likely be afraid of him. And given our past, I am not one who frightens easily. Shawn puts the shirt on, and then a pair of sunglasses. With those blue eyes concealed he becomes unrecognizable as the boy that was once one of my best friends. Hiding in plain sight, he fires up another cigarette and says, "Ready?"

Together, the three of us walk through the field of headstones until we reach my father's grave. A modest stone, it stands by itself at the end of a row. With me living so far away, and my mother's memory nowhere to be found, as if she never existed in his life at all, even in death he remains hopelessly alone.

I can still feel his pain, his fear, and it breaks my heart all over again.

Memories of the last time I saw my father's face come to me, and despite my best efforts to prevent it, my eyes fill with tears. The world blurs. Choking back emotion and wiping my eyes, I turn my back on the gravesite. "Sorry."

Suddenly there's a hand on my shoulder. Shawn. "Don't apologize."

"As it is we have to come back here tomorrow for the funeral," Max says. "Maybe we should leave for now and—"

"Yeah," I interrupt, facing them again. "I'm ready to go if you guys are."

"Where you two staying?" Shawn asks.

"I didn't get anything yet," I tell him.

"Normally I would've booked something ahead of time." Max shakes his head, disappointed in himself. "I wasn't thinking clearly, but I should've known better. This close to Cape Cod in summer, nobody's going to have vacancies."

"Is the Friendly still in business?"

Shawn's grinning, and I can't help but chuckle at the mere mention of it myself. A seedy little roadside motel in existence since the 1950s, the Friendly Motor Inn was a no-frills place with cheap rooms located on the outskirts of town, not far from Alex's childhood home. At one point or another nearly everyone eighteen or older took a girlfriend there for sex, because you could check in with cash and no questions asked. Back in the day, flopping at the Friendly Motor Inn—or the Friendly, as everyone called it—was a rite of passage. I'd been a few times myself, but never stayed the night. I didn't know anyone who had. Couple hours of sex then you were right back out the door so you could drop your girlfriend off and be home yourself before it got too late.

"Oh my God," Max says, fiddling with his phone. "Believe it or not, it is."

"No shit?"

Max faces his phone out so we can see the screen. "No shit."

"Sounds like a plan."

"Yeah," I say, "let's do it."

Max puts his phone away. "Since I'm the only one that's never been there, I suppose now's as good a time as any."

"If it's anything like it used to be, you don't know what you've been missing." I roll my eyes. "It'll be different actually *staying* there, though."

"Tell me about it," Shawn says. "I think my record was about three hours, and that included taking a shower."

I walk back to my father's stone, place my hand on it and silently tell him I love and miss him more than he knows. And then, ignoring the woods at the edge of the cemetery, the trees like sentries watching our every move, I turn back to the others.

"Come on." There's more to talk about, but no one wants to do it here. "Let's get the hell out of here."

* * *

As it turns out, the Friendly hasn't changed much. It remains dated and no-frills, the rooms outfitted with a double bed, coin-operated tube televisions (complete with rabbit ears), and the most basic accommodations imaginable.

When we were kids, it was owned by a man we knew simply as Reggie. An older guy, with sprigs of white hair jutting out from either side of his otherwise bald head, he chewed tobacco, was always drunk, and lived in a small apartment attached to the office with his Korean wife, a woman several years younger than he was. They operated the motel together, but ironically, neither was known for being particularly accommodating, much less friendly.

They're both long gone now, and we are checked in instead by a bored twentysomething woman who does her best to make sure there's still nothing friendly about the Friendly.

Because there are only two other people staying here, we get our own rooms. Shawn and I pay cash. Max uses American Express. Once settled in, we all meet in Shawn's room and decide to venture out in search of food.

"Hey," Shawn says, "I wonder if the Samoset Grill is still around?"

Five minutes later, we find out it's not. The building is there, but it's been completely redone and is now a family restaurant sitting on a nicely paved lot. Though it's not what we hoped for, it looks clean and relatively welcoming, and we're hungry, so in we go.

With memories of greasy burgers, clouds of cigarette smoke, and ripping the place off blind dancing in my head, what I find instead is a rather generic looking place with booths and a few tables. The kitchen is in back now and hidden from view, and the old magazine rack is no more.

"Jesus, it's a whole new place," Shawn says, looking around.

Some things stay the same. It's just usually not the ones you want to.

A hostess seats us in a booth and hands us three laminated menus before moving away. Max and I take one side. Shawn sits alone on the other.

"Can't believe the old place is gone," Shawn says.

"This is actually a lot nicer." Max opens his menu.

"Yeah, but the grill had…"

"Character," I say.

Shawn points at me. "Exactly."

"Well, at least the Friendly's still a fucking dump."

"The rooms look exactly the same, don't they?"

"Smell the same too," I add.

Max laughs lightly, flipping through the menu. "Yes, I noticed mine had a rather peculiar odor. If I'm not mistaken, regret, with a sprinkling of despair."

"That'd be it," Shawn says.

As they chat I glance at the menu but catch myself staring at Shawn. I know it's him, of course, but if I passed him on the street after all these years, I wouldn't recognize him. We've all gotten older, and we've all changed, but there's something about Shawn that's terribly damaged now. Far beyond that which Max and I have sustained. When he speaks, or if I look into his eyes, I see the old Shawn—the one I knew, he's still in there, in the same way that there are still parts of our younger versions in all of us—but it's different with him. There are pieces of Shawn missing. Who he is now is all that's left. Maybe that's true of all of us, and I'm just putting more on him because his looks have changed so drastically and he's done time in prison and been through God knows what else in the years since I've seen him. But I don't think so. We're all haunted, all of us broken. But those pieces of Shawn aren't just missing, they're dead.

"What?" he asks, having caught me staring.

"Nothing, sorry, I…" I return my attention to the menu. "Just zoned out there for a minute, I'm tired and hungry is all."

Once I decide what I want I put the menu aside. It's then that I notice we're the only customers here. I can only hope it's due to this being an odd time of day, somewhere between lunch and dinner, rather than bad food.

I stay quiet while Max tells Shawn about his husband and daughter, and then shows him the same photographs on his phone he showed me earlier. Shawn seems genuinely happy for Max, but there's something more there, and when he explains he too has children, two grown sons he hasn't seen since they were babies with a woman he hasn't spoken to in years, and four grandchildren he's never laid eyes on, it's evident why this subject is so painful for him.

"I'm sorry," Max says softly. "I didn't mean to—"

"There's nothing for you to be sorry about, man. I fucked up, you didn't."

"I fucked up plenty, Shawn, trust me."

"Even more reason to be proud of what you got now."

The idea of Shawn being a grandfather is the most sobering thing I've heard in quite a while. It puts things in perspective, and quickly.

"You've never even *seen* your grandkids?" Max asks.

Shawn guiltily shakes his head no. "Not a one."

"Well, maybe you could—"

"They're better off, Maxie."

"That's not true, you—"

"They're better off."

"Okay, what about you then?"

"I'm ashamed," he says evenly. "Okay?"

I see an opening and take it. "Look, maybe we should just—"

"That's not what I meant," Max interrupts. "Are *you* better off?"

"Max," I say, "let it go, huh?"

"I'm only trying to—"

"It's okay." Shawn looks down at the table. "It is what it is."

I suggest, calmly as possible, that we talk about something else.

"Cool," Shawn says. "What about you, Frankie Boy?"

I knew it was coming but still feel unprepared. Unlike Max, I have a feeling Shawn won't let it rest, but I stall for time anyway. "What about me?"

"You got a wife and kids?"

"No."

He arches an eyebrow. "No?"

"No."

"You divorced?"

"I've never been married."

"You're shitting me."

"I'm a high school teacher," I tell him. "I work a lot. I've had a couple serious relationships but nothing ever panned out for me in that department."

"And no kids either?"

I give him the stock answer. "None that I know of."

Shawn looks genuinely surprised, and more than a little disappointed. "Always figured you'd end up with the wife and kids, the dog, the whole bit."

"Honestly, so did I," Max says.

Thankfully, before I can say anything more about it, a middle-aged waitress arrives with three glasses of water, introduces herself as Wanda, and asks to take our orders. I've never been so happy to see a waitress in all my life.

Max gets a tuna salad on rye and a side salad. I go for a turkey club with fries and a Diet Coke, and Shawn orders a bacon cheeseburger with extra bacon and extra cheese, a large side of onion rings, and a bottle of Budweiser.

"Jesus," Max says, laughing. "Are you planning on having the heart attack right here at the table or later tonight?"

I'm grateful to see Shawn laugh too. "Fuck it, I smoke like a chimney, drink like a fish, and eat whatever the hell I want."

"In the shape you're in you can get away with it. I'm envious, actually."

"God, me too," I say. "Wish I could still eat like that."

"What the hell's the matter with you guys? Couple old farts. It's a fucking burger, for Christ's sake, calm down. Don't you get those at the nursing home?"

"They're not regularly on the menu, no," Max says.

"Soups," I tell him. "Mostly soups and porridges, but there's bingo twice a week, crafts every Wednesday, and we get to watch all the *Matlock* we want. So, you know, there's that."

It feels good to joke and laugh, even if just for a little while. For a brief moment we're kids again, alive in ways I haven't felt in a very long time. But it's not the same, and we know it. Alex is missing, and without him, so are we. Those people are gone and they're not coming back no matter how hard we try to pretend they are. People are dead, and we're fatally wounded, stumbling along and trying to make sense of things before we fall to dust along with them. Only the evil remains, the madness. It never lets go. It never lets us forget. We know that all too well, each of us, in our own ways. There can be no real peace, only learning to live with the knowledge that evil is never far and, given the chance, is ready to resume its place in our minds, hearts, and whatever's left of our souls. Once something is possible, once it's real, you can never escape it. Not really.

Not ever.

CHAPTER FOURTEEN
~1977~

EVERY SMALL TOWN had one. The outcast, the hermit, the strange and misunderstood pariah no one really knew but was deathly afraid of. Accounts of their alleged dark and disturbing offences swept through a community like a virus whispered from one resident to another. These tall tales could never be verified, of course, because the witness or person in the know was always a friend of a friend, a distant relative or someone no longer among the living, but those who told such stories always swore they were true. Eventually the person in question achieved a mythic, rather legendary status, and were no longer just odd, lost, antisocial, or shunned souls living on the periphery of society, but something far worse. The more involved the stories became, the more the person ceased to be wholly human, and were instead relegated to the realm of savage psychopathic killers and rapists, eaters of children, monsters, witches, demons and the like. In the end, despite all the dramatics, it was really just a rationalization for treating people different from themselves as second-class citizens. It often took the form of racism, classism, and simple abject cruelty, as it was usually aimed at people who were, for any number of immoral reasons, deemed different from, and therefore inferior to, the so-called norm. Regardless, the end result was the same. They were the *other*, and that made them evil. Such hideous creatures needed to be kept separate and apart from decent, God-fearing folk, and were to be feared and avoided at all costs. Those foolish enough to ignore the warnings lost their minds, souls, or maybe even their lives. Sometimes they simply went missing and were never seen or heard from again. And despite the fact that no one could be sure any of these alleged victims had ever actually existed, the stories persisted nonetheless. Eventually, they became fact.

In Samoset, that person was known as Mean Earl.

His real name was Earl Gordon Lopez, but I didn't know that then. I also had no idea that he was a former member of the United States Army, and a veteran of the Korean War. Earl was a direct descendant of the Wampanoag Tribe, and sadly, despite the area's rich First Peoples history, and the fact that our town and several others bore the names of their ancestors, at that point in my life, he was the only actual living Indian I'd ever seen outside of a Western on television. Many of the Wampanoag died in the early 1600s due to a bacterial epidemic believed to be smallpox, then nearly half of the surviving population were slaughtered from 1675 to 1676, during what became known as King Phillip's War. Many of the survivors were sold into slavery, while the rest were segregated and allowed to live in much of their traditional lands, but were also forced to assimilate. When I learned about the Wampanoag in school, the truth behind their history was largely denied or highly sanitized, and I was unaware of the realities of what had taken place until I was a college student. The horrible injustices suffered by native peoples were always set in the Wild West, in a different time and place. Here we were taught that the Pilgrims and Indians were friends and got along famously. But then where were they? Their names were everywhere. There were stories and statues, yet they themselves were largely absent as real, breathing, living human beings. I knew they existed, of course, but never saw them, and in my somewhat sheltered life at the time, I suppose it never occurred to me to question why an entire group of human beings were, for lack of a better word, missing so thoroughly from the landscape of my daily life. The harsh and inconvenient reality was that we were living in a place with a brutally violent past and an entitled, indifferent present that had been built atop their corpses, their blood, and their ravaged, largely forgotten history. Perhaps that was why so much darkness and underlying evil still seemed to lurk in the shadows of this ancient, and to the Wampanoag, sacred land.

As for Mean Earl, he was known as a strange and disagreeable loner, a man in his middle forties that owned and operated the only junkyard in town and was rarely seen beyond the confines of his property. I'd only seen him from a distance, but at well over six feet and weighing more than two hundred pounds, Mean Earl was a formidable and imposing figure. And of course the stories people told about him were terrifying.

I wasn't sure I believed them all, but being fourteen years old, and just as susceptible to urban legends and the hysteria that often accompanied them as anyone else, I wasn't sure I didn't either.

Mean Earl once killed a man in a bar fight. Beat him to death with his bare hands, then laughed about it while a bar room full of people looked on in horror. Because those who had witnessed it were so afraid of him, and his black magic, no one would testify against him, and he was never arrested for the crime. He snapped men's bones for the fun of it, strangled dogs and cats, and once murdered a lost child who mistakenly wandered into his junkyard. The animal bodies he burned in his incinerator. The child he buried under a pile of used car parts and old kitchen appliances. Some even claimed to know the exact location of the boy's grave but were too afraid to go and investigate. Even the cops feared him, so the stories went, because Mean Earl worshipped the Devil. He conducted all sorts of bizarre rituals in the dead of night, bathed in the blood of animals he'd butchered and sacrificed, or according to some stories, runaways and missing teenagers he'd kidnapped, tortured, and murdered. According to the legend, if you went to the junkyard at night you could hear the screams of Mean Earl's victims in the darkness all around you, echoing through the forest and along the dirt road leading in. If it was a full moon, you might even see some of their ghosts haunting the grounds, or the Devil himself, conjured during one of Earl's blasphemous moonlight ceremonies. Because Mean Earl had made a deal with Satan years before, you see, while in combat in Korea, where he first got his taste for killing and human blood. Hoping to survive the war, he made a bargain that would get him home safely. In return, for the remainder of his days, he would be a soldier for Satan, and gladly do his bidding without question or protest, regardless of what the Prince of Darkness demanded.

The junkyard, located at the end of a lonely road in a largely wooded area in the northern and less-populated part of town, was comprised of several acres and included an office and a small shack where Earl supposedly also lived. The entire place was surrounded by high chain-link fence, complete with barbed wire strung along the top. To us, at the time, this was a mysterious and dangerous compound, Mean Earl's literal lair, so venturing beyond those old metal gates was nearly as terrifying as the man himself.

It didn't help that the weather had started to shift. Though still warm, it had become quite overcast, the sun now hidden from view behind a series of dark clouds that had slowly rolled in along the horizon. A slight but steady breeze had picked up as well. There was a storming coming.

Given the circumstances, it seemed fitting.

With the junkyard about fifty yards in the distance, we stood off to the side of the road and scoped it out as best we could. It was quiet, and nothing was moving in there from what we could see, which from our perspective was just a bunch of trashed cars and countless heaps of throwaway items tossed aside into haphazard stacks in an attempt at order.

"You sure you want to do this?" Alex kept his voice low for fear Mean Earl might hear him somehow.

"No," I said. "But I'm doing it anyway."

"You know what people say, man."

I gave a defiant nod.

"You don't really believe all that nonsense, do you?" Max asked.

"Maybe I do and maybe I don't," Alex said. "Doesn't much matter, I'm not the one going in there."

"Fuck it," Shawn said. "I'll go with you, Frankie Boy."

"No. I'm going alone." I drew a deep breath. "You guys hang here."

"Why go by yourself?" Max said. "Shawn's willing to—"

"If I'm not back in half an hour tops, take off and get help. Got it?"

"What are you hoping he's going to know?" Max asked.

"I don't know for sure," I said. "But it's got to be more than we know now. If we're going back into those woods to try to find this thing, I want to know as much as I can about what we're up against before we do."

Shawn slapped me on the back. "You got some major league gonads, Frankie Boy, I'll give you that."

"Here." Alex slid a small penknife from his pocket. "Good thing Daniels didn't search us or make us empty our pockets, he would've taken it."

"Hell's he supposed to do with that?" Shawn said. "Clean his fingernails?"

"It's better than going in there with nothing, isn't it?" Alex's face flushed with embarrassment. "Fine, whatever then, he doesn't have to take it."

"It's cool," I said. "Let me have it just in case."

Alex handed me the knife. "Blade's small but really sharp."

"Thanks, man." I stuffed it into my pocket. "Hope I won't have to find out."

Max looked almost as worried as Alex. "Please be careful in there."

"Just remember," I said, heart racing as I started for the gates, "half an hour tops."

A minute later I had passed through the open gates and was standing amidst the piles of junk. Even in the open air, the area smelled of gasoline and grease. I looked back. The guys, huddled along the side of the road, were hiding behind some brush and small trees. Alex reached out, gave me a thumbs up.

With my heart pounding so hard in my chest I could hear it thumping, I scanned the place. Another sixty yards in, a dilapidated tow truck was parked out in front of a small ramshackle building. Above the only door an old white sign with faded black letters spelled out the word OFFICE.

A strange whistling sounded somewhere behind me, but I was so nervous by the time I realized it was one of the guys trying to alert me while sounding like some sort of bird, it was too late.

"*What do you want, boy?*"

I spun around to find Mean Earl standing right next to me. I'd never heard him coming, yet he was less than two feet away. It was as if he'd materialized out of thin air. My stomach clenched and my bowels followed. Certain I was about to empty my terror directly into my pants, I tried to respond but couldn't get any words out. Though my instinct was to run, my feet wouldn't budge.

Mean Earl, dressed in a ratty Army jacket, t-shirt, filthy jeans, and a pair of badly worn Dingo boots, towered over me, looking impossibly larger at close range than he had from a distance. His chest was broad, his shoulders wide, arms thick and powerful, his hands enormous, the fingers crooked and looking like they'd been broken numerous times. His face was smeared with grease, like he'd just gotten out from under a car or working on some engine, and his hair hung loose to just beyond his shoulders, black and straight and pushed straight back off of his brooding, chiseled face. In that moment I'd have sworn his dark eyes were black as coal as well, and held a cruelty beyond anything I'd ever before seen, but I was so frightened I couldn't be sure of anything other than my sudden urge to use a bathroom.

He squinted at me and cocked his head as if baffled. "You deaf?" he asked. His voice was deep and gravelly, like he'd just gargled crushed glass.

"No, sir," I managed, my voice trembling almost as bad as the rest of me.

"I asked what you want."

"I wanted to—to talk to you," I stammered.

Mean Earl watched me a while. "Were you planning on doing it today?"

"Sorry, I—need—I need to ask you—"

"You looking for work? I got nothing for you, if that's what this is about."

"I'm not looking for a job."

He spat on the ground, not far from my feet. It hit the dirt like a bullet. "How old are you, boy?"

"Fourteen."

"And just what in the hell's a fourteen-year-old white boy want with me?"

"I'm not a white boy. I'm Italian."

He scrunched his face up like he smelled something bad. "What?"

"I just meant they sometimes say I'm not white either, I—"

"There something wrong with you, boy?" He sized me up like he couldn't believe I was still standing there. "You slow, little soft in the head maybe?"

"No, sir," I answered, my knees shaking so badly I thought my legs might give out. All I could think about were the things people said about him, and here I was within his grasp and I'd already pissed him off.

He widened his stance, folded his arms across his chest, and glared down at me. "Then this is the last time I'm asking. What do you want?"

I cleared my throat and swallowed a huge pool of spit that had formed under my tongue. "I need your help."

"My *help*?"

"Yes, sir, your help."

"With what?"

A gentle rain began to fall. "That's what I want to talk to you about."

"Ain't you heard about me?" he asked.

I wanted to wipe my face but I still couldn't move, so I blinked the rain away from my eyes instead. "I don't think I...I don't believe all that."

Mean Earl's lips curled into something similar to a smile, but even that was terrifying, more like the way a dog twists its lips back away from its teeth before it rips into you. "Oh, you don't, huh?"

"It doesn't really matter," I said. "I still need your help."

He seemed to consider this a moment, but I couldn't be sure if I'd made him even angrier, or if what I was seeing in his expression was a modicum of respect.

"So just because you need something from me," he said, "you think I got to give it to you?"

"No, but I'm hoping you will." I couldn't take it anymore, and this time when I tried to move, I was able to lift my arm and wipe the rain from my face. I was still scared, but he hadn't tried to kill or even hurt me, so my fear started to lessen. "Will you?"

"I guess that depends on what kind of help you're looking for, boy."

"There's something going on in this town," I said. "Something bad."

"Lots of bad things go on in this town all the time, have for years, ain't nothing new." He uncrossed his arms and ran a hand through his hair, pushing it back and away from his forehead. His face was wet with rain but he didn't seem to notice or care. "What's any of it got to do with me?"

"Did you hear about the gypsy moths?" I asked. "The town's been spraying for them real early in the morning."

"You're here about a bunch of goddamn *moths*?"

It felt like I'd been standing there with him for hours. I had to get to what I'd come here for before he had enough and threw me out...or worse. "I think maybe it brought them here," I said.

Mean Earl pushed his hands into his jacket pockets and let out a long, heavy sigh. "It?"

"Says in the history books your people call it a *Chenoo*."

Something changed in his expression and demeanor when I said that word. It was subtle, but I noticed it.

"My people, huh?" he scoffed. "What in the hell would you know about *my people*?"

"I'm talking about a Wendigo."

"Don't come around here letting things fall out your mouth you know nothing about and don't understand, boy!"

It was the first time he'd raised his voice, and just like that the terror was back and coursing through me like a lightning strike. I wanted to run, but I held my ground. "That's why I'm here," I said.

"You think I'm something outta some movie or comic book?" he growled. "Mr. Big Chief Injun Man, is that it? Expect me to do a dance, smoke a peace pipe, and tell you the ways of the world and secrets of the universe? You're shining me on and wasting my time, you little racist pissant, now get on out of here and get back to your white boy bullshit before I bury my foot so deep in your ass they'll need a backhoe to dig it out."

"I'm sorry," I said, shaking. "I didn't mean to offend you. Honest I didn't. I just need to know more, to understand better, that's all. That's *all*, I swear."

The rage was still in his eyes, but the volume of his voice returned to what it had been before. "And why do you need to do that?"

"Because one's after my dad," I said, hating myself for being so frightened and feeling every bit as ridiculous as Mean Earl obviously thought I was. At that point I couldn't be sure if he was going to help me or tear me to shreds, so all I could do was be honest with him and hope for the best.

"I think it's after me too," I added. "It might even have something to do with the two high school kids that went missing."

Thunder rolled in the distance. The storm was moving closer.

Mean Earl gazed at the sky a moment, then returned his attention to me. "This ain't a game, boy."

"If I thought it was, do you think I'd risk coming here alone to ask for help?"

He stared at me but didn't respond.

"People say you worship the Devil out here," I told him.

"The Devil ain't got the balls to fuck with me."

"I believe you."

"I don't give two shits *what* you believe."

"I know," I said. "But can you help me anyway? Please."

"Your friends gonna stay put?"

I'd never even seen him glance in that direction, but somehow he knew they were there. "Yes, sir," I answered. "They won't cause any trouble. They're just waiting on me."

Mean Earl sighed again. "All right then, come on. We'll talk inside."

Panic grabbed hold of me all over again. "*Inside*?"

"See them clouds? Hear that thunder? There's a storm coming. I'd rather not be standing out in it when it gets here." Muttering and shaking his head, Mean Earl lumbered toward his office. "Stupid-ass little shit."

With a quick nervous wave to the others, I followed, hurrying through the rain in an effort to catch up to him.

* * * *

Inside, I was confronted by a small wooden counter area. A scarred and filthy sheet of plastic covered the entire surface, and an old metal cash register sat in the center of it, along with an ashtray full of cigarette butts and a chipped Boston Red Sox mug housing old pens and pencils. Everything here was old, bare and battered wood, the floor, the walls, even the ceiling. A musty smell hung in the air mixed in with the stench of oil and grease. Along the wall next to the door was the only window—which looked like it hadn't been washed in years—and a couple folding chairs. An ancient woodstove filled the back rear corner of the room, a pile of split wood stacked high in a bin alongside it. On the wall above hung another calendar, this one advertising a tool company and featuring a busty woman in a skimpy bikini and the highest heels I'd ever seen smiling seductively and holding a huge wrench in both hands like it was the most amazing thing she'd ever laid eyes on. A poster featuring Boston Bruins star and tough guy Stan Jonathan filled nearly the entire opposite wall, but the Playboy centerfold pinned to the wall above the chairs immediately got my laser-focused attention.

"Might wanna close your mouth and put your eyes back in your head."

I looked away, blushing.

Behind the counter, Mean Earl poured himself a mug of coffee from a pot on a small table. When he finished he rolled a stool out over near the chairs and plunked himself down on it. "Ain't you never seen tits and bush before, boy?"

"Sure," I said, still embarrassed but trying to play it cool. "Seen plenty, I—"

"Sit your ass down."

I sank onto the closest folding chair, and we both sat there for what seemed a long time. A scanner behind the counter crackled with static and the occasional garbled chatter of police, fireman, and paramedics, but otherwise there was only the sound of what had become a steady rain. Mean Earl stared at me with those dark eyes and occasionally sipped his coffee, but said nothing more. I tried to look anywhere but right at him, but it was difficult in such a small space. "You like Stan Jonathan?" I finally said, motioning to the poster.

He glanced at it and nodded. "He's not a big man, but he's tough as nails and he ain't afraid of nobody. I respect that."

"Yeah, he never backs down. Did you know he's an Indian too?" The minute I said it, I wished I hadn't. Once again my nerves had gotten the better of me. I guess I couldn't get my head around the fact that I was sitting there having a conversation with Mean Earl and he hadn't killed me yet. "He's from Canada."

"You don't say?"

"You probably—I guess you—probably already knew that."

"Yeah," Mean Earl said. "Probably did."

"I like hockey too. I watch the Bruins on channel 38 and—"

"You come here to talk sports?"

"No, sir."

His eyes narrowed behind a column of steam slowly rising from his mug. "Well, go on then, ain't got all day. I work for a living."

After his reaction the last time, I wasn't sure if I should say its name again. "It's after my dad," I said. "And I think it's after me too."

"How come you think that?"

"I saw a book at the library. It had a drawing in it."

"And it looked like what you seen?"

"I didn't see it. Not yet anyways. My dad did. So did a friend of mine."

Mean Earl sipped his coffee. "It looked like what *they* seen."

"Yes. It had antlers like a deer, but it stood on two feet like a man."

He sat back a bit, tilting the stool toward the counter. It creaked against his weight. "Long time ago, people and animals didn't look so different, like they do now. World was in balance then. I bet they don't teach you that in school."

I had no idea what he was talking about, so I just shook my head no.

"Don't matter," he said. "It ain't for you. That's the thing about the white man, he thinks *everything's* for him. When it ain't, he don't like it much. It scares him, offends him, and when the white man's offended, he gets pissed. Sooner or later, somebody's got to pay for all that anger, so the white man just smashes it all until it fits, until it *is* about him again. Then he feels safe, superior—hell—even righteous. All the rest, all that came before, he thinks it just goes away like it was never there in the first place. He tells himself and teaches his children it was all just a bunch of bullshit made up by stupid savages with ignorant ways and childlike beliefs. Truth is there was a whole other world here before the white man got to it, and it ain't gone nowhere. It just stepped back into the shadows is all, in ways the white man don't understand or know anything about. So he don't acknowledge it, because it don't fit into what he needs or wants to believe. Thing is, that don't mean it's not real."

Rain sprayed the window, startling me.

"Easy, boy," Mean Earl said, looking almost amused by how jumpy I was.

"My name's Frank," I told him. "Frank Molinari."

He looked at me like I'd lost my mind. "Who gives a shit?"

"Well, you never asked and—"

"What do you want from me, boy? Why you think I can help you?"

Still leery of him, I tried to answer carefully and in a way that wouldn't upset him. "Like I said, I thought maybe you'd know more about it."

His face went expressionless again, but he seemed to be gauging my intentions. He drank his coffee and waited a while before he finally responded. "Your daddy the one claimed he seen it at the paper company a while back?"

Jesus, I thought, *even Mean Earl heard about what my father saw at work. Was there anyone other than me that hadn't?*

"Yeah," I said, "that's him. People think he's crazy."

"It can break a man's mind easy as it can break his back."

"Am I right? Is it a...am I allowed to say it?"

"They're hunters," he said, ignoring my questions. "And they're hungry. Always hungry, you understand? *Always*. Their hunger don't end, not ever. It's what they do. It's *all* they do. They hunt and they eat. They don't, they waste away and get weak. They get smaller. Sometimes they sleep. Sometimes for days, sometimes months or even years, but when they wake up there ain't no stopping them. They *got* to feed."

"And they eat...*people*?"

"Right down past the bone to your soul," he said. "They got a hunger they can't stop feeding even for a little while. They're like a machine that way. Cold, no feelings, just needs to be fed. Kinda like them moths you were talking about, or a shark out swimming in the ocean."

"Why is it here in Samoset?" I asked.

"They've always been here. Been walking these lands since before Man was here and they'll be walking them long after we're all gone." Mean Earl righted the stool with another loud creak then placed his mug on the counter. "What your people haven't never understood is that this world and the spirit world ain't two totally separate things. They exist together, side-by-side, moving in and out of the other, like fog, you see? And the *Chenoo*...he walks in both."

"Can we get away from it?" I asked.

"Can't outrun them, not ever, because they won't stop no matter where you go or how far." He rose from the stool, took off his jacket and tossed it onto the counter. His short-sleeved t-shirt was tight and further showcased his physique. His was a thick and powerful build for any age, but particularly impressive for a man in his forties. "They're fast. I mean real fast. Faster than seems possible, and they got endurance for days. They can see and sense things we can't. It can hear the heartbeat of a mouse from miles away if it wants to. For all we know, it could be listening to us right now."

"I thought it was a monster," I said, "but just an animal."

"That sound like any animal you ever heard of?" He shook his head like I was the dumbest sonofabitch he'd ever encountered. "It's an evil spirit, boy."

A pang of fear shook me. I thought about the guys out there in the rain surrounded by forest, and hoped they were all right.

"It can use the weather, other animals or men, anything in the forest if it wants. It can control all that and use them like weapons to take down their prey." Mean Earl walked to the window, gazed out through the rain-blurred glass, and dug a pack of cigarettes from his t-shirt pocket. "Once it's on you, there ain't no safe place. Not inside or out."

"My dad's been hiding in our house mostly," I told him.

"That won't work for long. It can unlock doors, come right in whenever it damn well pleases. They been known to do that, eat everybody in the house then take it over for their own to hibernate in."

My head filled with visions of an antlered being creeping through the shadows of our house and stalking my father. A deeply unsettling current of fear fired through me. "Why does it want my father?" I asked. "Why does it want me? What did we do? Why us?"

"Thing about evil spirits is, sometimes they find you…and sometimes you find them." He shook a cigarette free of the pack. "They notice you, see what I'm saying? Sometimes they notice you noticing them, and that's all it takes. Once they do, once they lock on, they don't never let go."

I steeled myself as best I could, but I was terrified. I wanted to see my mother and father, to make sure they were all right. I wanted to see my friends, to know they weren't dead in the woods. I wanted to go home.

"Can we kill it?" I asked.

Mean Earl stabbed the cigarette into the corner of his mouth, returned the pack to his pocket, then dug a disposable lighter from his jeans. He hesitated a moment, as if he'd seen something outside, then lit the cigarette and took a long drag. He left the cigarette in his mouth and twirled the lighter between his fingers like doing so was second nature. He didn't even seem aware that he was doing it. Eventually, he slid the lighter back into his jeans. After another deep drag, he took the cigarette from his mouth and exhaled through his nose. "Only one way to kill it," he said. "Got to catch it when it's in its physical form and weak from hunger. Any other time you got no chance. You'll need a blade, pure silver. Its heart is ice and colder than anything you can imagine. If you can stab it in its heart—deep and hard—you can wound it enough to try to finish the job. But it ain't easy. It's got to be the heart. You cut off a hand or an arm or leg, it comes right back. Only way to truly wound it is by piercing the heart. Once that's done, you got to cut the heart out. *Out*, you understand? And you got to shatter it. Then you put all them shattered pieces into a silver box and bury it in holy, consecrated ground. The rest of the body you cut up into pieces, salt, and burn. Then you gather up them ashes and whatever else is left and you scatter them on the winds. If you can't do that, it's said you can cut it up and bury the remains, but you got to do it far away from where the heart is. You got to do it in as remote a wilderness as you can find, and make sure you bury it deep where nothing can dig it up or get to it. You don't do it exactly like that—and I mean *exactly*—it comes back, resurrects itself. Once it does, you got no chance. It's coming for you, and it *will* get you, because won't nothing stop it a second time."

I wanted to stand up and move around too, to get these thoughts and horrors under control and out of my head, but he'd told me to sit so I stayed put.

"There's something else," Mean Earl said, turning from the window and focusing on me again. "You'll find it deep in the woods, but usually not far from some kind of water. It uses sounds, so be careful. Growls, howling, screeches—all that—and it can imitate human voices too. It can trick you, pretending to be something or someone it ain't. Don't never listen to it. Not ever. If you do, it gets inside your head and it can take you over. Once it's got your soul, it'll run you down to death. It'll make you crazy and violent and evil as it is, and you'll be under its power until it uses everything it can of you. Then it gives power back to you and tosses you aside, but by then it's already gotten the life force it needed from you, and you're left holding the bag for all it's done. And won't nobody believe it was really the Chenoo working through you. It'll all be on you. They'll think you're crazy and evil because that's exactly what you was while it had hold of you. Never look into its eyes, boy, and never listen to a word it says."

Unable to stand it anymore, I got out of the chair. "You ever see one?"

Mean Earl slowly shook his head no. "But that don't mean I don't know it's there," he said evenly. "People think your father's crazy. Probably your friend that seen it too. They ain't. None of you is crazy. You might be doomed, but you ain't crazy."

"Do you think we're doomed?"

"Boy, sooner or later in this life, we're all doomed." He took a couple pulls on his cigarette. "But just like the Chenoo, we walk in both worlds too, and same as here, it's all in how you walk, and what you walk to and from that matters. You understand?"

"I think so," I said softly.

"Don't be afraid. I know it's hard, but try." He grimaced, as if he'd just remembered something. "Blood's what makes it stronger...bigger...it's how it grows. But fear...fear's what keeps it alive."

I didn't want to be afraid but I couldn't help it. I was terrified.

Squinting through the clouds of smoke drifting all around us, Mean Earl was back to studying me. "You got what you came here for?"

"Yes, sir," I said. "Thank you."

"Don't thank me, boy. Not for this." He returned his attention to the dirty, blurry window, and all that lived beyond it. "Storm's getting worse. Go fetch your friends and get on out of here now."

"I'm sorry I believed all those things people said about you."

"Got to be careful what you believe in this life, boy. And what you don't."

I made my way to the door. Part of me was afraid to go out there, and ironically, a man I'd been petrified of just moments before had become the only thing still making me feel safe. So much so I didn't want to leave that little shack without him. But I had no choice. I knew now what had to be done.

I wanted to say something more to Mean Earl. Though it seemed like I should, I couldn't find the words. Maybe they didn't exist. I saw him around town now and then over the next few years, but we never spoke again. He wasn't interested, and usually wouldn't make eye contact. He acknowledged me a couple times with a subtle nod or a knowing look, though even that was rare and always the extent of it. We knew what we knew, and that was it. I often fantasized he was my friend, and who knows, maybe in a way he was. All I knew for sure was that I'd remain grateful to him for the rest of my life.

"Go on, get. Ain't nothing else I can do for you."

Those were the last words Mean Earl ever said to me.

He wasn't looking, but I waved goodbye anyway.

Then I opened the door and stepped into the rain.

CHAPTER FIFTEEN

I REMEMBER RUNNING. Fast and hard and to the point where my lungs were burning and my legs felt like they might give out. I'd met the others at the tree line and together we ran back down the road, through the now heavy rain and away from the junkyard and Mean Earl and the thick woods surrounding us.

A mile or so away but still a fair distance from the more populated parts of town, we found ourselves huddled inside the remains of an old abandoned house. Built back in the 1800s, it was a single-story structure that had been abandoned and left to rot for decades. A hangout for older kids that used it as a secluded place to party, the house was gutted, had no windows or doors, the walls and beams were covered in graffiti, and there was trash and empty beer cans and liquor bottles everywhere. The roof was only partially intact, and the part that was had numerous holes and tears in it, so plenty of rain was getting through, but it beat being outside in all that chaos.

Drenched and dripping, we sought shelter as best we could and watched the storm. The wind had picked up, occasional forks of lightning stabbed an increasingly darkening sky, and thunder rumbled overhead as violent torrents of rain kept falling. There was something almost apocalyptic about it, but all I kept thinking about was everything Mean Earl had told me, especially how a Wendigo could manipulate the weather. Had it brought this storm about? Was it a show of power, a warning, or a harbinger of things to come? I couldn't be sure, but I'd told the others about it and given them a quick rundown of everything else I'd learned. For several minutes, no one had responded to any of it.

Alex knelt near the entrance, picked up an empty beer bottle and tossed it outside. "Man," he said above the din of rain. "We're gonna be here a while."

"It's just a summer storm," Max said. "Don't worry, it won't last long. They never do."

Shawn undid his bandana, pulled it off his head and wiped his face with it, his chest still heaving from our sprint. "I can't believe you talked to Mean Earl in his own place and lived to tell about it."

"Did he have a bunch of Devil stuff in there?" Alex asked.

"Nah, none of that shit's true," I said.

"Imagine that." Max rolled his eyes. He'd always cautioned us against believing many of the more outlandish stories people told about Mean Earl.

"He is pretty mean," I added. "But he's actually sort of a cool guy. He knew a lot about what's out there in those woods, just like I was hoping."

"And you believe these things he told you?" Max asked.

"Yeah, Max, I do."

Shawn shook the water free of his bandana, then tied it back around his head again. "I do too," he said.

"Alex?" Max asked.

Still kneeling, he gazed at the storm as the rain splashed and formed huge puddles and rivers that rushed along the sides of the road. "It doesn't make any difference what I believe. It's all for one, no matter what. Just like always."

"Of course," Max said. "I guess it just seems like we're a little...I don't know...*old* for this kind of thing, that's all."

"What kind of thing is that?" Shawn asked.

"Hunting monsters?"

"I don't care what it seems like," I said. "That thing's out there. It's real and it's coming for me, maybe for all of you. We can't hide and we can't run."

"Okay then." Shawn moved over next to Alex and leaned against what was left of the doorframe. "What's the plan?"

"We go back to where you saw it." I ran my hands through my soaked hair, pushing it back. The water ran down along my neck and between my shoulder blades, giving me an unexpected chill. "See if we find it out there, or if it finds us."

Thunder rolled, shaking the old house. The rain fell even harder than before, like maybe we'd angered it somehow.

"And then we kill the fucker."

Shawn went back to watching the rain. He didn't say it. No one did.

But we were all thinking it.

Or die trying.

* * * *

It was late afternoon when I got home. The storm had passed and dusk was coming soon, but the heat had risen again. The world was drying out.

Before night could fall, any trace of the rain would be long gone. There was no one in the house, so I checked outside and found my father on our small patio just beyond the glass sliders.

No longer dressed in his pajamas, robe, and slippers, he'd traded them for a short-sleeved shirt, khakis, and a pair of work boots. Staring down at the patio as if he'd forgotten what he was doing there, the Ouija board lay at his feet, snapped and broken into several pieces. The planchette had been tossed next to it, and he'd apparently stomped on it as it too was broken. In one hand he held a small can of lighter fluid, in the other a box of stick matches.

Though he'd obviously showered, shaved, and looked more like himself than he had in a long time, I still found myself approaching him cautiously, as if he were some sort of unpredictable wild animal. "Dad, what are you doing?"

The sound of my voice snapped him out of his trance but he didn't answer.

"Are you okay?" I asked. "Where's Mom?"

"Who knows?"

It sounded like maybe he did, but I let it go.

"Smashed it into pieces," he said, indicating the Ouija board. "Now I'm going to light it on fire and watch it burn into oblivion where it belongs."

"Did something else happen while I was gone?"

"It's in my head, son." His bottom lip trembled. "My *head*, and I—I need to get it out, do you understand? I need to get it the hell out of my head."

"I know what it is, Dad."

They're hunters.

"Don't say it. Not out loud. I think maybe it can hear us."

And they're hungry.

"It's been talking to me," he said. "It's been the one all along, using the Ouija board, this—this evil *thing* disguised as a toy. But I'm not listening anymore. I *can't*, not ever again. I don't want to hear what it has to say because it's trying to destroy us and—and I'm not going to let that happen."

He looked better but was acting the same. I was concerned he might hurt himself in such a state, which made me want to take the matches and lighter fluid away from him. But I had to let him do this. It was a ritual he needed to complete, and after all he'd been through, I had no right to stand in the way of that. So I stayed quiet as he sprayed the lighter fluid over the pieces. When he finished, he handed me the can.

"Be careful," I said, stepping back.

"It's too late for careful, Frankie Boy." He struck a match then dropped it.

The pieces caught fire quickly, and were soon consumed and emitting a horrible chemical-like stench.

"Burn, you sonofabitch," he muttered. "*Burn.*"

Afraid he was too close to the fire, I took hold of his wrist and guided my father a few steps away from the flames.

As he watched the fire he'd created, I looked to the woods instead. The overwhelming feeling that something was looking back returned, and this time, deep in my gut, I could sense how displeased it was with what it was witnessing.

It's an evil spirit, boy.

Shaken, I wanted nothing more than to go back inside, but Mean Earl's warnings kept replaying in my head.

There ain't no safe place, inside or out.

My father had gotten a shovel from the shed earlier and leaned it against the foundation. Using it, he stamped out the flames then broke the remains up even more with the edge of the shovel. "Got to let this cool down, then I'll bury it just past the tree line." He tossed the shovel onto the grass. "But right now, I don't know how safe it is for us to be out here, son."

It can unlock doors…

"You showered and got dressed," I said. "You look good, Dad."

"It was time. I'm still so tired but…I can't…"

"Have you eaten anything today?"

"It shouldn't be like this. I'm supposed to take care of you, I—"

"We're supposed to take care of each other," I told him, doing the best I could to keep my fear hidden. "And that's what we're doing. Okay?"

"I'm going to make this right." Eyes glistening with tears, he kissed my forehead. "It won't be perfect, but I'll make it right. You'll see."

"I know you will, Dad."

I put my arm around him, and together we went back inside.

Since I wasn't sure when my mother would be home, even though it was a little early for dinner, Dad admitted he hadn't eaten all day, so I got him situated in the living room then made us some hot dogs. I didn't know how to cook a lot of things but I managed those all right, and when I'd finished I put them on paper plates along with some potato chips, grabbed a couple bottles of root beer from the fridge, then joined him in the living room.

"With mustard and relish?" he asked, inspecting his hot dogs.

I did my best to put on a happy face. "Just the way you like them."

"Yes." He picked one up and admired it as if he'd never seen anything quite so magnificent. It was a sudden but wonderful glimpse of the old him, something I hadn't seen in a long while. "So they are. Thank you."

We ate dinner without saying much else. Though nothing had changed and the same horrible things continued to weigh on us and fill our heads, the chaos of it all actually quieted somewhat, and for a little while we were just a father and son having dinner together. Our eyes met at one point, and his expression indicated how much he was enjoying the food. It reminded me of how he'd always done such things, making big productions out of some silly drawing I'd done, a quiz at school I'd aced, or any number of my other minor achievements. He always made them out to be more important than they really were, and seeing this in my father again, even over something as trivial as a hot dog, made me realize maybe he wasn't so irrevocably broken after all. The man I knew and the father I loved was still there. He was drowning, but he was still alive, still fighting to stay above the surface and certain destruction.

"Those were, without a doubt, two of the finest hot dogs I've ever had," he said once we'd finished. "I can't remember the last time I enjoyed a meal quite that much."

I wiped a smear of mustard from my mouth. "They were pretty good, weren't they?"

"They certainly were." He tried to smile but I could tell it was difficult for him, this man that had smiled so effortlessly my entire life. "Frankie Boy, I want you to know how sorry I am, I—"

"*Dad*," I said, placing my hand on his shoulder. "It's okay. We're in this together and we'll get through it together."

He nodded, though he hardly seemed convinced. "You're becoming a fine young man, son, and I'm proud of you. No matter what happens, I want you to know that."

"Thanks, Dad."

"You're right, we'll...we'll get through this. One way or another, we will."

"Do you know where Mom is?" I asked.

With a defeated sigh, he shook his head no.

"She'll probably be home soon. Why don't you try to get some rest?"

"I don't know if I could sleep, I...I'm so tired but...maybe I could lie down a while, try to take a nap."

"Go ahead," I told him. "I'll be all right."

He stood up and walked toward their bedroom. "When your mother gets home tell her to wake me up, okay?"

"I will," I said. "But, Dad, can I ask you something?"

"Sure."

"What happened today that made you decide to burn the Ouija board?"

He didn't answer right away. For several seconds he just stood there, shoulders slumped and head bowed. "It told me something," he eventually said. "So I have to be ready, can't be wandering around the house like this anymore."

"What did it tell you?"

"It's a secret."

"Can't you tell me?"

"No," he said. "But when the time's right, you'll know. I promise, son."

I knew he wouldn't go any further, so I didn't push it. "Okay."

"I love you, Frankie Boy, more than anything in the whole world."

My father had told me countless times how much he loved me, but there was something troubling about it this time because I'd never before heard him say it with such profound sorrow.

"I love you too," I said.

And then he was gone.

I sat there a while, waiting and hoping he'd drift off to sleep. After a few minutes, I tossed the paper plates and bottles in the trash, then went to the hutch in the living room where my parents kept their good silver service. I found the silverware in the middle drawer. It had belonged to my mother's side of the family for a couple generations, and although it was given to my parents on their wedding day, it was quite ornate and we rarely used any of it.

There were several knives, though none sharp or with serrated edges. They weren't small—eight or nine inches from butt of the handle to tip of the blade—but were essentially large fancy butter knives. I selected one, got a good grip and held it up. Even the end of the blade was rounded and dull. It wasn't remotely impressive as a weapon.

It was, however, pure silver.

I slid the drawer closed then went quickly to my bedroom, where I hid the knife in my desk drawer. I was about to call Shawn to let him know about it when I heard the front door close, so I ventured back out to the kitchen.

My mother stood at the counter in a short and low-cut yellow dress, a pair of white Keds, and an apparently new purse with a huge sunflower on it slung over one shoulder. She quickly rifled through a smile pile of mail, muttered something then tossed it all aside. As she headed for the fridge, she saw me in the doorway and came to an abrupt halt. "Jesus!" she said breathlessly, a hand to her heart. "Will you *stop* doing that? Every time I turn around in this house lately, there you are like some sort of hall monitor or something."

Obviously drunk, and worse than last time, she giggled, shook her head and staggered to the refrigerator. I didn't say a word as she found a bottle of Coca-Cola, nearly dropped it, then slapped it on the counter. After managing to get a small glass from the cupboard, she decided to stare at me a while, hands on her hips. "What?"

"Nothing, I just didn't know where you were," I said. "I was worried."

"My son, ever the worrier!" she said, waving her arms dramatically.

"Did you drive home from…wherever?" I asked.

"Yes, I drove home, and I'm just fine. Thank you for your concern. Now, since you *still* don't seem to have a firm grasp on how things work, let's go over them again, shall we? You are not the parent here, Frankie Boy. I am."

"Then why don't you try acting like it?"

Any drunken humor she'd found in the situation to that point vanished immediately. From the look in her glassy eyes I thought she might actually hit me. Instead she staggered a bit closer and said, "I'm curious. Have you said the same to your father? No, of course you haven't. I'm the only one with whom you're so unforgiving. I alone receive the honor of having such lofty expectations placed upon me, or, for that matter, *any* expectations whatsoever."

"Where were you, Mom?" I asked.

"None of your goddamn business," she snapped. "*That's* where I was."

I indicated her scant dress without trying to look directly at it because it was painfully obvious she wasn't wearing anything underneath it. "Is that new?"

"Yes!" she said in a purposely exaggerated and melodramatic tone. "What a scandal! I'm wearing a new outfit!"

"Were you out with that guy from the other day?"

"No, I was not," she said, suddenly giggling again. "Mr. Prosecutor."

I didn't want to know anything more. "Do you need coffee or something?"

"Coffee's the last thing I need," she said. "But if you stop being such an insufferable little bore and go fetch me the bottle of whiskey in the other room, I'll whip us up something for dinner. How's that sound?"

"Dad and I already ate."

"Oh. Well, then…"

"If you care, Dad got rid of the Ouija board. He won't be doing…that… anymore. He even took a shower and shaved and got dressed."

She seemed genuinely shocked. "Really?"

"He was still wicked tired so he's in bed now getting some rest, but he's trying. He's really trying, Mom."

"So am I." Her expression turned serious. In seconds she'd gone from giggling to the verge of tears. "More than you know."

I wanted to believe her, and I suppose in some sense I did. But it didn't help. I still desperately needed my mother, and she was nowhere in sight. "I have a lot to offer, you know," she said, furiously digging her cigarettes from her purse. "I have dreams just like everybody else. This may come as a huge shock to you, but I have wants and desires and a hope for some kind of life I can be proud of and happy in the same as anyone. Don't you think I want those things too? Look at me. I'm an educated and intelligent woman. Sometimes men even think I'm beautiful. I know you think I'm some ancient relic, but I'm still relatively young, goddamn it." As she lit her cigarette then threw her purse on the counter, she lost her balance and crashed into the kitchen table. Somehow managing to remain upright, she yanked a chair out and sat down. "Let me tell you something, Frankie Boy, and I suggest you listen very carefully. There are two kinds of men in this life. There are wolves and there are sheep. And you know what? It's all bullshit because the end result for women is the same. The sheep, he devours his victim just like the wolf does, don't kid yourself. He just does it slower, over time, and with a pathetic and allegedly loving grin on his face. Sometimes, the sheep even drives a woman to the wolves. And the wolves, well, they're wolves, so we all know how that goes. Either way, it's the slaughterhouse for us girls, isn't it? So you might as well be a wolf and at least be the kind of man that has enough mercy to take down your prey as quickly and viciously as possible. The other way, the sheep's way, is so terribly *cruel*."

My mother had begun to cry, and her dark eyeliner was running and forming little spots beneath her eyes. She kicked off her Keds, sending one halfway across the room, then stabbed the cigarette into the corner of her mouth and left it there. "Be a good kid," she said drunkenly. "Go get me that bottle."

I walked over to the table, gave her a hug and kissed her cheek, then started down the hallway toward my bedroom.

"Go get it yourself."

CHAPTER SIXTEEN

THE NIGHT THAT followed was one of the longest of my life. I didn't get much sleep, other than the occasional catnap when exhaustion won out and I'd nod off. Even then, I'd come awake with a start only moments later, still sitting up on my bed, a flashlight in one hand and the silver knife in the other. Scared as I was, I couldn't help but feel a bit ridiculous, but everything was suspect now—each creak or shifting of the house, every burst of wind, every sound and drifting shadow—even my own thoughts seemed intent on sabotaging any hope of rest or peace. I imagined Mean Earl in his little shack, drinking his coffee and living with all the things he knew, that knowledge twisting through his brain like a slowly slithering snake. I thought about Shawn, Max, and Alex and if they were beyond sleeping through the night now too. I even wondered about Perry Jenkins and Keith Dickinson, and if we'd ever know what happened to them.

It all led me back to the evil spirit in the nearby forest. Listening to my thoughts and starving for human flesh and vulnerable souls, it darted through the dark woods at impossible speeds, getting closer and closer to our house. And then, just as it reached the edge of our backyard, it stopped…watched…waited.

I closed my eyes and imagined moonlight breaking through the trees to reveal the Wendigo's antlered silhouette. All around it, the gypsy moths fed, devouring our little town bit by bit.

Terrified as I was, maybe if I killed this thing our lives would go back to the way they were before my father got sick and my mother became someone else, before that hideous demon showed itself and the gypsy moths invaded Samoset. People always said turning back time was impossible, but I had to believe they were wrong because that's exactly what I needed to do.

When Sunday morning finally arrived, I went to the bathroom, got dressed, then snuck through the house, hoping to get out before my parents realized I was gone. Before all this began we would've gone to Mass in a few hours, but we hadn't been to church in months, so I was confident I could get out undetected.

Dad was nowhere in sight and likely still asleep in the bedroom. My mother I found passed out on the couch, an empty glass and whiskey bottle on the floor nearby. Barefoot but still in her dress from the night before, she was lying on her stomach and snoring softly. Although it was supposed to be another scorcher, it was a bit chilly in the house, so I covered her with an old afghan draped across the back of the couch, then picked up the glass and bottle and put them in the sink in the kitchen.

After eating a package of Pop-Tarts, I took a long look out the back door. The burned remains of the Ouija board were still there. I considered burying them but was too scared to go into the woods alone, so I quietly slipped outside and made a beeline for the street.

I knew Max would have to go to church with his parents—there was no way out of it for him—so I decided to go to Shawn's house first. Like Alex's mother and Rafe, Shawn's parents didn't go to church, so he'd be around and I wouldn't be interrupting anything or have to risk getting him in trouble.

When I got there, even though it was only a little after seven-thirty, Mr. O'Hara was out in the front yard in an Adirondack chair strumming an acoustic guitar. "Youngblood," he said with a smile. "How you doing on this fine Sunday morning, you doing all right?"

Rather than answer that question I simply replied, "Hi, Mr. O'Hara."

"Cop a squat." He motioned to the chair next to him with a cock of his head. "Shawn's already up, said you guys had some important stuff going down today. Usually can't get that dude out of bed on a Sunday morning without detonating a thermonuclear device, so it must be serious."

"We're just hanging out." I'd stuck the knife in the waistband of my shorts and covered it with a long t-shirt, so as I sat next to him I had to adjust my position to prevent it from digging into me. "We're going over Alex's house."

"Hey," he said, strumming his guitar, "thought we were going to see *Star Wars* yesterday, but Shawn said you fellas were up to some top-secret stuff and couldn't make it. If you want, we'll check it out next weekend, yeah?"

"Yeah," I said, "that'd be cool."

Until recently, going to see *Star Wars* and the anticipation of what magic it might hold had been vitally important to me. Now, only a few weeks later, the entire thing could not have seemed more trivial and inconsequential.

Mr. O'Hara abruptly stopped playing his guitar, as if he'd just thought of something. "You okay, youngblood?"

"Yeah, I—I'm okay."

"Got a lot of weight on those shoulders?" He waited, expecting a response. When I didn't give him one, he went back to strumming his guitar. "Just do me a solid, okay? If you ever need to talk about anything, I'm around."

"Thanks," I said, trying to smile.

"You bet. Got to look out for one another, or what the hell good are we?" He winked then began to play Neil Young's "Old Man."

"How's it going with the invasion?" I asked.

"The invasion," he said, laughing lightly. "The resistance is underway, youngblood, well underway and going good as can be expected. We killed a whole bunch of the little bastards so far. I'll tell you what, though, they don't go easy. Me and the boys got some more to do come Monday, but we're winning. Another week or two, we ought to be seeing the last of them. We'll kill the rest or drive them out, don't make any difference either way, they just got to go."

Before I could say anything more, Shawn came out of the house. As he approached us we exchanged glances and I gave him a subtle nod. "What's up, man?" he said. "You ready?"

"Yeah," I stood up. "See you later, Mr. O'Hara."

"Later, little dudes. Have fun."

He was still playing "Old Man" and started singing the lyrics as Shawn and I walked across the yard, down the driveway and into the street.

"You get it?" Shawn asked.

"It's tucked in my shorts."

"Good. Alex is waiting on us. Max is going to meet us there when he gets out of church and the fuck away from his parents. Then we'll figure out how we're going to do this." He checked back over his shoulder to make certain we'd gotten far enough for him to light a cigarette. "Jesus, Frankie Boy, you look like shit. You sleep at all last night?"

"Not much," I told him.

"Me neither." He rolled a Camel between his lips, fired it up, then broke into a quick rendition of "Tossin' and Turnin'." "*I couldn't sleep at all last night!*"

He was trying to make me laugh and lighten the mood, but I just didn't have it in me. "I'd rather listen to your old man sing Neil Young."

"Fine, then let me show you some dance moves I've been working on."

"Fuck that, I've seen you dance, go ahead and sing."

As we kept walking, we fell quiet, and I wanted to tell him about what was going on with my mother. I just didn't know how to start. Part of me didn't want him to know, but I felt like if I didn't talk to somebody about it I was going to snap. Then again, it was bad enough everyone thought my father had gone crazy, I wasn't sure I should let anyone—even my best friends—know that my mother had become someone I no longer recognized either.

"You think anything will ever be the same again?" I asked instead.

Shawn came to an abrupt stop and considered me a second, like he was thinking it over. "How do you mean?"

"You know," I said, "like back to the way they were before."

Drawing deeply on his cigarette, Shawn exhaled two streams of smoke from his nostrils. Like a dragon. Or maybe somebody ready to help slay one.

"No."

Turned out he was right.

* * * *

"What the hell is this?" Alex looked from me to Shawn then back again. "You guys made fun of my knife and you show up with *this*? At least mine could cut or stab somebody. What the fuck are we gonna do with this? *Butter* the thing?"

"The weapon has to be solid silver," I said. "It's all I've got."

"Back off, man!" Alex brandished the knife dramatically. "I got this and a tub of margarine and I'll fucking use them! You just try me, tough guy!"

Shawn laughed but turned away in the hopes I wouldn't see him.

"You got anything better?" I asked him.

"Do Wendigo's like toast?" Alex held the knife up again. "Because a loaf of Wonder Bread and this savage sword of Conan you got here should cover his breakfast needs pretty good. We didn't kill him, but he's wicked full so, you know, everything's fine now. Jesus, dude, you'd be better off with a fork."

This time I laughed too. "Okay, *dickhead*, you got any better ideas then?"

"You sure it's got to be solid silver?" Shawn asked. "Can't be part?"

"Mean Earl said it had to be pure silver."

"Then what the hell are we gonna do? Alex is right. We can't go back into the woods with that." Shawn scratched his head. "Is there any way we could make it better?"

I looked to Alex. As we all stood out in front of his house, the sun steadily rising higher in the sky and the heat ramping up, something finally dawned in his eyes. "Yeah," he said. "Maybe there is. Come on."

We followed him around the side of the house to the tool shed out back. Rafe was sitting in a lawn chair in front of it, tinkering with an old car part he had balanced in his lap. He looked up as we rounded the corner, a cigarette dangling from his mouth, his eyes hidden behind his black sunglasses.

"Rafe," Alex said, "can you take a look at this?"

He put the car part on the ground and took the knife. Turning it slowly in his hands, he studied it as if he'd never seen anything like it before. In typical Rafe fashion, he didn't say a word.

"Can you make that sharper?" Alex asked. "Like, a lot sharper, I mean."

Rafe gazed up at him, expressionless.

"Thing is, I don't want Mom to know anything about it." Alex glanced at the house as if to make sure his mother wasn't lurking nearby. "And I can't tell you why I need you to do it. It's important, though. I promise we won't hurt ourselves or anybody else with it, but we need it today, as soon as possible."

Rafe's head slowly panned from Alex, to me, to Shawn.

"I know what you're thinking," Alex said. "It's not a very responsible thing for you to do, right? That's true, I'm not gonna lie. But can you do it anyway?"

With a deep sigh, Rafe returned his attention to the knife, the pomade in his pompadour glistening in the sunlight. "Give me an hour."

* * * *

Apparently my mom wasn't the only one spending her Sunday morning sleeping off a Saturday night drunk, because Alex's mother had not gotten up yet either. Spared having to deal with what Max often called her *incessant charm*, rather than going inside and risking waking her, we stayed outside in front of the house, killing time and waiting to see what Rafe could come up with. Whatever he was doing involved some sort of machine, as an on and off grinding noise emanated from the tool shed out back, followed by the occasional clanging sound of metal on metal. I was sure it was only a matter of time before it woke Alex's mother, but it wasn't she who emerged from the house. It was Ronica.

Though not quite nine yet, she was already in a bikini, a large beach towel slung over her shoulder. A cassette player/recorder dangled from one hand and she held a tube of suntan lotion in the other. Her hair was up and in a ponytail, a pair of mirrored sunglasses concealed her eyes, and she was barefoot. A leather ankle bracelet adorned with little silver bells jingled softly as she strode seductively from the patio and into the weed-infested yard.

"Jesus," Shawn muttered, watching her approach. "Now *that's* a bikini."

Ronica flashed her dazzling smile then threw the towel down and flattened it out, making sure to bend over directly in front of us. "What's up, you guys?"

"Holy shit," Shawn whispered to me. "I just popped a mega-rod."

I was in lust with Ronica as much as anyone, but with everything else going on I wasn't in the mood for her bullshit. Fond as I was of her, she was a distraction we didn't need right now.

As if sensing this, she focused on me and she stretched out on her towel. "Frankie Boy, rub some lotion on my back for me?" She held out the tube. "It's already sunny and *so* hot. I can just imagine how bad it's going to be later."

"Thanks, I'm all set," I said, noticing how Alex had his nose buried in a wrestling magazine and was doing his best to ignore his sister's games.

"Seriously?" Shocked, Ronica pulled her sunglasses off and frowned. "How am I supposed to reach my back?"

"I'll do it." Shawn pulled his shirt off, tucked it into the back of his shorts, and made it a point to puff up his chest. "No problem-o, happy to."

Ronica rolled her eyes. "I didn't ask you."

"What the hell's the difference?"

"Frankie Boy's a gentleman. You're a total perv. *That's* the difference."

"Okay, that's fair. Just the same, I think we better go ahead and get you protected from the sun's powerful rays." Shawn pointed a reprimanding finger at her. "Sunburns are nothing to take lightly, young lady."

With a dramatic sigh she rolled onto her stomach, bent one leg at the knee and pointed her toes in the air. "Fine," she said, holding the tube up behind her head. "Just hurry up, don't touch anything you're not supposed to and try not to be such a nerd about it."

As Shawn joined Ronica on the towel I sat down next to Alex. "Is that the issue that's got the story on Tony Garea and Larry Zbyzsko?" I asked.

Alex nodded. "Yeah, says they're gonna be in a big tag team tournament for the belts later this year. I bet they win it if they can get by Tanaka and Fuji. Those fucking guys always cheat."

"So," Ronica said, "what's going on with you boys anyway?"

When no one else answered, I said, "Nothing, we're just hanging out."

Shawn squirted lotion on the back of her shoulders and started rubbing it in, but Ronica stopped him by rolling onto her side so she could face us.

"You guys are up to no good," she said. "I can tell. Know how? I *invented* being up to no good. I know it when I see it. And I see it."

"It's none of your beeswax," Alex mumbled.

"It kinda is though."

Alex looked up from his magazine. "How you figure?"

"If you get yourselves in some sort of trouble," she said, "and knowing you guys, you probably will, I'll be the one that has to get you out of it. You'll have to come to me, because Mom will murder you."

"Nobody asked for your help, Ronica."

"Not yet anyway." She smiled as she rolled back onto her stomach. "But we'll see."

Shawn resumed rubbing lotion on her. "It'd probably be a lot easier if I undid your top so I could get maximum coverage here."

"Oh my God," she said, laughing. "Work around it."

"Okay, but I'm not responsible for any tan lines."

"Where's Maxie?" Ronica asked.

"Church," I said.

"Oh, right, how could I forget?"

"He's meeting us here when he gets out."

"Good, because whatever you're up to, he's got more sense than all three of you put together."

"Shut the fuck up, Ronica." Alex tossed the magazine aside and stood up. "You don't even know what you're talking about."

"Wow," she giggled. "*Somebody's* in a mood."

I picked up the magazine and flipped through the pages, doing my best to stay out of it. But it would be another hour or more before Max got here, and I had no idea how we were going to fill that much time and still avoid Ronica's suspicions. I knew we could tell her, bring her into it, and she'd likely go along if for no reasons other than morbid curiosity and what she'd consider entertainment value, but I didn't want her involved. It was obvious from Alex's behavior he didn't either. I knew he was trying to protect her the only way he knew how, and I guess in my own way I was too.

Alex went inside, so I read the magazine and tried to concentrate on that, but it was really hot out in the direct sunlight, so I took my shirt off and reclined back on the grass. Hands behind my head, I closed my eyes. I'd already tanned an even deep brown, as I did every summer, but if I was going to roast, I figured I might as well get even darker in the process.

"Okay, your back's good," I heard Shawn say. "But I should probably get your legs too. Any exposed area, really, they're all at risk."

It was a while later when I felt someone shaking me awake.

Shawn was standing over me. His hand was extended but he was barely discernable with the sun blinding me. "What?" I said groggily.

"You fell asleep," he said. "Come on."

I took his hand and he pulled me to my feet. As I rubbed my eyes and waited for the sunspots to dissipate, I saw Ronica was still on her towel, but lying on her back now. I couldn't be sure, but she looked like she'd drifted off too.

"I know, it's fucking ridiculous how hot she is," Shawn said, using my chin as a handle to turn my head in the other direction. "But look, I think he's done."

Alex was at the corner of the house with Rafe. He looked back and waved us over, so we hurried across the yard and joined them.

"Any luck?" I asked.

Rafe responded by lighting a Lucky Strike and taking a quick drag.

"You tell me." Alex handed me the knife.

It now came to a fine point and both sides of the blade were sharp as a razor. It wasn't exactly pristine, in that there were numerous scratches and a couple small chips missing on either side of the blade, but the transformation was amazing. "Wow," I said. "That's incredible."

"*Damn*, Rafe," Shawn said, looking equally impressed. "You're the man."

Rafe shrugged and took another drag on his cigarette.

"Thanks," Alex told him. "It stays between us, I promise."

"Yeah," I said. "Thank you, Rafe."

Like the Fonz, he gave us two thumbs up then turned and strode back to his lawn chair and sat down. Stretching out his legs in front of him, he retrieved the car part he'd been holding when we first got there, and resumed tinkering with that.

"You should probably go in and get that dude a beer," Shawn said. "That's one of the most amazing fucking things I've ever seen."

It was then that we saw Max running toward the property. I could tell from the look on his face something was wrong, and that he'd probably run the entire way, which was not like him.

We ran across the yard and met him just as he stopped and doubled over, hands on his knees and his chest heaving with each breath.

"What's going on?" I asked. "Are you okay?"

Max nodded and held up a finger. After a moment, he managed to get a response out. "I came as fast as I could."

"What happened?" Shawn said. "What's wrong?"

"It's the only thing anybody was talking about at church," he gasped, still struggling to regain his breath. "They found them, you guys. Perry and Keith, they found them."

We all stood there, stunned. We might've even been relieved, but from Max's expression, we all knew there was something more. And it wasn't good.

"They're dead."

CHAPTER SEVENTEEN

LOCATED IN WESTERN Massachusetts, the town of Ware had a population of about ten thousand people and was home to the Quabbin Reservoir, the largest body of inland water in the state and, despite being nearly seventy miles away, the primary water source for the city of Boston. According to FBI statistics, Ware also had one of the higher crime rates in the commonwealth, but no one could have anticipated the bizarre and grisly events that took place there in the summer of 1977.

A few days before Perry Jenkins and Keith Dickinson went missing, a gold 1972 Oldsmobile Cutlass was reported stolen by its owner to the Samoset Police. Parked in the owner's driveway, it had apparently been hotwired and taken at some point during the night. It didn't turn up until a few days later, when it was found over one hundred miles away in an empty lot in the town of Ware.

The police officers on scene immediately noticed an awful stench emanating from the trunk of the abandoned car, and upon forcing it open, discovered the bloated and disfigured nude body of eighteen-year-old Keith Dickinson.

The teenager's eyes, tongue, throat, and genitals had been torn out, and the rest of his body had not only been grotesquely mutilated and partially skinned, there were signs it had been cannibalized as well.

Later that same day, a young man matching Perry Jenkins' description was seen by multiple witnesses at various locations around Ware, including a convenience store where he attempted to use the restroom and was asked to leave by the manager due to his peculiar behavior. Others described him as looking disheveled to the point of appearing homeless and acting deranged, as if he were suffering from severe mental illness.

Just before noon, Jenkins purchased a bus ticket to New York City. When the clerk noticed the wrinkled bills the bleary-eyed teenager used to pay were stained with blood, he called the police. They arrived a few moments later but Jenkins, and his bus, had already left the station.

The bus had only made it a few blocks however, when the driver and other passengers became alarmed by a filthy and erratic teenager with long black hair staggering up and down the aisle and screaming in a language no one was able to understand. Worried for the safety of his passengers, the driver stopped the bus, radioed for help, and attempted to subdue the young man.

Witnesses reported Jenkins claimed a demon was inside his skull, that he couldn't get it out and it was making him do horrible things. At one point he began to growl like an animal, and when the driver attempted to calm him down, Jenkins suddenly produced a large hunting knife from his jeans and told him he needed to devour human flesh to stay alive.

The passengers, in a panic, watched as Jenkins slashed the driver's arm.

Bleeding profusely, the driver fled the bus but Jenkins followed, catching him on the street. By then the police had arrived on scene with weapons drawn, and instructed Jenkins to drop the knife. Refusing to comply, he continued screaming about demonic possession and his need to devour human flesh.

The showdown came to an end when Jenkins, still brandishing the knife, continued to ignore the police's instructions, and in what one witness described as sounding like he was speaking in tongues, lunged for the nearest officer.

Perry Jenkins was shot dead at the scene. He was eighteen years old.

It was later reported that Jenkins and Dickinson, who were seasoned car thieves, stole the Cutlass in Samoset then set off across the state, heading west on a crime spree that lasted several days. The subsequent coroner's report showed that Keith Dickinson had been dead for more than a day when his body was found, but that he'd been tortured, mutilated, and partially skinned and consumed while still alive. In fact, there was every indication Jenkins had been gradually feeding on the corpse.

Both Jenkins and Dickinson had extensive juvenile criminal records, and were known violent drug and alcohol abusers, so this was the official explanation given for what took place. What authorities didn't know was that despite Perry and Keith's penchant for such things, Jenkins was neither suffering from mental illness nor was he under the influence of a drug-fueled rage.

The truth behind what had actually taken place was much worse.

And well beyond even their worst nightmares.

On that hot Sunday morning, at the edge of Alex and Ronica's property, while we didn't have all the gory details quite yet, we did our best to take in the news of their deaths as best we could.

But even we didn't yet know the full extent of what we were up against.

"I can't believe it," Max said after a period of awkward silence. "They found Keith in the trunk of the car they stole."

"They were best friends," Alex said. "Why would Perry kill Keith?"

"Because he was a psycho fuck-face and Keith was a scumbag piece of shit with the brains of a patio brick?" Shawn looked at each of us in turn. "What, are we supposed to feel bad now because they're dead? Fuck those dickheads. They've been beating the snot out of us since we were like— what—six, seven? You guys hated those twats as much as I did."

Max sighed and sat on the curb. "That doesn't mean we wanted them to die, Shawn. Jesus."

"Are you sure, *Mary*?" Shawn snapped. "You're upset they died now, is that it, you pussy-ass faggot? You fucking queer!"

"Stop it, Shawn," Alex said softly. "What the fuck, man?"

Max bowed his head but didn't respond.

"Those assholes treated us like shit and said that kind of stuff to Max every fucking time they saw him—you know, when they weren't too busy beating the living daylights out of him. I'm—"

"We get it," I said. "But stop it, all right? Just stop."

Shawn crouched down in front of Max. "Dude, you know I—"

"It's fine, don't worry about it." Max smiled gently. "I appreciate what you're trying to say, and you're not wrong. But maybe Alex isn't either, know what I mean?"

Shawn gave him a playful slap on the arm. "I'm sorry, Maxie. I just can't pretend I'm bummed those motherfuckers are gone."

"The cops shot Perry," Alex said, rescuing him. "Man, that's nuts."

"Not before he killed and mutilated Keith," Max added.

"Fuck, he mutilated him too?"

"That's what people were saying, his body was mutilated."

"Crazy shit," Alex said. "But at least we were wrong about the Wendigo."

"*Wrong*?" I said. "What the hell are you talking about?"

"If they made it to the other end of the state, then whatever was in the woods didn't kill them, Frankie Boy. They got away like we did, right?"

I saw Ronica sit up on her towel. She was watching us, and I was afraid she might come over and ask what was going on. "I told you what Mean Earl said," I reminded him. "It can break a man's mind as easily as his back. It got into Perry's head, took him over and used him. That's why he killed Keith, that's why he was acting crazy."

"He still doesn't buy all this." Shawn stood up out of his crouch.

Max wiped sweat from his forehead with the back of his hand. "I have to admit I'm beginning to wonder if it matters *what* we believe."

"You know what?" I said, my patience gone. "I'm done trying to convince anybody what we're dealing with here. I'm going after it."

"Hey, man," Alex said, extending his hand, palm down. "You don't have to convince me of shit because it doesn't matter if I believe as much of this as you do. I'm still in. *All* in, I told you that."

"Absolutely," Max said as he stood and put his hand on top of Alex's.

I let my hand rest atop theirs. "Okay then."

Shawn put his in last. He didn't have to say anything more.

Although I was focused on them, I still had an eye on Ronica. "We have to make sure this all stays with us and only us," I said. "There's no telling what we might find out there."

"Or what we might bring back," Shawn said.

I hadn't thought of that, but it sent a shiver through me despite the heat. "The only thing we're bringing back is that fucking thing's shattered heart."

We dropped our hands, and Alex said, "Don't worry. I'll take care of my sister and make sure she stays out of this. One thing, though. I'm not going into those woods empty-handed."

"Me neither." Shawn lit a cigarette. "The rest of us need weapons too."

Alex combed some hair from his eyes with his fingers. "I'll handle it."

"Get everything together," I said. "Then meet me out in front of Clancy's in half an hour. I'm gonna spend the rest of my birthday money."

When you're fourteen you think you'll live forever.

Even when there's a good chance you won't.

CHAPTER EIGHTEEN

ONE OF THE older establishments in Samoset, Clancy's originally opened in the 1930s, and the ice cream parlor had remained in the same family ever since. Known for delicious homemade ice cream and a vintage soda fountain, it sported a checkerboard floor, old-style high-backed wood booths, ornate ceiling fans, and a counter with retro stools. It was like stepping back in time to a romanticized past otherwise only occasionally glimpsed in old movies.

By the time I slipped through the door and escaped the blistering heat for the air-conditioning inside, I'd walked halfway across town and was dripping sweat.

Two middle-aged men sat at one end of the counter eating hot fudge sundaes and chatting while the third-generation owner, Peter Clancy, a rotund little man with thinning blond hair and dark eyes, finished preparing a milkshake. At the other end of the counter, Officer Bishop, who was not only the lone black cop on the force at the time but the only nonwhite policeman the town had ever had, awaited his order. As the radio on his belt crackled loudly, he reached down and silenced it before acknowledging me with a restrained but warm smile. Although he'd been a cop in town for a couple years, we'd never had any personal interaction before. What little I knew of him was that he was a tall and physically formidable man, but unlike Officer Daniels and most of the other cops in town, he carried himself in an affable, approachable manner.

With the vintage ceiling fans slowly rotating overhead and circulating the cool air, I approached the counter and waited.

"What can I get you, pal?" Mr. Clancy asked, looking over his shoulder at me as he finished Officer Bishop's order.

"Four milkshakes, please, three chocolate and one strawberry."

"Just be a minute," he said.

Officer Bishop plucked a few napkins from a holder on the counter and held them out for me, motioning to my forehead. "Getting awfully hot out there," he said. "You've got quite a sweat going."

I took the napkins and wiped my forehead and face. "Thanks."

As I dropped the napkins in a trash barrel at the end of the counter, Mr. Clancy slid a tall paper cup over to Officer Bishop. "Here you go, Nathan," he said. "One vanilla milkshake."

Bishop thanked him and reached for the milkshake. As he turned from the counter, he lost his grip on the cup, and before he or I could catch it, the cup hit the floor and the contents exploded forth, leaving a sizeable puddle and spraying milk and vanilla ice cream everywhere.

"Oh, wow," Bishop said, clearly mortified. "Sorry, Pete, it slipped right out of my hand."

The two men at the end of the counter burst into laughter but made no move to help. One elbowed the other and said, "That's what you get for ordering a white man's drink, Nathan!"

While the men laughed uproariously, I stepped back and out of the way as Mr. Clancy came around the counter and started cleaning the mess. "Don't even worry about it," he said. "These things happen. I'll make another one real quick."

Officer Bishop had a spray of milk and ice cream across the front of his uniform, so I grabbed some napkins and gave them to him, returning the favor.

"Appreciate it," he said, wiping himself off.

As he looked over at the men, it was evident he'd found their attempt at humor, if that's really what it was, very offensive. I had too, and I could tell Mr. Clancy was uncomfortable and trying to pretend he hadn't heard it. Not knowing what to do, I waited to see what would happen next. But rather than engage or even respond to them, Officer Bishop instead turned to me and smiled.

"Almost got you too, son, sorry about that."

Before I could respond, I heard the other guy at the counter say, "Hell, if *that's* your son, his momma's got some serious explaining to do!"

More ugly laughter followed.

"It's okay," I told him. "It missed me."

"That's the Molinari kid," one of the men said. "Way his momma's been parading her ass around town lately, she's got a lot of explaining to do anyway."

My heart sank. Was this how it was going to be from now on? Were people going to keep insulting and making fun of my parents everywhere I went? Did everyone in town see our family as nothing more than a laughing stock, the punchline to their sordid jokes?

My anger rising, I suddenly felt the forest running through me, its whispers beckoning me. "What'd you say about my mother?" I asked through gritted teeth.

"Uh oh, look out, Vernon," one man chuckled. "He's gonna kick your butt!"

Fists at my side, I stepped toward them. "Say it again, you racist asshole."

The one called Vernon slid down off his stool and hitched his jeans up under his enormous belly. "I ought to wash that filthy mouth out with soap."

"You think I'm afraid of you?" The knife in my waistband dug into my side, reminding me it was there. "You're just a loudmouth tub of shit."

Officer Bishop stepped between me and the men. "All right, that's about enough of that now." He motioned to the stool. "Sit down, Vernon."

Vernon stayed where he was, glaring at me.

"I said, *sit down*."

"Aw, hell, Nathan," Vernon whined, plopping himself back onto the stool. "We're just having some fun and joking around is all."

"It's *Officer Bishop*," he corrected him. "My friends call me Nathan."

"That boy needs to watch the way he talks to me, I'm a grown man."

"Eat your ice cream and mind your business."

Muttering awkwardly, Vernon returned his attention to his sundae.

"And you," he said to me, "go wait outside."

"What about my milkshakes?" I asked, still seething.

"I'll bring them out to you, now go on."

"But I didn't pay for them yet."

Officer Bishop pointed to the door. "Go."

I gave the men at the counter a dirty look then shuffled back outside into the heat and sat at one of the tables out front.

Flashes of the forest and a horrific blur of something that wasn't human darting rapidly between the trees blinked across my mind's eye.

Through the front window I saw Officer Bishop standing close to the two men. I couldn't hear what he was saying, but if the expressions on their faces were any indication, they weren't too happy about it.

A moment later Bishop emerged with a cardboard tray holding my four milkshakes. "You okay?" he asked.

Before I could answer him Vernon burst through the door, visibly upset. "I don't know what in the *hell* makes you think you can talk to me like that," he said, pointing a finger at Bishop. "But I'll tell you this, *Officer* Bishop, I'm going straight to the chief to file a complaint against your black ass!"

"You do that, Vernon," Bishop said evenly. "But you watch your tone with me, or my *black ass* is going to give you something to be really upset about. And when you drive out of here you make real sure you do it safely and responsibly, you read me? So much as screech your tires and you'll be filing your complaint from the inside of a cell."

"Yeah, well we—we'll just see about that!" Face flushed, Vernon stomped over to his pickup truck, climbed in, and slammed shut the door. But when he pulled out, he did so slowly.

Once he was gone Bishop handed me the milkshakes. "Here," he said, taking a quick look around. "You're not going to drink all them yourself, are you?"

"No, sir, I'm waiting on my friends." I placed the tray on the table. "Are you gonna be in trouble now?"

"It'll be fine." Bishop waved at the air as if swatting away a small bug. "No one listens to that fool. If you're smart—and I'm sure you are—you won't either."

"What did you say to him that got him so mad?"

"That's between me and him, nothing for you to worry about." He winked then wiped some sweat from his brow. "Sure is a hot one today."

"Didn't you get another milkshake?" I asked.

"Pete's making it now. He's going to run it out to me."

"What do I owe you for these?"

"It's on me."

"Thanks," I said, shocked. "I have money. You didn't have to do that."

"I wanted to. Nobody ought to talk about another man's mother like that."

"It's not true. What he said, it isn't true."

"I know." Bishop smiled. "Vernon's an idiot, don't worry about it."

"I'm Frank Molinari." I offered my hand. "My friends call me Frankie Boy."

"Nathan Bishop," he said as we shook.

Something more than a fond handshake passed between us. I wasn't sure what it was at first because I hadn't felt it in a while, but once I knew, I latched on. It was relief. The kind a kid feels when they know they can count on an adult to not only do what's right, but to do it with genuine kindness and concern. The sort of relief a kid feels knowing it's all right to be the kid in the equation because they're in the presence of an adult that's got their back and is equipped to do so. Though he was probably only about ten years older than I was, word around town was he was a decorated combat Vietnam vet, and he looked the part. Like the hero in a war movie. Between that and his kindness, I found safety, a chance to take a deep breath. And I took it.

It was then that I realized I wanted desperately to tell him what was happening, what I knew, what me and the guys were about to do—all of it—yet I knew I couldn't. I wanted to believe if I did Officer Bishop could save me, rescue me—us—from all of this and somehow make it right. *If you're in trouble tell a policeman.* That's what I'd been taught since I was a little kid.

If only it had been that simple.

"Your friends better hurry up," he said as Mr. Clancy came out, handed him his milkshake, then hurried back inside. "Those are going to melt before they get here."

"They're coming any minute," I said.

"All right, you take care then." Officer Bishop stabbed a straw through the hole in the plastic cover and strolled over to his cruiser. "Stay out of trouble."

"I will."

He started to get in his car then hesitated, his eyes still trained on me. "You sure you're all right, son?"

"Yes, sir," I lied.

"There anything else you want to tell me?"

I knew by the way he asked that he had sensed there was.

"Nah, I'm okay."

"Are you sure about that?"

I nodded.

"Well, if that changes, you let me know, all right?" Officer Bishop turned up the radio on his belt, listening to a call coming through it a moment, and then took another sip of his milkshake. "See you around, Frankie Boy."

Once in his car, he gave me a quick wave then drove off.

Alone now, with the sun beating down on me, I pulled one of the chocolate shakes from the tray, pushed a straw through the top and took a sip.

Behind me, through the window, I saw Mr. Clancy busying himself at the counter, a look of disgust and guilt on his face as Vernon's friend rambled on in an animated fashion, probably about Officer Bishop.

I turned away, and focused on a couple trees across the street, the lower part of the trunks painted white. Everything else looked in place, like always, the quaint little town all around me intact and existing as it always had. But that paint told the real truth, because beneath the surface of our lovely little town there was a slow rot taking over. Maybe it had always been there and I'd just never noticed it before. Maybe that's why the gypsy moths had really come, not to destroy our town, but to cleanse it. That darkness—the corruption in our souls—is what they'd come to devour, and without even realizing it, we were doing everything in our power to stop them from saving us.

We were too busy feeding on each other.

While the Wendigo fed on our fear.
And those gypsy moths fed on us all.

* * * *

Blurred by waves of rippling heat rising from the pavement, they strode toward me. Shoulder-to-shoulder, gaits slow but deliberate and faces stoic, Shawn held a club fashioned from wood he'd made in shop the year before, Max carried a scarred baseball bat, and Alex had his knapsack and a canteen over his shoulder, and a slingshot he'd had for years protruding from the pocket of his shorts. Baby-faced warriors ready for battle, they joined me at the table.

"Cool, milkshakes!" Alex said suddenly. "Did you get me a strawberry?"

And just like that, we were us again.

"Yeah," I said, plucking it from the tray and handing it to him.

Shawn and Max happily helped themselves to theirs.

Alex beaming in a way he seldom did, and all of us laughing and enjoying those shakes under a merciless sun, made for a memory I knew I'd never forget. What I didn't know was that I'd be unable to duplicate it for the remainder of my life. In that moment we managed to forget about what was still to come, and reverted back to being carefree fourteen-year-old boys. There was something undeniably magical about that.

It was also quite fragile, because the moment our milkshakes were gone, so was the moment.

"Okay," Shawn said, his game face back on, "if Officer Daniels or any other pain in the ass tries to mess with us, we're on our way back from playing some baseball. Don't even try to hide the bat, Max. The rest of us can keep our shit undercover easy."

For good measure, Alex stuffed his slingshot deeper into his pocket.

"Just stick to the story no matter what," Shawn added.

Nobody else said anything, so I tossed my cup into the trash and headed for the street. "Let's go."

Ten minutes or so later we found ourselves at a crossroad.

To the left was the beach, mobbed and bustling. On any other Sunday summer afternoon that's where we'd have been too, swimming and cooling off in the ocean with everyone else.

To the right was my street, our little house about halfway up. I glanced in that direction, wondered if I'd ever walk that street or see the inside of that house or my parents again.

Straight ahead lay the forest. I'd never feared it. Now I felt nothing but.

Alex's canteen dangled at his hip from a strap he'd slung across his chest. He pulled it free, and after unscrewing the top, took a swig of water. As we passed it between us, we all took small quick sips, careful not to drink too much since we had no idea how long we might have to make it last.

"Okay," I said. "This is it."

"Last chance to forget all this and go swimming," Max said, forcing a grin.

With a quick look around to make sure the coast was clear, Shawn slid the club from the waistband of his shorts and held it down against his leg. He didn't say anything. He didn't have to. Like always, he just quietly and confidently took the lead.

And as he headed into the woods, we followed.

CHAPTER NINETEEN
~2017~

NOT LONG AFTER dark, a light rain begins to fall. With dinner sitting in the pit of my stomach like a brick, I throw some water on my face, change my shirt, and step out of my room to find Shawn in the parking lot covering his bike with a tarp. Once he finishes he retrieves a case of beer from the pavement, and since his room is adjacent to mine, heads toward me.

"Where's Max?" he asks.

"In his room, said he wanted to call home."

Shawn joins me under the modest tin awning that runs the length of the motel. It provides a bit of cover from the rain but not much. Old metal chairs painted green are positioned next to all the room doors, so he puts his beer down on one and sits in another. "Figured it'd be a slow night," he says. "So I went out and grabbed something to help pass the time."

"Beer?"

"Works like a charm. Want one?"

"Just one," I say. "I'm going for a drive."

"Have a seat." Tearing open the box, he pulls a can of Budweiser free and tosses it to me. "You don't want to miss out on this spectacular view of the state highway."

"God forbid." I sit down and open the can as Shawn gets one for himself. Never been much of a beer drinker, but it's nice and cold and feels good going down. Despite the gentle rain, the temperature hasn't dropped much and it looks like we're in for a muggy and oppressively hot night.

"So where you headed, man?"

"Thought maybe I'd go see Ronica," I tell him.

"God *damn* that girl was the balls, wasn't she?" Shawn smiles fondly then something else seems to occur to him. "You sure you want to bother her the night before her baby brother's funeral?"

"When we spoke on the phone, I told her I'd be by to see her tonight."

Shawn sips his beer. "I'd go with you but it'll be hard enough tomorrow, so if you don't mind I'm gonna sit here and get shit-faced."

"Do what you need to do."

We're quiet for a while. The rain and steady buzz of cars racing along the highway in the distance fills the silence. "Remember that time we scared the shit out of Tracy Davenport?" Shawn chuckles softly.

"Literally," I say.

"Yup, sprayed a *big* ole shit right in her pants." He drinks some beer. "I wonder whatever happened to her. Probably some dude's wife, somebody's mother—hell, grandmother—funny to think about her like that, isn't it?"

Truth is I haven't thought about her in years, but that night we frightened her has stayed with me. Only it doesn't seem so funny anymore. Rather than say anything else about it, I take another sip of beer.

"We're a long way from those days, Frankie Boy, a long goddamn way."

"Like a whole other life."

"Yeah, it really was." Shawn gives me a sideways glance. "Know who I was thinking about today? Marcy Rayland."

His girlfriend through most of high school, I remember her as a vivacious cheerleader he had a volatile, on-again off-again relationship with for most of our teenage years. The year after everything happened, 1978, our first year of high school, that's when they'd met.

"I should've married that girl," he says. "She wanted to, you know."

"Not surprised, for a while there I thought you might."

"She's a nurse," he tells me. "Been married for years, got four kids."

"How'd you find out all that?"

"I know I don't exactly look like the social media type," Shawn says. "But even I can figure out how to use Facebook."

"She never left town, huh?"

"Nope, far as I could tell she never did. I was gonna look her up, but I figure why disrupt her life, you know? Don't seem right."

"You could just say hello, Shawn, you don't have to run away with her."

"I'm probably the last person she'd want to see after all these years." He takes a long drink. "Not that I blame her. Hell, I can't even stand me most days."

I press the cold can against my forehead. It feels soothing. "Little while after graduation she called me. You'd already left town and I was headed for college. She kept asking where you were. I told her I didn't know and that you just got on your bike and took off."

"That old Honda I had back then. What a piece of shit."

"I don't think she believed me."

"Yeah," he says, "I bet not." Having already finished his beer, he crushes the can, drops it next to his chair then gets another one. "She was one of the good ones, though. Didn't know what I had until it was gone, story of my life."

"That day you left I figured we'd see each other again at some point."

Shawn holds his beer out. "We did."

I tap it but with less enthusiasm than he probably would've liked.

"What about you?" Shawn asks. "You ever think about Lauren…what the hell was her last name? I can't remember."

"Nilsson."

"Right, Nilsson."

"Sure," I admit. "Now and then I do."

He doesn't know that the real love of my life was a woman I met in college and lived with for more than a year, but I feel no need to tell him. What would be the point?

"Ever track her down?" he asks.

"No, never have."

"What about Jill McCorkle? You dated her a while."

"Jill dated everybody, Shawn."

"Not me."

"You had sex with her under the bleachers junior year."

"True, but it wasn't technically a date."

"We were only an item for about a week."

"That was a record for her, though. Jill was a major league punchboard."

"That's cold." I finish my beer, place it on the ground. "We were just kids."

"Want to know what happened to her?"

I look at him, an eyebrow raised. "Find her on Facebook too, did you?"

"She's this big religious nut now, all judgmental and holier than thou, one of those." Shawn laughs, has more to drink. "Fucking perfect, right? Nobody had more fun than that bitch and now she's trying to ruin it for everybody else."

I stand and stretch, suddenly reminded of every ache and pain I have whenever it rains. Of all the people I thought might be living in the past, Shawn is not one of them. I know that's not really what he's doing, though. He's only grasping at whatever he can get hold of that doesn't involve the horror of that summer, and although we spent the next four years trying desperately to convince ourselves none of it happened and live something resembling normal lives, evidently for now, this sort of reminiscing will do.

"I'm heading out."

"Why do you think Alex did it?"

His question hits me like a bat to the knees. I knew he'd ask it at some point, I just hadn't expected it now. "I don't know," I answer. "Maybe Ronica can shed some light on that, but I don't think Alex had an easy time all these years."

"Not many of us did." Shawn stares at his beer can. "The day I took off, I figured I'd be back at some point, you know? I knew it'd be a good long while, but I never thought it'd be this long."

I don't know what to say or how to console him. Glad as I am to see him and Max, I never wanted to come back here. Not then, not now.

He pauses to finish his second beer. "I thought I'd see him again."

"I know. It's okay."

"No, it's not." He takes it out on the can, crushing it like the first, and then reaches for another. "I never even talked to Alex again. And now he's in a box."

"But we don't know why he—"

"How do we know it's not back?"

"We don't." I step out from under the awning and into the rain. "A lot of shit happened, Shawn. Shit I've spent most of my life pretending didn't. We were fourteen, man. We did the best we could. We all did. Christ, we still do."

"Yeah, no shit." Shawn opens his beer and takes a long pull. "Because all those years ago the Devil came to town, Frankie Boy, and that motherfucker looked us right in the eye. It took more from you than anyone, so you tell me. How in the *fuck* do we live with that?"

The secrets locked in my head fall through my mind like the rain all around me. The horror, the fear, the violence, and the loss; it's all there, pulling me under, strangling me like always. Softly, and with a lump in my throat, I give him the only answer I've ever had.

"I have no idea."

* * * *

With the address Ronica gave me on the phone entered into my GPS, I travel the lonely and largely empty streets of Samoset. Night fell a while ago. It's still relatively early evening, but feels much later. As I drive through the rain towards my destination, the biggest change I see in town is the economic shift. Always a working-class burg, Samoset now looks more depressed and generally less affluent. The only areas that look the same, if not more prosperous, are the few neighborhoods we used to consider the rich parts of town when we were kids. Like most of the country these days, the gulf between the haves and the have-nots is significantly wider than it once was. It's more obvious, and profane. Those who had little, or some, have less. Those who had plenty have even more. When we were kids we were taught to fear the invisible but very real boundaries between the neighborhoods in town. I can only imagine how much more deeply drawn those lines must be today.

Rolling past several recognizable landmarks, I feel sentimentality mixed in with the constant state of apprehension that's had hold of me since I got here, and as I stop at a red light, I realize I'm in a familiar area. Across from me are the old train tracks. Ronica's new address is less than a five-minute drive from where she grew up with Alex.

With everything she had going for her, and as much of a force of nature we believed her to be, in all these years that's as far as Ronica got. It's not so unusual, I suppose, and there's certainly nothing wrong with it, yet I can't help but feel sorry for her. Poised to conquer the world, in the end, she never even made it out of Samoset. I wonder if that's how she wanted it, or if something changed.

Maybe everything did.

When the light turns green I cross the tracks and take a left, leaving the bigger and brightly lit street for a darker, winding and more rural road. I follow it for a half mile or so, the headlights carving two long pools into the thick darkness ahead while offering a peripheral glimpse of the woods on either side of me.

Don't look... Keep your eyes straight ahead... Don't look at the woods...

I do my best to focus on the classic rock station I've got the radio tuned to, but there's already a tightness spreading across my chest. Gripping the wheel, I press the gas and increase speed, covering as much ground as quickly as I can. But even with the trees blurred and mostly concealed in darkness, I can't escape the feeling that the forest is closing in on me. Like a noose, it tightens little by little until my heart smashes against the wall of my chest and the muscles in my neck constrict, sending sharp pains up into the back of my skull. Despite the car's air-conditioning, I break into a sweat and my body begins to shake so violently I'm afraid I might lose control of myself and the car.

"Breathe," I whisper. There are no houses, no other cars, nothing. *Where the hell is this place?* "You're all right, you're safe. Breathe...*breathe*..."

As I rocket through the night, eyes locked on the road, I'm surrounded by a darkness I know is alive and aware of my terror. Like the unseen things hidden within it, the night—*this* night—is a predator. And once again, it's hunting me.

The GPS signals my destination is located just beyond the next left. I slow the car and lean closer to the windshield, squinting for a better look just as a sign finally comes into view. Following the instructions, I turn onto a dirt road, passing the lighted sign that reads: *Pinewood Court*. Still shaking, I pass a dark trailer marked OFFICE then follow the road into a small mobile home park. This place didn't exist when I lived in town, but from the rundown appearance of the trailers it's clearly far from a new development, and most certainly a low-income district.

I find Ronica's trailer at the end of the third row of homes, a double-wide job with an old Ford and a relatively new Chevy pickup in the driveway. I park on the side of the road, across from the driveway, and run my hands over my face and into my hair. Though I'm still sweating and my heart is racing, I feel myself inching away from the precipice of a total meltdown.

After shutting off the car, I get out and hurry along the driveway to the three wood steps attached to the side of the trailer. With a quick look behind me to be certain no one is there or approaching from the darkness, I climb the steps and knock on the door. A dull nightlight illuminates a black mat beneath my feet that features a grinning cartoon cat. It reads: *Purr-fectly Welcome!*

Nervous as I am to see Ronica after all these years, the idea of remaining outside and vulnerable in the dark makes me even more anxious, so I'm grateful when I hear movement inside and the door slowly opens.

A thirtysomething man with thinning dark hair and a beard that hangs a few inches below his chin stands before me. Tall, well-built, and dressed in work boots, jeans, and a sleeveless Alice in Chains t-shirt, he stares at me tentatively.

"I'm Frank," I say through the still-closed screen door. "Frank Molinari."

Upon hearing my name the man relaxes his posture. "Come in," he says, opening and holding the screen door for me. "My mom's expecting you."

His mom? Jesus Christ.

I step directly into a kitchen. Beyond it is a narrow hallway I assume leads to the bedrooms and bathroom. To my right is a living room. There is little light here, mostly from the kitchen stove, and a strong odor of potpourri masks the underlying smell of booze and cigarettes in the air. An old air-conditioner rattles and groans in a window on the far kitchen wall, and a couple real cats are lying next to the table. One is asleep, sprawled out on its back. The other looks up at me with a bored expression but doesn't otherwise move.

The man closes both doors behind me and thrusts a meaty hand in my direction. "I'm Dennis—Denny."

My hand disappears into his as we shake. Despite the size of his hand, his grip is actually quite gentle. "I'm very sorry for your loss."

"Thank you, sir," he says solemnly, then releases my hand. "Uncle Alex used to talk about you and his other buddies from when he was a kid now and then. He said you guys were real tight."

I don't know why this surprises and moves me, but it does. "We were very close right through high school, yes." I take a subtle glance around but don't see anyone else. "How's your mother holding up?"

"Well as can be expected, I guess." He motions to the living room. "You can go on in and see her. I'll leave you guys alone."

Denny crosses the kitchen then slips down the hallway and out of sight.

In the living room is a couch bookended by two small tables. A flat screen is mounted on the wall, and a fake fireplace heater sits beneath it. Across from the couch is a recliner, its back facing me.

It's then I realize Ronica's been sitting in it all along.

In two short strides I'm in the living room, and though I can see half a silhouette that I'm certain is her, I still can't make her out due to the lack of light in the room. Her silhouette lifts a small bottle and drinks from it. I move around to the couch and finally see her, though still in shadow.

"Ronica," I say softly, unsure if I should go to her or stay where I am. "Hi."

"Frankie Boy," a raspy female voice answers.

"God, I—I'm so sorry."

She doesn't respond right away. "I used an Internet site to track you down," she finally says. "Once I had your number I punched it into my phone three times before I let it go through. After all these years, I..."

"I'm sorry if I was awkward when you called, I just—"

"*You*? Hey, Frankie Boy, it's me, Ronica, you know, Alex's sister? From a million years ago, remember? Yeah, Alex is dead."

Her words are spiked with long-suffering anger, and who can blame her? "I would've come earlier but—"

"Don't worry about it," she says.

Slowly deflating, I lower myself onto the couch, hands in my lap. I know it's an idiotic question, but I need to ask it anyway. "Are you all right?"

Ronica reaches for a pack of cigarettes and a book of matches on a freestanding ashtray positioned to the left of the recliner. "We're planting my kid brother in the ground tomorrow. So no, I don't think I am, actually. Not that it matters. The world keeps right on spinning whether I'm all right or not."

I wish she'd sit forward, out of the shadows, so I can see her. "Is there anything I can do, anything you need?"

A match flares to life with a hiss. As she brings it to the cigarette in her mouth, the flame partially illuminates her face. I glimpse tired, heavily made-up eyes, a hand with short fingernails covered in chipped black polish, and a bit of dark hair hanging along the side of her face. She shakes the match to darkness as the head of her cigarette burns bright orange. Tossing the spent match into the ashtray, Ronica sits backs and exhales a cloud of smoke that hangs in the air between us like an apparition. "I've got to give these fucking things up," she says through a sigh. "Nobody smokes anymore."

"Max and Shawn are both in town," I tell her. "They wanted me to let you know they'll see you tomorrow. They would've come too but we didn't want to—"

"It's hard to believe you're sitting here." She draws on her cigarette. "You were eighteen and I was twenty the last time I saw you, that makes it thirty-eight years. Doesn't seem possible, does it? Then again, a lot of things have been hard to believe around here lately. Sometimes I wonder if it's all a bad dream."

Neither of us says anything for a moment, and I wonder now if I should've come. Desperately searching for something to break the uncomfortable silence, I say, "So that's your son?"

"Can you believe it?" she asks. "He insisted on staying with me tonight. I told him to go home to his wife and kids, but he won't leave my side."

"That's good. He's looking out for you."

"He's thirty-four, had him when I was twenty-two. That means he's old enough now to have been our father back when you and I knew each other. How crazy is that?" She tilts her head back and exhales a stream of smoke at the ceiling. "Want to really blow your mind? I've got two grandbabies now, ten and seven. I'm a goddamn grandmother."

Ronica's cigarette hand emerges from the shadows and points to a crude mantel above the fireplace that features a framed photograph of two little girls, the younger one sporting a huge toothless smile. Unlike Denny, who bears little resemblance, I can see traces of her in both of her grandchildren's faces.

But it is the photograph next to them that catches my eye.

Denny standing next to a man I know immediately is Alex. Their arms are around each other, and both are smiling. Denny broadly, Alex with the same sad little grin he had when I knew him. In the photograph he looks to be in his middle to late forties. He wears a ratty-looking baseball cap, but the hair I can see has turned gray. Salt-and-pepper stubble covers his gaunt, heavily lined face, and his eyes appear dulled from what I presume is years of drug and alcohol abuse. But there's no mistaking who it is. A lump forms in my throat, and as my eyes fill I can only hope the shadows will conceal me as well as they're hiding Ronica.

"His father's never been in the mix," she says. "I've been married and divorced twice, and had my share of boyfriends, God knows, but none of them were ever much good for Denny. He was always a good kid, though. Still is, I don't know what I'd do without him."

I know it's her, but she doesn't sound much like the Ronica I once knew, and it's jarring. There's a weight to her voice that only time, age, and tragedy can bring.

"This is hard on him too," she says. "Alex was good to him, there for him in ways other guys weren't, you know? Most days Alex had a hard enough time getting himself through the day, but he tried as best he could with Denny, he really did. He was the closest thing to a dad my son's ever going to know."

I let her words sit a while before asking if Alex had any kids of his own.

"No," she says, and as soon as I'm sure she has no plans to elaborate further, she does just that. "Do you remember Vanessa Bennett?"

It takes me a few seconds, but I do. "You mean from high school? Skinny, kind of shy? Blonde hair? Braces?"

"Yeah, she was a year behind you guys."

Alex rarely dated in high school and never had a steady girlfriend the entire time I knew him, but Vanessa stands out in my memories because Alex took her to our senior prom. "Yes," I say. "I remember Vanessa."

"Alex married her a couple years after she graduated," Ronica says. "He was working for the cable company doing installs and repairs and Vanessa got a job as a cashier over at Stop & Shop. They had a nice little cottage not far from the beach. It's the only time I ever saw my brother happy. I mean *really* happy. When I think about it I just...I don't know...it chokes me up."

I glance at the photo of him again without being too obvious about it. The man staring back, though smiling, looks anything but happy. He's hopeless and broken. His eyes tell me so.

A flash of him covered in blood comes to me then fades.

"Were they still together or..."

"Their marriage lasted about five years," Ronica explains. "She was a sweet kid, and they were good together. Far as my brother was concerned, the sun rose and set on that girl. I'm pretty sure she's the only woman he ever loved. Then she got sick, cancer. They both went through hell, but Alex was so good, so strong through the whole thing, right until the end. He never let her see his pain, his fear. When Vanessa died it was in his arms. It broke his heart. He was never the same, never recovered."

She reaches to the floor next to the recliner, comes back with the bottle of beer again and takes a long drink.

"He hardly even dated after that," Ronica continues. "Maybe a hookup here or there but never anything serious. And he started drinking a lot, doing drugs. A few years later he hurt his back at work and had to go on disability. He was in a lot of pain so his doctor put him on Oxys. When the whole opioid thing got out of control, they wouldn't prescribe it anymore, even for people like Alex, addicts that needed it. So he eventually wound up on fucking heroin, like a lot around here have."

"Christ," I say.

"Wasn't much left of him by then, but he hung on best he could."

"I'm so sorry," I say, trying to imagine my old friend living that life and damning myself for being nowhere near any of it. "I had no idea he—"

"Of course not, why would you?"

Her response hits me like a punch to the gut. She's not wrong, and it's not as if I don't deserve it, but it still hurts. "Ronica, I—"

"Hey," she says, cutting me off. "Is what it is, right? It's been almost forty years, little silly to start explaining ourselves at this point, don't you think?"

I don't feel like she's the one I need to explain myself to, but Alex is dead. Ronica's all I've got.

"I had to go, Ronica. I couldn't stay here."

"I know," she says in a softer tone. "With everything that happened I know how hard it was for you. I remember. Do you still see your mother at all?"

"She died a few years ago."

"Sorry." She drinks more beer. "Have any family? A wife, kids?"

"Never married," I tell her. "No kids."

She turns in the chair enough for me to make out the side of her face. "You're all alone?"

I nod.

"Never saw that for you."

"Not sure I did either, but it's okay. I'm used to it."

Except for the hum of the air-conditioner, the quiet returns. She finishes her cigarette, crushes it in the ashtray, then sits forward into the sparse light. As Ronica's eyes meet mine, she slowly rises to her feet.

She's significantly older, of course, and I can see a bit of her mother in her in the way the years have taken a toll. But she's mesmerizing as ever. Her hair is shorter now—a messy, slightly long pixie cut framing her face and dyed jet black—and she still has a body most women half her age would kill for.

As she closes the gap between us I stand too, and she draws me in for a hug. As we hold each other tight, I'm reminded of the countless times I've remembered her, fantasized about her, and the things we'd say and do if our paths ever crossed again. Nearly forty years later, this is not how I imagined it.

Few things ever are.

She smells of beer and cigarettes, but her hair has a pleasant scent, and her body feels good against mine. Even though it's been a while since I've had close physical contact with a woman, there is little erotic about our hug. We're riddled with too much sorrow and pain, too many scars for that. And yet, it's the most purely intimate moment we've ever shared.

Her lips press against my cheek, then she releases me.

I stand there a moment, unsure of what to do with myself.

Ronica walks to the kitchen, places her now empty beer bottle on the table, then grabs two more from the refrigerator. As she saunters back, she steps over the slumbering cats, and hands me a beer.

I don't really want it, but rather than offend her, I take it. Although I'm not looking forward to the drive out of here, my nerves are almost settled, and maybe a beer before I go will relax me enough so I won't have another panic attack.

If that's what it was.

The only window in this part of the trailer is the one over the sink in the kitchen. After handing me a beer, Ronica takes hers and drifts over to it. The light from the stove better reveals her outfit of black jeans, a yellow top with spaghetti straps, and her bare feet. As she gazes out at the night, I find myself taking her and all of this in like a dream. Can I really be here after all this time? Is Alex really dead and gone? Dizzying as it is maddening, I chug my beer as long-ago memories begin to fire, sending me hurtling back through time in a tempest of horror and regret.

"We didn't mean to abandon Alex," I say. "*I* didn't mean to."

Ronica's head snaps in my direction like the sound of my voice has startled her. Cocking a hip, she holds her bottle down against her leg as if concealing a weapon. Her eyes, red from crying, search mine, but I've got nothing for her. Only screams and horror from a past she still doesn't know or understand, a past that from the moment her brother and I ventured into the woods four decades ago has informed every breath I take, every thought I have, every sleepless night I've endured, and every nightmare I've ever known since.

"And yet," Ronica says evenly, "that's exactly what you all did."

"I had to get out. I *had* to. I don't know how I lasted as long as I did."

"He knew you and Max were going to college, but when Shawn left he was so lost, so alone. Even when he was with Vanessa he talked about you guys like he was some sort of guardian, like he'd been left in charge of something. Not long after Vanessa's death, Rafe was killed in that fucking El Camino he loved so much. Driving too fast one night, lost control and hit a cluster of trees."

I don't say it, but that strikes me as how Rafe would've wanted to go out. "I'm sorry to hear that. He was the coolest, and I know he and Alex were close."

In his way, Rafe saved us all. Only no one knows it. He didn't even know.

"We lost Mom a few years ago, liver issues from all the booze. She tried to get well but it was too late, the damage was done. Through it all Alex was sure you'd be back at some point, all of you. Even if not permanently, he really believed you'd be back. He died believing it."

"Ronica, you don't understand—"

"Yeah, that's what he used to say. Because no matter how much he missed you guys, and how bad he thought you'd left him behind, he always defended you. Much as it hurt him, he'd defend you. And whenever I asked him why, he said I didn't understand." She takes a long drink from the bottle and leaves the window to lean against the table. "I know something happened with you guys that day you all went off together with that knife Rafe made for you. Yeah, didn't think I knew that, did you? Trust me, baby, by then I'd already perfected lying out in a bikini and not missing a goddamn thing. My brother left our house that day with you guys, and when he came back he wasn't the same kid. None of you were. You'd changed, and not for the better. Every weakness Alex had, every bit of sorrow and pain and fear he ever carried inside him, was worse. And he never got a break after that day, not really. Even when he did it was ripped away from him the way Vanessa was. But don't worry, Frankie Boy, he kept your secrets safe and sound. Even when he'd get drunk and really stoned, even when he was strung out on heroin so bad he didn't know where the hell he was, he never told me. He said he couldn't, and when I'd ask him why, he'd say because he was cursed. You all were. It was just a matter of degrees, he'd say. You believe that shit? Yeah, I'm thinking you do."

"I'm sorry," I say. It's all I have left that means anything, and it's not even close to enough. "Sometimes knowing things is worse than not knowing them."

She arches an eyebrow. "Is that supposed to be poetic?"

"It's just the truth."

"Convenient as it may be, right?"

I don't want a showdown, never did, it's not why I'm here, so I return to the couch and sit down. If only we could be back in that old Volkswagen she had when were teenagers, flying along dark roads and laughing, our eyes meeting in the rearview mirror and hoping the night would never end. In my mind's eye I see her running along the sand on the beach that night. She was so alive, so strong. My God, we were all invincible.

"Did he leave a note?" I ask quietly.

"You mean before he shot up one last time, took his belt, hanged himself in his bedroom closet and died alone?" Ronica's voice breaks as her face twists with pain. "Yes, he left a note."

I bow my head.

"He said goodbye, and that he was sorry. There wasn't anything about your precious little secrets in it, don't worry. Matter of fact, there wasn't anything about you or Max or Shawn in it at all. Why the fuck would there be? None of you were a part of my brother's life. You all saw to that."

"Is that why you think I'm here, to make sure he didn't—"

"I don't know, Frankie Boy, is it?" Ronica wipes her eyes, finishes the beer, then plunks it angrily on the kitchen table. "You tell me."

The truth is I'm not entirely sure myself. Part of me needs to know if Alex's death had anything to do with the past, and if what we fought all those years ago has somehow come back. But it's more than that. I want to make sense of it all, to find forgiveness and to put it to bed once and for all. Or maybe I'm just a tired and lonely man limping toward old age, still afraid of the dark and grasping at straws.

Redemption is always elusive. It can't be any other way.

"What happened that day, Frankie Boy?"

Death…that's what happened that day…

"It was a bad summer," I say, knowing this isn't enough.

"Sure was. Son of Sam was shooting up New York City. We had a peeper running around town looking in windows, the whole Perry Jenkins and Keith Dickinson thing, those goddamn gypsy moths, and then your father…" She stops herself, but it's too late. "Is that why you've never had children?" An odd dawning crosses her face. "My God, that's it, isn't it? That's why you're alone."

"Mental illness is often hereditary," I tell her.

Ronica comes to me, places a hand on the side of my face, and then slowly slides it to my neck and down onto my shoulder. She can't figure out if she loves or hates me, and I know exactly how she feels.

"I'm sorry," she says softly.

"For the love of God, please don't apologize to me, Ronica." I put my hand on hers. "Not tonight."

"We all just get the lives we're dealt, don't we?" She sighs and moves away, shaking her head and laughing lightly, though there's not a thing humorous or joyful about it. "Maybe it really is that simple."

I don't think she's wrong, but it's not quite that cut and dry either.

"Remember how I wanted to go to Hollywood and be a movie star?"

"Like Raquel Welch," I say.

She smiles, and this time, though it's laced with regret, it's genuine. "Yeah," she says, choking up again. "Like Raquel Welch."

I don't ask because I already know the answer.

"Never got there," she says anyway. "Now look at me, I've spent my life working the line at the paper factory for a couple bucks over minimum wage just like every other loser in this fucking shit town. It's my own damn fault, though, no one else's. When it came down to it, I didn't have the guts to leave."

"You had the guts. You had more guts than anyone I've ever known."

"Just looked that way," she says. "I was as scared to chase my dreams as everyone else around here. I was just better at hiding it. Maybe that's why they call them dreams." Though pushing sixty, Ronica defiantly strikes a pose reminiscent of her younger self. She pulls it off seamlessly: hands on hips, head cocked slightly to the side, back straight, breasts straining against the thin fabric of her top. "It takes a lifetime to dream about a life worth having, but only a minute or two to burn it all down."

A memory of Alex and me as kids hits me. Stumbling down the street, arms around each other and laughing with an abandon reserved for the young.

"Doesn't seem fair," she says.

"That's because it's not."

Somewhere in the distance, thunder rolls and rumbles.

"Once, not so long ago, Alex crashed here for the night. He shot up in the bathroom, and then he sat right on that couch and drank until he passed out. At one point I asked him what happened that summer day, I wanted to know why he came home all beat up, why he was so haunted after that, why you guys were so different. You were all carrying something you hadn't been before, and it was weighing you down. It was obvious something bad had happened and that it bothered him. It'd been fucking with his head for years. Like I said, he never gave away your secrets, but do you want to know what he *did* tell me? He said monsters really do exist. He wouldn't say anything else, no matter how drunk or high he got, just that. I always assumed he was using the word *monster* metaphorically. But I've never been sure. Does it matter, Frankie Boy?"

"Not anymore."

"Is that all you're going to give me?"

"You don't want more. Trust me."

Ronica nods and closes her eyes. A teardrop rolls the length of her face. "He was so sweet, so lost," she says, the words hitching in her throat. "I really don't think Alex wanted to die. He just didn't know how to keep on living."

She looks vulnerable, destroyed. And I've never felt more useless.

When I close my eyes it is Alex's face I see, looking back at me from long ago. I want to believe he's telling us it's all right now, that everything is okay and there's no reason to be afraid because he's seen the other side and knows that what's waiting for us has nothing to do with the evil that claimed and bound us to it when we were kids. But what if it's like Ronica said, and this is all just a bad dream? What if we're dead or dying in those dark woods right now? What if this is a nightmare conjured in a slowly dying mind, one that's struggling to imagine a future that never was and never will be?

When I return to the here and now, it's just us, but I still can't be sure.

Nothing's changed. And in a way, everything has.

I join Ronica in the kitchen, and we embrace again.

"It wasn't supposed to be like this," she says, her breath hot in my ear.

In the dim light of Ronica's kitchen, I hold her tight and watch the darkness through the window over the sink. I can't heal her. I can't even heal myself. So I just keep my arms around her and hope she'll soon stop shaking.

More thunder, this time closer, and then a heavier rain drums the trailer.

I know when I leave here and step out into that rain the same threatening darkness will be waiting for me. I'm in no hurry, but can't hold Ronica forever. When I let her go, to my surprise, she continues clinging to me, holding on even tighter than before. Slowly, I put my arms around her again.

Hard as we try, we can never absolve each other of our sins or stop the storms that rage within us both.

But for a short while at least, we do find a little shelter.

CHAPTER TWENTY
~1977~

SUNLIGHT CUT THROUGH the treetops in crisscrossing golden beams that gave the forest an otherworldly, magical look. The forest floor was covered in a bed of pine needles, uneven and populated with gnarled roots and occasional drop-offs. The terrain was not a friendly one, and the deeper we went the worse it got.

As we reached the section of woods near my house, the area where we'd last seen Perry and Keith and where Shawn had his sighting, the heat remained thick and oppressive, though slightly more tolerable than being out in the open. While Max, Alex, and I began searching for clues to what might have happened here, I noticed Shawn looking back in the direction from which we'd come.

"What is it?" I asked. "What's wrong?"

"I thought I heard something back there."

That got the attention of Max and Alex, who stopped what they were doing and took up position on either side of me.

"Like what?" Max asked.

"Like somebody following us," Shawn muttered. "Guess I was wrong."

"Are you sure?"

"No, but I don't see anything."

"Me neither," Alex said.

I looked and listened as well. The forest was still and, with the exception of some birdsongs, quiet.

Max gave him a quick pat on the shoulder. "Maybe it's just nerves?"

"Yeah, maybe," Shawn said, though he looked skeptical.

After a moment we resumed scouring the area. The problem was that none of us were sure exactly what we were looking for or hoped to find, so after a while, when we didn't come across anything unusual, we gave up.

"If this is where it got to Perry and Keith, there's no evidence," Alex said. "Doesn't look any different than the last time we were here."

"Shawn," I said, "where was it when you saw it?"

"There." He pointed to the spot. "Right next to that big bastard."

Wiping sweat from my face, I walked over to the base of the large pine he'd indicated and crouched down. No tracks, nothing disturbed. I next checked the tree itself, but found no scratches, broken branches, or anything to suggest there had ever been something that large anywhere near this place.

"It's like it was never here."

"We've been in these woods a million times," Shawn said. "Except for the other day, I've never felt spooked out here. But I'm feeling it again. It's different now, not like before. Almost like there's something...I don't know...*wrong*. You guys getting it too?"

We didn't have to answer. Everyone felt it, a dread hanging in the air so heavily it was palpable. Like something had died here in an evil and horrifically violent manner and the residue of that carnage was not only lingering somehow, but spreading and growing stronger.

"There's something evil in these woods." I stood up and looked around again. "And it knows we're here."

Rather than respond, Shawn hocked a loogie at a nearby tree. It hit the trunk then hung there, dangling grotesquely.

"*God* that is so fucking revolting," Max said with a sigh.

"Thanks." Shawn grinned. "Appreciate it."

"Jesus H," Alex said, laughing. "You could lay floor tiles with that shit."

As the others attempted to calm their nerves with jokes and laughter, something else drew my attention: several gypsy moths gathered halfway up the tree trunk, partly camouflaged and motionless.

"Let's go." I pushed forward. "Keep your eyes open."

A couple minutes later we reached the section of forest that ran parallel to my backyard. Through the branches and shrubs was my house, only thirty or so yards away. Coming home this way numerous times over the years had worn a narrow path right to our property, so I followed it like I had countless times in the past. This time, however, I stopped at the tree line and scanned the lot.

The charred pile of Ouija board remains were still there, but the shovel my father tossed on the lawn was nowhere to be seen. As my eyes drifted up to the glass sliders, I wondered what my dad was doing in there now. How many days and nights over the last year had he stood in front of them and gazed into the woods? How many times had the Wendigo been gazing back from this very spot? The bright sunshine bearing down on the sliders made it impossible to see beyond them into the house, so at that point anyone could've been standing there...or no one at all.

I turned away, not knowing for sure if I'd ever see or return to my home again, and continued deeper into the woods. The others trailed behind me, no one speaking or joking now, but quiet and focused on the forest instead.

We'd gone a couple miles when Alex finally said, "Not trying to be a dick, but we've been walking for almost an hour and we haven't seen a thing."

When I stopped, everyone else did too, and we all stood there trying to figure out what to do next. For the first time I felt like maybe I'd been wrong about all this. Were we just a bunch of stupid kids chasing something that didn't even exist?

"We don't exactly have a plan for where this fucking thing is," Shawn said, removing his sunglasses long enough to wipe his face with his bandana. Once finished, he tied it around his head again, then dug his lighter and cigarettes from his shorts. "We got miles of woods out here. We could keep walking until after dark and still wouldn't cover all of them."

Max blanched. "I, for one, do not want to be here after dark."

"We may not have any choice," I said.

Alex took a swig from his canteen then passed it to me. "I brought a flashlight just in case," he said, indicating one on his belt.

As I took a drink I noticed the others exchanging troubled glances. I was losing them. They were already doubting the point of all this. And maybe they were right.

I handed Max the canteen and looked in the direction we were headed. In another mile or two we'd run into the Samoset Quarry. An old granite quarry abandoned not long after World War II, it was privately owned land and off-limits, but people frequently trespassed there anyway. Over the years it had become a place to party and hangout for older teens, college kids, and young adults. As was the case with many depleted quarries, the huge holes left behind filled with water and eventually formed a large and dangerous quarry lake that was at some points more than two hundred feet deep. Despite the danger, or because of it, the quarry had been an attraction for years. It wasn't as popular as the beaches, but it was out of the way, a lot harder to get to and far more private, which was appealing to some. Kids often dared each other to leap from the rock cliffs to the lake below, and for years, every summer, at least one or two people drowned out there. As a result, the cops had cracked down on the partying and congregating, and these days it was a far less travelled area, even in the summer months.

I was thinking about the fact that there were a lot of places to hide there, when something up ahead caught my eye. Heart pounding my chest, I slid my sunglasses off and pointed. "You guys...*look*."

No one said anything, but I knew they'd seen them too.

We moved quickly between the trees, stopping short of another big pine. Upright and leaning severely to the left, its massive branches were sprawled out overhead like giant wings. But our focus was closer to the ground, and on the things hanging from a much lower branch.

Just out of reach, and fastened with what appeared to be some sort of primitive wood twine, several sets of deer antlers, smooth and bleached white from the sun, dangled above our heads.

Max was suddenly standing next to me. "Are those real?"

I nodded.

Shawn circled the tree, searching for more.

"Is that normal?" Max asked. "I mean, is that something hunters do?"

Alex made a face. "Why the hell would hunters do that?"

"I have no idea." Using the tip of the baseball bat, Max poked the antlers, causing them to sway and click against each other like some horrible wind chime. "But it shouldn't exactly come as a shock that I'm not up on the dos and don'ts of hunting."

"Hunters didn't do this," I said, watching the forest now.

"No." Alex looked up at them, his face a mask of confusion. "They didn't."

"It's a message, a sign...a warning maybe."

"From the—"

"Don't say its name." I let a hand fall to the knife on my belt.

"Frankie Boy, for God's sake, I—"

"It knows we're here." Shawn stabbed a cigarette into his mouth and lit it quickly. "And it's telling us what's waiting for us if we keep going."

"Death," I said.

Max took a quick drink of water, then handed the canteen back to Alex. "How are you two coming up with all that from some antlers in a tree?"

I could tell from Alex's face he already knew, but he wasn't about to say it.

An eerie silence fell over the forest. Even the birds had stopped singing. The sun was noticeably lower in the sky and beginning its descent. Night was only a few hours away.

"Notice how many of them there are?" Shawn said.

He looked up, counted them. "Jesus."

"Exactly," Shawn said, but his eyes were on me. "Four."

I drew a deep breath, let it out slowly. "There are four of us."

I couldn't see it. None of us could. But we all felt it.
Right down to the pits of our stomachs.
The Wendigo was in this forest with us. And it was close.

CHAPTER TWENTY-ONE

A CHAIN-LINK FENCE seven feet high stood before us. Attached to the center of it was a bright orange sign with black letters that read: PRIVATE PROPERTY! NO TRESPASSING! VIOLATORS WILL BE PROSECUTED! Beyond it was a stretch of forest leading to the quarry.

Nothing felt real anymore. The forest appeared more ominous than usual, like it was not only watching, but stalking us too, ready to come alive and crash down on us at any moment. We were all hot and tired from walking, and now I felt disoriented as well, as if I'd been drugged. The sun, beautiful when we'd set out, was dying, the beams of gold gone, replaced by dull light bleeding through the canopy of treetops overhead. It was as if we'd left the confines of the usual world and stepped through a portal that deposited us on an alien planet. I knew these woods—we all did—and yet it felt like I'd never been here before.

Shawn was watching the forest behind us again, his sunglasses resting atop his head. Whatever he heard earlier, or thought he heard, he'd apparently heard again. His eyes scanned the trees, a look of deep concern on his face. Dropping into a crouch, he sniffed the air like he smelled something unusual. "Come on, Shawn, what's with the Davey Crockett bullshit?" Alex said. "Is there somebody following us or not?"

"I don't know." Shawn stood up and flashed Alex a cross look. "And fuck you, man. If there's somebody back there we don't need them coming up on us."

"If you're worried about it, let's go back and see what's—"

"Shawn," Max said, sliding between them with his usual subtlety, "what did you hear?"

"Movement, okay? And I thought I smelled something. Soap or aftershave or something, I—I don't know, all right?" He shook his head and paced around in a circle like he was becoming as disoriented and detached from reality as I felt. "But there's nothing there, I...I'm just..."

A hot breeze blew through the trees, gone as suddenly as it arrived.

"Mean Earl said it fucks with your mind," I said. "Maybe that's what's happening now because I don't feel right."

"Me either." Shawn shook his arms, like he was trying to loosen up his muscles. "I'm so *tired* all of a sudden."

I knew exactly what he meant. Despite the fear, confusion, and tension firing through me, I knew if I were to lie down right then and there I'd go to sleep immediately. "Something's happening," I said.

"I feel it too." Max swung the baseball bat back and forth lazily at his feet, as if trying to figure out what to do with it. "I'm a little sick to my stomach."

"Yeah," Shawn agreed, "nauseous, right?"

Max nodded.

"You guys are letting this shit go to your heads," Alex said. "I don't feel a thing except hot. You know why? Because it's fucking hot out. Now, are we going over this fence or what?"

It can use the weather, other animals or men, anything in the forest...

"It's using everything around us," I told them.

Once it's on you, there ain't no safe place...

Alex pointed to the fence. "We going or should we turn back?"

A sudden and horrific shriek sounded in the distance. Shrill and howl-like, it was an otherworldly cry similar to the call of a coyote. But this had come from a much larger creature. The kind of sound that shook you to your core because it tapped into something primordial and horrific, it was not only a reminder, but a warning that it was not the prey. We were.

It uses sounds. Growls, howling, screeches...

"Fuckin' hell was that?" Shawn said, the blood draining from his face.

"Don't listen to it," I told them. "It's trying to frighten us."

Max wiped sweat from his brow. "It's succeeding."

Alex approached the fence, watching the forest beyond it where the wail originated from. Struggling to make sense of what we'd all heard, I could almost see the gears turning in his head as he tried to come up with an animal to assign it to. "It's just..."

It can imitate voices too...

"Whatever you hear, don't listen," I said.

It can trick you if you're not careful...

"Maybe we should go back," Max said. "Maybe we should just go back."

Don't listen to it. Not ever.

"No." I shook my head in an attempt to clear the cobwebs. It didn't really work, but I forced myself toward the fence anyway. "Let's go."

Alex still looked baffled, but he went first anyway, maybe to prove a point. Regardless, he scaled the fence quickly, and as he dropped down on the other side, he shrugged like it was no big deal.

"Go," Shawn said, cocking his head toward the fence. "I'll watch our backs until you guys are over."

After a couple deep breaths, Max went next.

Once he'd made it, I joined him and Alex on the other side.

With a final look at the woods behind us, Shawn climbed the fence, the chain-link rattling and shaking against his weight.

Ahead lay a stretch of woods leading to the quarry…

And whatever had made that terrifying screech.

* * * *

With Shawn in the lead, Max and me in the middle, and Alex pulling up the rear, we trudged slowly but purposefully through the thick brush and trees. The forest was much denser here, so it was hard to see anything clearly more than a few feet ahead of us. There was also less light, which reminded me of walking through the haunted house attractions that popped up in town every Halloween, where you knew it was only a matter of time before something horrifying lurched out at you as if from nowhere. Only there was nothing fun about this fear.

The shriek had not sounded again, but its memory stayed with me. Hard as I tried to focus on the forest in front of us, my mind kept drifting to Perry and Keith and conjuring various possible scenarios of what had taken place here, each one more grotesque and terrifying than the last.

As we broke through the last patch of thick brush, it gave way to a path which led through the final stretch of forest before the quarry. More wide-open now, our visibility improved dramatically, and once again the woods became immense, the trees towering above us.

"Do you hear that?" Max suddenly pulled up short and stumbled to a stop. A spasm-like smile scurried across his face, and he looked like he was about to lose his mind. "Please tell me you guys hear that."

I slowly shook my head no.

Eyes locked on the forest before us, Max cocked his head to the side and scowled as if in pain. "Laughing, you—you seriously don't hear it?"

"What in the *fuck* are you talking about?" Alex snapped. "You hear laughing?"

Max put a visibly trembling hand to his mouth. "You don't?"

"What kind of laughing?" I asked.

"Like a…child…a…a little *child*."

"Don't listen. It's not real. Look at me, Max."

He did.

"*It's not real.*"

"I know, I…I know." Max looked around as if to be sure. "It stopped, I…I think it stopped."

We kept moving, following the forest along what quickly became a narrow path. To our left, another stretch of woods; to the right, a severe drop off of slanted forest through which glimpses of the quarry lake below could be seen beyond the trees. Ahead of us was the final bit of woods leading up to the granite cliffs.

It was then that the stench hit us. Somewhere between rotting garbage, decayed flesh, and the pungent odor of filthy wet fur, it swept through the air around us in great rushing waves.

"I'm gonna fucking barf," Shawn said. "What the hell is that stink?"

"An animal probably died nearby." Alex brought a hand to his nose. "From the smell I'd say it's been rotting in the sun for a while."

Max suddenly bent at the waist and threw up.

Ahead, the ground slanted upward, leading to a summit where forest became granite. The sun was even lower now, but the heat still rippled up ahead, rising from the ground in waves just like it had from the street back in town. Everything beyond it looked blurred and in motion. Combined with the smells of Max's vomit and the strange stench filling the air, my stomach turned, and as a sharp pain rifled through my abdomen, I doubled over and barfed too.

Shawn, preoccupied by something he had clearly seen at the summit that no one else had, moved toward it. Slowly at first, and then he pulled the club from his belt and began to run, letting out a howl that sounded like a war cry.

"Shawn!" Alex called. "Wait up!"

Max dropped to his knees. "Everything's spinning," he gasped.

I knew exactly what he meant, and closed my eyes in an attempt to stop it, but within seconds I felt myself tilting and swaying, and by the time I opened my eyes it was too late. I'd stumbled ahead, too close to the edge of the path, and was suddenly falling through the air. Violently impacting with the ground, I rolled down the embankment toward the lake below.

Somewhere in the distance I heard Max calling my name. But he sounded impossibly far away, as if he were shouting to me from the distant end of a long tunnel.

The world tumbled all around me, trees and sky and forest floor spinning and turning again and again as I smashed across rocks and roots and branches, rolling faster and faster through the woods. If I didn't crash directly into a tree along the way, I'd eventually roll off the ledge and take a significant fall into the lake below. I threw my arms out and almost caught a tree, but couldn't get a strong enough grip and momentum painfully tore my hands free. Continuing to roll down the ridge, I braced myself for the sudden sensation of falling off the ledge and descending through the air in a twisted freefall, when my legs suddenly snagged on a tree. The back of my knees hit the trunk in a way that slowed then spun me around before I finally slid to a stop.

Bruised, cut, scraped, scratched, and out of breath, with the taste of vomit still coating my mouth, I sunk my hands into the pine needles on the ground until I'd found purchase, then pulled myself up and raised my knees to my chest.

I lay there with my ears ringing and that terrible odor still drifting all around me. In the distance I heard frantic voices, but they quickly faded. As I looked up the path from which I'd fallen, despite the tears in my eyes I could see someone standing there looking down at me.

Realizing I was no longer in danger of rolling the rest of the way to the lake below, I ignored the pain and forced myself to my hands and knees. Still trying to catch my breath, I looked again.

At first I thought it might be Shawn, but it wasn't.

It wasn't Max or Alex either.

What stood on that ridge looking down at me was not human.

Tall and gangly, with limbs that appeared unnaturally long in relation to the rest of its body, its head was proportional but narrow and skeletal, with sunken black eyes and a snout that came nearly to a point. As it raised its clawed hands to the heavens, it threw back its head and let out another terrifying screech.

The sound echoed through the trees, down the ridge, and struck me like a punch to the center of my chest. Despite being drenched in sweat, an icy chill shot straight up my back. Horrified, and struggling to maintain some semblance of sanity, I wiped my eyes and blinked until my vision cleared completely.

When I looked again, the creature was gone.

I tried to stand, but a sharp pain stabbed my temple then fanned out across my forehead, and I collapsed down onto my stomach. As darkness closed in around me, more screams followed...human, and very far away.

* * * *

I don't know where I am, but I can hear water dripping. Slow and steady, the drips hit something hard, perhaps a porcelain sink. It is that sound I hone in on, as I find a peculiar comfort in its rhythm and consistency. The sound focuses me, brings me back toward consciousness...or something similar.

"I'm not a monster."

The voice is familiar but echoes and sounds like it's been electronically manipulated somehow. I realize I am lying on my back on a cold and cracked cement floor. I want to sit up but my body won't respond. I can only turn my head from side to side enough to see that I'm in what appears to be an abandoned building of some sort. The walls are cement like the floor, and there are no windows. Yet there is light. Artificial light, but I cannot figure out the source or where it's coming from. Am I in a bunker?

As my head lolls to the right, the direction in which I think the voice came from, I see someone sitting in the corner. They're partially concealed in shadow, but I see now that it's Perry Jenkins. I recognize what little of his face I can see through the long dark hair hanging in front of it. But there's something wrong. He's not...right...

"I'm not a monster," *he says again.* "I just didn't believe in nothin'. Not even me. That's what they do. They kill it in you. Everything you believe, they kill it. You know that the same as I do. Don't you, Frankie Boy?"

"Help me." *My voice is raspy and raw, like I've been screaming for hours.*

"I can't," *Perry says.* "No one can."

"What's happening to me?"

"It's taking you. It's been happening for a very long time."

The dripping increases, becomes a bit louder.

"What should I do?"

Perry reaches up and pulls his hair aside, revealing more of his face.

At first I think he's smiling, but it's not that at all. His lips are gone, gnawed off, accentuating his bloody teeth and raw gums.

It is not water dripping into a sink, but blood leaking from his horrifying mouth onto the floor.

I turn away. I don't want to see his face, it frightens and repulses me.

I hear shuffling and know he's slithering toward me. I won't look at him—I won't—but I can smell and hear and feel him as his cold dead hands touch me, and his sour breath, like the exhale of an open grave, pulses against my face.

"You should scream," *Perry says,* "for mercy that will never come."

And as he licks me, his tongue cool and dry like leather sliding across my cheek, I do just that. But it only excites him, and soon the licking turns to biting, and his teeth sink deep into my flesh.

As Perry tears loose a chunk of meat from my face, his rumbling laugher rises to a fever pitch. I scream again, this time in pain, and at the sight of antlers that burst from his skull like gnarled bony fingers lunging for my eyes.

* * * *

Light returned slowly. It was dim and not as bright as before, and as I found myself next to the same tree that had stopped my fall, I realized that dusk had nearly arrived.

Frantic to get out of there and find the others, I got on all-fours and crawled back up the ridge as quickly as I could. Though I slipped and slid a few times, I managed to maintain my balance until I'd reached the path and rolled back onto relatively even ground. Above me, the sky was growing dark. Night was still maybe half an hour or so away, but it was coming and coming fast. With labored breath, and still lightheaded, I got back to my feet.

Somehow, the knife was still in my belt and hadn't fallen free. Ignoring some dizziness and the pain coursing throughout my body, I ran for the quarry.

As I reached the path's summit, and pine needles and dirt turned to granite, I saw the walls of stone. Those near the cliffs were covered in graffiti. People had been painting on them for years. A flat shelf leading to the edge of the first drop to the lake lay directly before me.

Max lay in the center of it on his back, the baseball bat next to him. At first glance it looked as if he'd been dropped there from some higher elevation, but as I scrambled over to him, I saw that he was awake and staring up at the sky.

"You okay?" I said, sliding next to him on my knees. I looked around quickly but saw no sign of Shawn, Alex, or the creature. "Are you all right?"

His eyes rolled back to me, but he didn't move or say anything.

"Max," I said, taking hold of his shoulders. "What happened?"

He stared at me, mouth open and eyes blank. I'd never seen him look that way. There was no sign of physical damage, but it was as if something deep inside him had shut off, and this was all that was left.

"Are you hurt?" I asked. "Can you get up, can you stand?"

"I saw it," he whispered. "Frankie Boy, I...I *saw* it."

"I did too, at the top of the ridge."

Slowly, he pressed an index finger to his lips. "Shh, it might hear you."

"Where is it?" I said in a loud whisper. "Where are Shawn and Alex?"

"I don't know. Help me up."

I did, but he was still wobbly, so I held onto him. "What happened, Max?"

"I was running, and then it was like I hit a wall that wasn't there, I—I don't remember anything else until you were standing over me."

I reached down, picked up the bat, and handed it to him. "We've got to find them." I knew he heard and understood me, but still seemed out of it. "*Max*," I said. "We've got to find them!"

Though he was obviously disoriented, he nodded and held the bat up higher, as if to show me he'd regained his strength.

I pulled the knife free and, holding it blade-down, started across the first granite platform. With Max close behind me, we jumped from one slab to the next until we reached the second cliff. As we dropped down onto another huge shelf of stone, I noticed something red near the edge.

"That's Shawn's bandana," Max said before I could.

I crouched down and grabbed it, shaking with fear and anger.

"My God," Max said. "What's happening?"

Craning my neck, I looked down to the lake, which was at least a hundred feet below, but there was no sign of Shawn, Alex, or anyone else in the water. I stuffed his bandana into my waistband.

"Shawn!" I screamed, the sound of my voice echoing along the walls of the stone cliffs. "Alex!"

"We have to go for help," Max said when no answer came.

"We are the help."

He gave a reluctant nod. "It's going to be dark soon, and Alex has the only flashlight."

I crossed back over to the next shelf of rock, and from this slightly higher position, was able to see a good portion of the forest in one direction, and a third cliff in the other.

"Oh no, oh—oh no," I heard Max say from not far behind me.

He'd seen them too.

Standing near the edge of the third cliff was Shawn, his back to us. He'd taken his shirt off at some point and dropped it at his feet. Arms at his side, in one hand he held the club. It was stained with crimson.

Lying a few feet away, motionless and bloodied, was Alex.

CHAPTER TWENTY-TWO

SHAWN STARED OFF over the ledge, beyond the lake below and into the miles of forest in the distance. His eyes were dull and lifeless, his face expressionless and flecked with blood. Bare chest and stomach glistening with sweat, he stood motionless, the bloody club held down at his side.

While Max knelt next to Alex to check on him, I'd stepped in front of Shawn, putting myself between him and the edge of the cliff.

"Jesus," Max said, "are you okay?"

I heard Alex groan. Glancing down quickly, I saw Max helping him up into a sitting position. "Shawn," I said, focusing on him again. "I need you to give me the club now."

"It's not safe," he answered in monotone, his eyes looking right through me. "It's not...safe."

Slowly, I reached down and took hold of the club. To my surprise, he let me take it. Gently placing a hand on his shoulder, I guided him several steps away from the edge. "Is he all right?" I asked, looking back over my shoulder. "Alex, are you all right?"

"No, he's not *fucking* all right," Max said, spitting the words at me. "Look at his face!"

Although conscious and sitting up, Alex's nose was bleeding profusely from both nostrils, and a large welt had formed over his left eye that was already swelling and badly bruised. "I'm okay," he said groggily. "I just— I—I'm okay."

Max got back to his feet and closed on Shawn. Whatever state he'd been in previously was gone, and although he was back to himself, I'd never seen him show such rage. "You attacked Alex? Are you out of your *fucking* mind?"

"Take it easy," I said, holding a hand out to stop him from getting any closer. I didn't know if whatever had gotten into Shawn still had a hold of him and I was now afraid maybe it had its claws in Max. "Just hold on and—"

"What the fuck is happening?" Max began to tremble, and his eyes filled with tears. His body slumped, as if he were about to drop to his knees, but he remained upright. "What the fuck is happening!"

"I'm sorry," Shawn said, his face twisting with pain and regret. "I didn't mean to hurt you, Alex, I would never do that, you know I wouldn't, I—I didn't mean to—"

"What's happening to us?"

"I don't know, Maxie," Shawn said desperately. "I don't know."

"You were running," Alex said. "I chased after you, and when I found you up here you turned around and looked at me, but you looked like you didn't know who I was. I started to say something and your eyes went all crazy and you started swinging on me with the club. Before I knew it I was on the ground."

Shawn pushed by me and crouched down next to Alex, who flinched at first but then seemed to accept that he no longer posed a threat. "I'm sorry, man, I—I'm so fucking sorry! I didn't know what I was doing, I—"

"You could've killed him," Max said. "It's a miracle you didn't."

On the verge of tears, Shawn leaned in and kissed the top of Alex's head. "Last thing I remember," he said as he got to his feet, "I was running up the ridge and I—I started hearing these voices. They weren't human, and I didn't want to listen because they were saying things—bad things, man, I mean *really* bad things—but I couldn't make them stop. It was like they were ripping me apart from the inside. I had this pain in my head and I—I thought if it didn't stop it was gonna kill me. The voices kept telling me to hurt you. They said they'd stop the pain if I hurt you and—Jesus Christ, I—"

"It was that thing," Alex said softly, his previous skepticism gone. He looked up at me, blood still running from his nose in twin streams. "I saw it too, Frankie Boy."

I handed him Shawn's bandana. "Now we all have."

A brief wind blew through the trees behind us, sounding like a thousand whispers rushing over us at once. It brought with it that awful stench, and suddenly I was staggering, disoriented and lightheaded again.

With a horrible grimace, Shawn covered his ears and dropped to his knees. "No," he gasped. "*Stop…*"

"It's coming!" Alex said, still pressing the bandana to his nose as he scurried away from the edge of the shelf. "It's coming!"

"No." Horrified, Max pointed over my shoulder. "It's here."

The club in one hand and the knife in the other, I stumbled forward, following Max's finger to the shelf of granite above us. Ears ringing, stomach heaving, and vision blurred, I pushed through the terror and forced myself to look at something human beings were never meant or equipped to see.

The Wendigo stood leering down at us, its hideously emaciated body swaying, and a long string of drool hanging from its mouth. The creature had no lips. They'd been chewed off, as it had apparently devoured them in its ravenous hunger and rage. It was starving and weak, vulnerable. This was our chance.

A nightmare, a goddamn nightmare, and damned by God it most certainly was, the creature looked like something straight from the depths of Hell. No longer a flash or a fleeting vision gone in the blink of an eye, a nearly forgotten distant dream or a blurred hallucination in the dead of night, it was as real as the rest of us, right out in the open and bathed in the dying light.

It no longer wanted to hide. It wanted us to see. And it wanted to feed.

Unseen things moved beneath its sparse flesh, making odd clicking sounds like those of insects. As the creature swayed faster, the terrible sounds transformed into those of flesh tearing and splitting, bones breaking, and viscera popping and gushing from open wounds.

In the distance I heard faint music, strange and antiquated, drifting across the treetops and lake below, sounding as if it were coming from some terribly old phonograph hidden deep in the forest. Or a remote past I had never known.

Then the Wendigo's eyes rolled from black to red, and it lunged for us.

My mind shattering, I watched it leap forward off the edge of the shelf and into the air. In the split-second I had to react, I froze, paralyzed with terror. A voice called out—I think it was Max—but the actual words didn't register, and suddenly, from my right side, something else flew into my line of vision.

Shawn had launched himself into midair between me and it.

As their two bodies collided then rammed into mine, they took my legs out from beneath me and I crashed to the granite so hard it knocked the wind out of me. They flew right over me, and I came back up onto my hands and knees in time to see their tangled bodies tumble to the very edge of the cliff where Max was standing. He swung the bat down onto the creature's back, but couldn't slow their momentum. They slammed into him, and Max stumbled back, twisted around, and tried to find some footing. But it was too late.

With a look of panic and horror, his mouth open in a silent scream, Max fell from the edge of the cliff.

Still groggy, Alex scuttled on his belly to the precipice and hung his head over the edge, reaching for him as if he were still there. "Max!"

As I regained my feet, the air returned to my lungs, and I saw Shawn on his knees, the Wendigo standing before him, swaying and drooling.

Realizing I still had his club, I called his name then tossed it to him.

In one fluid motion, Shawn caught it, bounced up to his feet, and swung with all his might. The blow connected, but the thing simply swatted it aside with one hand then swiped at Shawn with the other. Its claws tore across his bare chest, ripping through the flesh and leaving bloody trails in their wake.

Crying out, Shawn fell to his knees, dropped the club, and clutched at his wounds. Looming over him, the thing raised its arms above its head and let out another horrifying screech.

Alex rolled away from the edge of the cliff with his hands over his ears, and though the sound was deafening at such close range and shook me like a blow to the face, I ignored every instinct telling me to run.

Gripping the silver knife as hard as I could, I charged instead.

I only made it a step or two before it snatched me by the throat and effortlessly lifted me off my feet. Holding me there, it pulled me so close I could feel and smell its cold putrid breath.

Kicking and flailing about, I tried to break free but couldn't. The feel of its clawed hand on me was revolting—icy and corpselike—and its grip so powerful, it only became tighter the harder I struggled. No longer able to breathe, I let go of the knife, and frantically using both hands, tried to pry the fingers loose and break its grip. Had it wanted to, it could've snapped my neck, but it wanted me to suffer. I could see that in its demonic, blood-red eyes. It preferred to strangle me, to choke the life from me until it crushed my windpipe and I died in its grasp.

It drew me closer, and as our faces nearly touched, a single thread of drool rolled and dangled from its horrible mouth. As its spittle hit my cheek and slithered down along my jawline, I thought for sure I'd vomit again, but I went still and limp instead. With my legs no longer kicking and my arms dangling lifelessly at my sides, my vision began to leave me, and I could no longer hear anything.

Except for that strange old music coming from the forest…

* * * *

The music…I can still hear the music. But it's closer now, louder.

In a series of flashes, a montage of images fire across my mind's eye at speeds so rapid-fire fast I can barely discern one from the next. But it's all there, everything that's happened that has led me to this place and time, to this day that has now become night. Each person and every circumstance unfolds before me, collapses like the house of cards it is and always has been.

Sitting on the floor like the child I am, I contemplate the black-and-white tiles organized into a giant checkerboard beneath me and wonder why I'm here and what this all means. Next to me, a dog-eared comic book from four years ago...1973...I recognize it as the one I read before, the issue Alex has.

The Uncanny X-Men...Issue #140...The Savage Fury of Wen-Di-Go!

But the creature depicted on the cover looks nothing like it. I want to say it's wrong and that this isn't how it really is, but there's no one there to explain this to. I don't understand why exactly, I only know I don't want to touch the comic book or even look at it anymore.

The music continues to play, this dated and scratchy instrumental tune my grandparents might have listened to in their youths. And although it is much closer than before, I still cannot figure out where this peculiar music is coming from. Why is it so unsettling? Why does it frighten and repel me so? The sound of it is like millions of insects scurrying over my skin, up the back of my neck and into my hair, down across my face and into my mouth and eyes and ears. It makes me want to hurt myself, to tear at my own flesh.

There is no one else in the room. No furniture, nothing on the bare white walls, no fixtures on the white ceiling. There are no doors. There is only me, this floor, the comic book, my visions, and this eerie godforsaken music.

Maybe they know more than they're telling us.

When I close my eyes in an attempt to shut it all out and off, it is an odd mist I see, spraying from the back of an old pickup truck.

They could be spraying damn near anything.

There is something...more...but I don't want to open my eyes, even when it all fades to black and I am alone in the darkness. There is something else here now. I can feel it all around me.

"Do you hear it?" a deep male voice says.

It reminds me of one of those cheesy announcers on TV, only...

"Within the music...beneath the music...do you hear it?"

This voice doesn't belong to anyone friendly.

"Do you feel it?"

I throw back my head and open my eyes.

It is snowing in the room, the flakes falling and swirling all around me.

"Did you really think it would be so silly?" the disembodied voice asks. "Like comic books or drive-in horror movies, teenage boys fighting monsters?"

It is then that I realize this isn't snow at all.

"Did you really think that's what's happening?"

These are not snowflakes tickling my face and body.

"Are you too afraid to believe, little boy?"
They are gypsy moths falling from the ceiling, swarming me.
"Are you too afraid to see the truth, to know *the truth?"*
Feeding on me...
"Tell us what you see, Frankie Boy."
Devouring me...
"Beyond the veil, to the place we have brought you to."
I'm lost, drowning in this evil.
"Tell us what you see."
Nothing...emptiness...a black sky under which anything is possible but nothing matters.
"What is there with you?"
I can't see it through this mass of tiny wings and bodies and bottomless black eyes.
"But..."
But it sees me.

* * * *

I struggled to turn away from those hideous red eyes but I couldn't move my head. More drool dribbled across my face as darkness rose, creeping slowly from the bottom of my eyes and ushering me toward what would soon be death.

A sudden clanging sound snapped me back into consciousness. The grip on my throat eased and I was able to get in at least some breath. Before I could figure out what was happening the clang sounded again, and this time the Wendigo's head snapped to the side and a chunk of flesh stuck to its skull flew free. A third clang sounded and I was falling, released from its claws. As I crashed to the granite, gasping for breath, another clang sounded and it bent to the side and stumbled.

Through the growing darkness, someone emerged from behind the creature, swinging a shovel. It swept past and connected with the Wendigo's side again. This time the person wielding the shovel brought it up, smashing it under the creature's chin with another loud clang.

That blow sent its back arching, and as it swiped at the air with its claws, it toppled over backwards to the ground.

From the shadows stepped my father, out of breath and with the bloody shovel clutched in both hands.

"Dad," I said, choking out the word, my hands rubbing my throat and neck.

That's who Shawn had heard. He'd been following us the whole time.

"Are you all right, son?"

Before I could answer, the creature leapt to its feet and closed on my father. He tried to swing the shovel again but it was too late. The entire thing looked as if it was happening in slow-motion, and though I reached for him, I knew it was a futile attempt.

The Wendigo bit into my father's shoulder with a horrible crunching sound, shaking its head like a wolf tearing into a kill, and ripped free a bloody chunk of meat.

My father screamed and rammed the shovel into the beast's midsection. As it stabbed into the thing and burst out its back with a gut-wrenchingly wet sound, the Wendigo let out another screech and began to thrash about violently.

Even as I called his name, I knew how bad it was. I knew.

Slumped over and gushing blood, he looked at me and tried to smile. My father was already dying but his focus was on comforting me.

Something flew by me with a strange whizzing sound, and the creature, struck in one of its eyes, reared back and screeched again.

Seething, I frantically looked around for the knife and found it a few feet away where I'd dropped it, right next to Alex, who had gotten to one knee and just fired a rock with his slingshot. I sprang to my feet, and as Shawn rushed by me in the opposite direction, the club raised, Alex grabbed the knife and tossed it to me.

I caught it and closed on the creature.

My father, with what strength he had left, swung the shovel again, this time hitting the thing full in the face. It collapsed in a heap, and Shawn pounced on it, raining down blows with the club and screaming like a banshee.

I joined him, stabbing the Wendigo again and again. The rage building with each thrust, I repeatedly tried for the heart, but it was jerking around and trying to ward us off with its claws, so I hit it as hard as I could wherever I could.

Suddenly Alex was there too, stomping on the creature with the heel of his foot, smashing down into its neck and face.

We pummeled it until it stopped fighting back, and lay there staring up at us through its bloody wounds as if hoping for mercy.

Please, it seemed to be saying, *stop*.

Don't listen to it.

I looked over at my father. He was down on one knee, had dropped the shovel and was trying desperately to apply pressure to his wound with both hands. But the blood kept coming, running between his fingers and drenching his chest and stomach in crimson.

As Shawn and Alex stood there out of breath, I turned back to the creature and its now pleading eyes.

Don't listen to it.

"Oh my God," I heard Alex say. "Mr. Molinari, you—you're hurt bad! We got to get out of here, we—we got to get him help!"

Not ever.

I straddled the fallen creature.

Clutching the knife with both hands, I raised it over my head.

"Do it," my father said, his voice gurgling with the blood that was bubbling up into the back of his throat. "Do it, Frankie Boy, now while it's weak. *Do it.*"

I slammed the blade down into its chest. The thing screeched a final time, reaching for me with its claws, but I yanked the knife free and brought it down again. Blood and bile burst from its mouth, and this time, it lay still.

Alex and I both took a step toward my father, but he held a bloody hand up to stop us. "No," he said, wincing. "Don't touch me, it's got me now and I know what happens from here. So do you."

"Dad, no, we can—"

"You listen to me, son." He motioned to the creature. "Finish it now."

A cold darkness swept through me. I looked out at the forest in the distance, beyond the lake. I wanted to cry. I wanted to hug my dad one last time. I wanted to kiss his cheek and tell him how much I loved him and how I'd never forget him.

Instead, I knelt next to the creature.

And cut its fucking heart out.

* * * *

It was almost totally dark. Alex switched the flashlight on.

The pool of light revealed it was roughly the size of a man's fist and resembled a dark crystal or perhaps a sculpted piece of dirty ice with a silver knife protruding from it. The creature let out something between a growl and a moan, then had a seizure and went quiet.

"We got to get down to the lake," Shawn said flatly. "Max…"

Alex swept the flashlight toward the edge of the cliff. "He fell but he's okay. I think he—he's okay. I saw him hit and come up, and then he was swimming."

"Got to get down to the lake," Shawn mumbled again. "He could be hurt."

I took the flashlight from Shawn, brought it around to my father and took a few steps closer to him. Shaking uncontrollably, I tried not to cry, but I'd never seen anyone bleeding so badly, and I could tell he was getting groggy, losing whatever light still burned in him.

"You knew, didn't you," I said.

It wasn't a question, but he answered anyway. "It would've killed them and taken you like it did that other boy. It was tormenting me, telling me it was you it wanted and how it was bringing you to it, luring you out here. I couldn't...I couldn't let that happen."

"Why did it want me?" I asked. "Why did it do this to us?"

"It's not what you think. Nothing is what you think it is, what you see or hear, none of it. It never is, son. It never was. We're not supposed to see certain things. Not supposed to know certain things. Once I did, I doomed us both, and I'm sorry. The factory, it's a lie, there's more there than paper."

He was growing delusional. "We have to get you to a hospital."

"No," he said. "I'd never make it, and even if I did, I'd be in this thing's clutches. It'd stay alive in me, do you understand? It has to die, Frankie Boy. Here and now, it has to die...and so do I."

Tears streamed my face, and I couldn't stop shaking. "What do I—what do I do, Dad? What do I do, what—what am I supposed to *do*?"

"Live your life, son. All of you boys—you're good boys—you go live your lives." My father coughed, and blood washed over his bottom lip onto his chin. "None of you were ever here, understand? None of this even happened, okay? They'll find my body in the lake, drowned and banged up from probably hitting rocks or the side of the cliff. It won't matter because I'm just a crazy old man that saw things and acted nuts before he finally killed himself, see? And that...that *thing*...it'll be gone in me. They'll never find its body because you're going to do what you have to do to make sure that demon never comes back. You hear me, son?"

I nodded.

"I love you. Always know that. Always. And you tell your mother I never stopped loving her, not ever." He flinched in pain and coughed again, but through it all, he managed another weak smile. "You and your mom and me, our family, it's all that ever meant anything to me, son. It's all I ever needed, and we had it once, didn't we? Didn't we have it once, Frankie Boy?"

I didn't answer. I didn't have to. He knew from the look in my eyes what I knew and felt and believed and would always carry in my heart. We both did.

"Shine the light," Shawn called from the edge of the cliff. "I'm going over. We got to find Max."

"Not yet," my father said. "Get out of the way, Shawn."

We didn't know what he meant.

Until the creature rose to its feet and, staggering about with what little life remained in it, lunged for me.

With speed and strength I didn't think my father still possessed, he rose and charged. Slamming into the Wendigo, he wrapped his arms around it, and took them both over the edge of the cliff into darkness.

CHAPTER TWENTY-THREE

AS NIGHT FULLY descended over the quarry and forest, the heat finally broke and the temperature dropped considerably, but everything remained unnaturally quiet. In shock, exhausted and broken, we crossed the granite slabs and shelves until we reached the far side of the quarry, and then followed the forest down a steep incline to the lake below. With only the single flashlight to lead the way, and a treacherous terrain to contend with, it took the better part of an hour before we reached the shore.

We found Max collapsed and lying on his stomach in the dirt just beyond the reaches of the lake. As well as could be expected, he'd suffered no serious physical injuries, but was so traumatized that even after we found him and he realized we were all alive, it took him a while before he or anyone else said anything. When Max finally did speak, it was measured and unusually lethargic, as if he'd been sedated.

"I heard another big splash," he said, his pale face partially lit with the flashlight beam Alex had aimed at him. "But I didn't see anything, and then it went quiet."

We all knew what had to be done, and what still lay ahead, and after everything that happened, we were beyond being affected by it. The evil was defeated, my father was a dead hero who had saved our lives, and the night was alive. Nothing would or could ever be the same.

No one asked me if I was all right. None of us asked that of each other.

Of course we weren't all right.

I moved closer to the lake, and placed the heart on the first flat rock I came across. The others joined me there, and together, Shawn, Alex, Max, and I stood over it a moment. It seemed such a small and silly thing after all that had taken place, this strange and impossible abomination that resembled a dirty chunk of ice.

Alex held the light on it.

Together, we stomped the heart until it shattered.

Each time I crashed my heel down onto it I saw my father's face, heard his voice, and remembered what it felt like to be near him. And each time I slammed my heel down harder, and with more vengeance.

When it was done, I gave Alex a quick nod.

He handed me the flashlight then removed an old silver cigar box from his knapsack. I recognized it as one he'd had in his bedroom that he used to keep loose change in. Gathering the pieces of the heart, Alex carefully placed them inside then closed the box and returned it to his knapsack.

Shawn was the first to break away, moving past me and into the darkness.

"Over here," he said a moment later.

I swept the flashlight in his direction.

At the edge of the lake, the dark silhouette of a body floated face-down. He already had a hold of it by the leg and was dragging it from the water.

Max and Alex helped him. I stayed where I was, shining the light.

The creature's body, limp and twisted, lay on the shore of the lake now, all of us staring at it in disbelief and horror. Even dead it was disturbing, perhaps more so. Its presence continued to warp and pervert any sense of reality we'd once known, and although I didn't want to touch it, I knew it was time to do what Mean Earl had instructed.

"You bring the salt?" I asked.

Alex gave his knapsack a pat. "Snagged some Morton's from the pantry."

"Let's finish it."

My memories of the next couple hours are vague at best, but I know we dragged the creature to the woods. I know we took turns using the knife, and I know we dismembered and salted the pieces. I know, using the shovel my father had brought to disable it, we took turns digging and buried the remains. No one said anything. No one objected or complained. All of us threw up at least once during the process, overtaken by the stench and pure barbarism of what we were doing, but we didn't stop until it was over.

There was no sign of my father's body.

It wouldn't be discovered until the following afternoon, when a pair of hikers noticed his bloated remains drifting across the surface of the lake and notified the authorities.

That night I stood at the bank of the lake for a very long time, stared out into the darkness and let the tears come. I wanted to swim out there, find him and take him home. Put him to rest. But that couldn't happen. It had to play out as my father said. Deep down I knew that, but leaving him there was the hardest thing I'd ever done.

The guys waited, giving me as much time as I needed. I don't know for sure how long I stood there, but eventually I wiped away my tears, turned my back on the lake, and let them know I was ready.

As the woods returned to normal, alive again with animal and insect sounds, like soldiers behind enemy lines after dark, we quietly and methodically made our way back across the quarry and through the forest toward home. It took much longer than it normally would have, and wasn't easy getting through the pitch-black woods with only one flashlight and being as mentally, emotionally, and physically exhausted as we were, but we made it through.

It was very late when we emerged from the forest and congregated under a streetlight not far from my house. In better light it was impossible to ignore our wounds and the ragged look of us, but we were still in shock. Emotionless and detached, outwardly we looked like a bunch of zombies. The turmoil was inside us now, burning like a fever.

Shawn still hadn't put his shirt back on, and while the scratches he'd suffered across his chest had stopped bleeding and started to scab over, they still looked quite painful. He sat on the curb, lit his last cigarette, then crushed the empty pack and tossed it aside. "Where are we doing it, Frankie Boy?"

"It has to be consecrated ground," I said listlessly. "Sacred."

Alex took the box from his knapsack. "Like holy ground, right?"

I nodded. "I know a place."

At that time of night everything was deathly quiet in town, like the entire world had fallen asleep. We walked the empty streets of Samoset until we'd reached Saint Anthony's, the Catholic church in town. In all the times I'd come here for Mass, or gone to the rectory for one of the dances they were sponsoring, I never could've imagined the day would come when I'd be standing on church property in the middle of the night with my friends, looking for a spot to bury the shattered heart of a legendary creature. Even then, it felt more like a horrible dream than anything even remotely real.

As I gazed for a moment at the old stone church, I remembered the strange music in the forest. Had that simply been in my head?

Do you really think that's what's happening?

Across the street from the church was a small private cemetery. One of the oldest burial grounds in Samoset, it housed only six headstones. Each marked the grave of a deceased priest that had died while assigned to Saint Anthony's, and spanned a timeframe from the late 1800s to the early 1900s. The last priest to be buried there was in 1919, and from that point forward, clergy were interred elsewhere.

Rarely attended to and barely paid even passing interest by most, this was the perfect spot. Holy, consecrated ground we could disturb and bury the box in without anyone ever noticing or even realizing we'd done it.

Using my father's bloody shovel, I dug a small hole in the right rear corner of the cemetery. When I'd gotten about three feet deep, I stopped, and Alex handed me the silver box.

I quickly dropped it in.

"Do we have to say anything?" Max asked.

"Yeah," Shawn said, and then spit into the hole. "Fuck you."

Alex put a hand on my shoulder. "Want me to cover it?"

"I got it."

With each shovel of dirt I sent back into that hole, the box became less visible, and so did the horror it contained. Once filled, I patted down the dirt with the shovel then handed it to Shawn and walked away. I didn't stop until I'd reached the opposite side of the street, and the long shadow of the church.

I'd been a member of this parish my whole life, yet somehow, in the darkness of that strange and ethereal night, while I still felt a connection to God, I no longer felt connected to what I'd always believed was His house. I wanted to—*needed* to even—but I felt nothing.

"Frankie Boy?"

It was Max that had spoken, but Alex and Shawn were behind me as well. Beaten down and exhausted, like me, this night had left them profoundly altered and stripped of things they'd never get back. For reasons I didn't understand then and likely never would, that created both a deeper bond and a wider chasm between us. I wanted them by my side, and I wanted to be by theirs, but at the same time, part of me never wanted to see them again.

Max hugged me, and as I hugged him back, Alex and Shawn hugged us both. We remained that way for what seemed a very long time.

"Is it done?" Alex asked when we finally let each other go.

It was done, but it would never be over, not really.

"Yeah," I answered. "I think so."

"Then let's go home."

CHAPTER TWENTY-FOUR

THERE ARE MOMENTS in time that come to us briefly and tenderly, like a gentle misting rain. They are often profound, defining moments in our lives, yet we rarely notice them long enough to remember. Unconsciously, we relegate them to the loneliest corners of our minds, casting them into a wasteland of forgotten and discarded memories we seldom acknowledge and sometimes don't even realize still exist. If never revisited, it is there that those wondrous moments go to die. Can you remember the final time you went outside to play as a child? Or the final time you and your childhood friends were together without a care in the world? Can you remember, when you were old enough to understand, the first time anyone told you they loved you? Can you remember the first time you told them? Can you remember the first time you realized how beautiful a sunset was? How about the first time you told a lie, or someone lied to you? Or the first time you ever hurt someone's feelings, or they hurt yours? When was the first time the unconditional love of an animal touched your soul? Can you remember? It's not because we don't want to, because once brought to our attention we most certainly do. Why then, do these things elude us so?

One such instance I do remember, and with a startling clarity I ironically sometimes wish I didn't. That night in the forest, at the quarry, and later at the church graveyard, was the final time any of us were children.

When we went our separate ways that night, our childhoods died.

The next time we were together, even though it was only a few days later, the kids we'd been were gone. We were adults, like it or not.

When I snuck into the house that night, my mother was passed out on the couch in the den. Maybe she'd fallen asleep waiting up for me or my father. I don't know and I never asked. I simply went to my room and undressed. Naked, I climbed into bed and slipped beneath the covers. I lay there staring at the ceiling, the horrors of everything that had taken place earlier replaying in my mind. Not only had I lost my father, I was certain I'd also lost my mind. And a very real and tangible part of me was dying along with both. A part I still needed, just as I still needed him. I knew then nothing would ever be normal or usual again. But then, I wasn't sure it ever had been.

Hoping to make as little noise as possible, I wept into my pillow until all I had left were quiet whimpers and groans. I never cried that violently before, and never have since.

In the morning, my mother came into my room. I let her think she was waking me even though I hadn't slept at all.

"My God," she said, hand to chest. "What happened to your throat?"

It was sore, my neck had gone stiff, and during the night black and purple bruises had appeared. "I got in a fight."

"A *fight*?" she said as if the very concept was inconceivable. "Who were you fighting with?"

"A kid I know, okay? It's no big deal."

"Are you all right?"

"I'm fine. It's just some bruises."

"They look painful."

"They are. What did you want, Mom?"

She drew a deep breath, let it out slowly. "Your father didn't come home last night. He wasn't here when I got home and I haven't heard from him."

I just looked at her.

"Did you hear what I said? Your father's been out all night."

I still didn't know what to say. Maybe I didn't want to know.

I never stopped loving my mother, but I realized then—as she stood trembling with what I assumed was fear, guilt, regret, and anger, her hair mussed and her clothes wrinkled and disheveled—that I hadn't liked her in a very long time. Had she felt the same way about me, and perhaps she did, I wouldn't have blamed her. When was the exact moment that happened to us, me and the woman from whom I came, who forged me inside her body and gave me life?

I'm still not sure.

Another moment lost in time.

The days that followed didn't get any easier, though things did play out exactly as my father said they would. His body was found the following day. In his pocket the police found a suicide note sealed inside a small plastic zip-lock sandwich bag. He could no longer take the things he was hearing and seeing, it read, and he loved us and would one day see us again.

As I suspected, my father had known all along. He'd been preparing to die for some time, and somehow knew that's what this would come to. All that time he'd been planning to save me, and he was trying to ready not only me, but himself. The whole time, he'd been in mourning.

After my mother identified the body she came home, sat me down at the kitchen table, and explained my father had died. He jumped from the quarry cliffs and drowned, she told me. He loved us very much, but he was sick. It wasn't anyone's fault—certainly not mine—so I must never blame myself, she said.

Only about twenty people attended my father's funeral.

The following day two stone-faced men in black suits and dark sunglasses pulled up in front of our house in a big black sedan. My mother met with them outside, and I watched from the window while they spoke. To this day I don't know who they were or what they said to her, but the whole thing lasted about five minutes, and then they were gone. Looking stunned, my mother stood there a while, even after they left. When she finally came inside she was shaken and had tears in her eyes, but assured me they were agents from the insurance company that had come to let her know that suicide was not covered by my father's life insurance policy. I wasn't sure I believed her, and I knew she could tell, but that's where she left it. We never discussed it further, but those strange men frightened me, and I was worried they might come back.

They never did.

In the weeks and months that followed, we went from being the family in town with the crazy father who saw monsters, to the family in town with the crazy father that killed himself. There weren't a lot of suicides in Samoset, especially back then, and though people had drowned at the quarry before, no one had ever killed themselves there. My father was falsely labeled the first.

Later that fall, they caught the peeping tom. It turned out to be Officer Daniels, of all people. He was apparently peeking in windows whenever he was on the nightshift. He was arrested and lost his job but never did any time for it. He moved away not long after. I don't know whatever became of him.

I spent the next four years in town living at home with my mother. She switched jobs again, this time taking a position in Boston for higher pay. She didn't date anyone and rarely went anywhere unless she had to. Her drinking got worse, and she started taking pills to help her sleep. It was like living with a ghost. I sensed her presence but rarely saw or interacted with her. When I did it was only in the most facile and absolutely necessary ways. We tried, but we just couldn't get back what we had before that summer of '77.

As for me, I got my first real job. I started high school. I dated girls. I played sports. I had bad dreams. The guys and I remained close, but that night hung over us like the nightmare it was. After a while we pretended none of it really happened, and that it was all just stupid kid stuff. We knew the truth, of course, but sometimes a lie is easier. So we just stopped talking about it.

By junior year we all had other friends too, and sort of wandered into our own little cliques the way high school kids do, but I was never as close to my other friends as I was to Shawn, Max, and Alex. The stigma of being the guy whose father was crazy and killed himself stayed with me through those years, and led to more than one fistfight. But like so much else, I learned to live with it. I counted the days until I could put Samoset in my rearview, studied hard and got the best grades I could. When I landed a full scholarship to a small college in upstate New York, I took it.

I only came back to Samoset when I had to, usually in the summers and for vacation breaks. While in college I fell in love. We were together for a while but ultimately it didn't work out. I made sure of that, I suppose.

After I graduated and got my license, I took a job at a high school near Syracuse. Although I felt terribly alone, I also felt free. If my father's afflictions were ever to become mine, I wouldn't make anyone else suffer with or because of them.

My mother sold the house and moved away less than a year after I graduated college. I didn't return to town to see her off, and she never came to see me where I lived. She called right before she left Samoset, and told me she planned to go out to the west coast and start her life over. That's how she put it. "I want to start over."

She deserved that as much as I did, and I genuinely wished her well.

Over the years we spoke on the phone now and then. Our conversations were brief and inconsequential, but always cordial.

We never saw each other again.

I think of her often. I miss her.

I miss my dad too, and the life we all shared before that awful summer. Sometimes I wonder if things were really as good as I remember them, or if the cracks in our lives had started much earlier and I just didn't realize it because I was a kid. It's hard to say, and I guess I'll never know for sure, but I've learned that sometimes more than one thing can be real. Like monsters and mental illness, horrifying visions and eerie music in the forest, factories and businesses both genuine and more than they appear to be, nightmares and memories, and menacing men in black suits that drive cars with government plates.

I still have the nightmares, and suspect I always will, but I choose to remember the times before those nightmares as good ones, when we were a typical happy little family, and I had the best friends in the world. A family and friends the likes of which I'd never know again. Not acquaintances or people I occasionally socialized with. Not colleagues I was fond of and whose company I enjoyed away from work from time to time. They were real family and genuine friends, and neither came with any of the bullshit and stress and pressure being an adult in the real world so cruelly demands of us all. But who's to say that wasn't the real world and everything since has been the lie? Either way, those were the purest and most innocent times of my life, and I remember the first moment to the last. No one can ever take them away from me. Only the years can rob me of them, and perhaps one day they will.

Then, like all the others, they'll be mere precious moments, never truly gone, just forever lost in time.

CHAPTER TWENTY-FIVE
~2017~

IT RAINS THE day of Alex's funeral. It begins slow and misty, then turns to a drizzle. Finally, it becomes a steady downpour. While at its worst, I'm sheltered in my car, which is parked across the street from the house I grew up in. It has vinyl siding now, and an addition has been added to the side of the house. Two large SUVs and a pickup truck fill the half-circle driveway, which has survived but is now paved rather than gravel, as it once was. It's nicer now, our old house, and surely worth a great deal more money than when we lived there. But I can still see it the way it once was, still feel us here and the traces we left behind. I'm alive, yet my ghost resides here too, bound by echoes of laughter and somber tears, faded shadows and gentle whispers, reminiscences of good times and bad, all of it—all of us—still lurking behind a gray sheet of callous rain.

When I close my eyes, a vision from long ago comes to me.

A very young boy sits on the kitchen floor watching his parents hold each other close and dance with a silly and joyful abandon. And he laughs too, the little boy. They're happy, this family, together and alive and unafraid.

I hope it's a real memory, and not my mind trying to protect me. Maybe my mother and father sent it to me just then, a gift from what once was to what now is, and, perhaps, to what might still one day be possible for me.

At fifty-four, I'm older than my father was when he died.

"Frank," Shawn says from the passenger seat. "We better get going."

For a moment, I'd forgotten he was there. I nod, start the car.

Glancing at the rearview, I see Max smiling at me from the backseat. I want to smile back, but I just can't seem to find one.

"Yeah," I say softly, and slowly pull away.

I don't look back.

* * * *

Alex was a lapsed Catholic, so Ronica decided he wouldn't have wanted a religious ceremony. Thus, there is no Mass. This spares us of not only having to listen to some well-meaning priest who didn't know Alex eulogize him, it also allows us to avoid Saint Anthony's and the thing we buried next door. For that, I am eternally grateful, as I'm sure Max and Shawn are.

The funeral is a small and uneventful affair. There are only a handful of people in attendance, including us: Ronica, her son (who is shaved and in full dress uniform, as we later learn he served two tours in Iraq a few years prior and is still active National Guard), and four other people I don't know or recognize. This shouldn't surprise me, I guess, but it does. More people should care.

God damn you for doing this, Alex. And God damn me for losing you.

Although Max and Shawn and I were here only a day ago, it feels as if we're in an entirely different place now. Maybe it's the rain, or the shiny new casket of wood and metal perched over a fresh grave where only a tarp resided before. It's real now. Alex is truly gone.

Like the others, we huddle beneath umbrellas as the funeral home director solemnly asks if anyone would like to say anything.

"We love you, Alex," Ronica says, weeping uncontrollably. "We love you."

Her voice is barely audible above the rain.

"May you find the peace in God's arms you never could in life," her son says. "Thank you for being my uncle."

Max chokes up, clears his throat, and despite the rain, slides his sunglasses on. I put my arm around him. Shawn does the same.

From the corner of my eye I see Shawn's bottom lip quivering as his eyes fill with tears. I suspect crying is not something he has allowed himself to do in a very long time. As he glances at me I look away, so as not to embarrass him.

Ronica lays a single flower on her brother's casket, then is escorted off by her son to a waiting car near the gates of the cemetery.

Everyone else just wanders away, as if mistakenly.

And then it's just the three of us.

I place my hand on the casket and, in a whisper, say goodbye.

Shawn lights a cigarette and walks away, quickly wiping his eyes as Max leans over the casket, kisses it, then lays his cheek against it.

I give him a moment, then go to him and gently place a hand on his back. "Come on," I say. "Let's get out of the rain."

* * * *

Ronica's son is a member of the local VFW, so we all meet back at the hall in town, which looks more or less like it did when we lived here. Bare bones and basic, there are cafeteria-style tables and chairs scattered throughout a large open area, with a kitchen in back.

By the time we get there, everyone else has already arrived and taken their seats at a long table in the center of the room that is covered with a white linen cloth and set with plates, silver, and glassware. They look to us in unison like the outsiders we've become, but try to appear as cordial as possible.

Ronica rises from her chair and slowly approaches us. She kisses and hugs me first, and I feel her trembling. We don't say anything, because we've already done that. But when she lets me go, she turns to Shawn, and with tears in her eyes, places a hand on either side of his face.

They embrace for a long time, whispering things to each other no one else can or needs to hear.

Finally, she looks to Max.

"Maxie," she says, her tears falling now and her face both a smile and a grimace. "My God, *Maxie*, look at you."

He begins to cry. As they embrace, Shawn and I leave them.

The anger and resentment Ronica showed with me is no longer evident now, and I'm glad. She has every right to feel those things, I'm just happy she directed them at me rather than Shawn and Max.

Eventually we join the others at the table. A couple of older women in aprons bring carafes of coffee and water, along with a large tray of scrambled eggs and plates of bacon, sausage, and toast.

The food reminds me it is only midmorning. It already feels like midnight.

No one eats. Everybody just stares at their empty plates.

"To Alex," Shawn says, raising his coffee.

We all raise our drinks too.

"To Alex…"

* * * *

When it's time to leave, Ronica walks us to the exit. After another round of long hugs, she wipes her eyes then takes something from her purse. "Do you guys remember that Polaroid camera my mom and Rafe got me for my sixteenth birthday?" she asks.

I do remember the big clunky camera she had and how it shot out instant photographs we'd sit and watch develop right before our eyes. It was one of the most amazing things we'd ever seen, and was very expensive at the time.

"Yes," Max answers for us. "You had so much fun with that thing."

"Do you remember those glamor shots you took of me?" she says.

"How could I forget, *darling*?" Max winks. "Do you remember the ones you took of me?"

"Of course I do, *darling*."

"I looked even more glamorous in that boa than you did."

Albeit briefly, Ronica actually laughs, and I'm sure I have never loved Max more. Even after all these years, and on the day she buried her brother, he's still able to pull it off. Their connection was always special, and for one wonderful moment, it still is.

"The first picture I ever took with it was of you guys," she tells us as she pushes the item she retrieved from her purse into my hand. "Alex saved it all these years. I found it in with his things. He would've wanted you to have it."

The minute I lay eyes on it I remember the exact moment it was taken. The four of us smile back at me from so very long ago, standing side-by-side in her front yard, our arms around each other. We were laughing at the moment Ronica pressed the button.

"My God," Max says, looking over my shoulder at it. "We're so young."

Shawn says nothing, but he does smile fondly then reach down and touch the photograph, as if doing so might somehow make it more real.

Taken only weeks before that summer of '77, I look into our eyes and realize none of us have any idea what lies ahead, and how drastically our world is about to change. Despite that, or perhaps because of it, although grainy and stained, it is one of the most beautiful and moving things I have ever seen.

It blurs before my eyes, and for the first time today, I break.

I cry for Alex. I cry for us all.

And as we group hug near that exit door, I cry for those lost teenagers running on a beach through the dark of night, laughing, out of breath and so certain of their immortality nothing could ever stop them. I cry for Ronica's gorgeous and mischievous eyes in the rearview of that awful little Volkswagen Bug, and how I wished that night would never end. I cry for my mother sitting alone at the kitchen table, and for my father desperately wandering the house in his bathrobe.

Max and Shawn and I say goodbye for the final time back at the motel. We promise to keep in touch, but who can be sure if we will or just really want to?

It's a typically awkward masculine farewell, with plenty of long and strong handshakes, some quick hugs, muttered though heartfelt words, and a lot of uncomfortable silences. We don't want to go our separate ways again, yet can't wait to do just that. I don't know why it has to be like that, but I suppose that's why they say you can never go home again. Maybe because the home you're trying to go back to no longer exists any more than the people you hope to see there do.

Later, after they've gone and I'm alone in my car, I look at the photograph again, grateful they allowed me to keep it. As the rain drums the roof and sluices along the windows and windshield, for some reason I think of the moths that invaded Samoset that summer. Just like the caterpillars that completed their cycle of life with a metamorphosis into gypsy moths, something similar happened to the boys in that picture. Though persecuted, we came full circle. Some of us made it, some of us didn't. But we were there. We faced our monsters, and though we paid a terrible price and could no longer exist exactly as we had previously, we made it through the transformative storm.

These days, when I awaken from a bad dream, hopeful it will finally be my last, I still cry for those boys. In the solitude of my little apartment, I cry for the children we were back then, and the mysteries and darkness we endured not only then, but now. Sometimes, though, when I remember how magical, frightening, and heartbreaking it is to be a child, it also occurs to me what a blessing it is to be an adult with a childhood to remember at all. However complicated and riddled with screeching monsters it may be.

It is then that I smile for those boys, for who we were, who we dreamed we might one day be, and for those lucky enough to still be here, for who we are and still aspire to one day become.

I find comfort in that.

The same as I found comfort that last day in Samoset, as I drove off through the rain, away from a town I knew I'd never return to. I took that old photograph and stuck it up under the visor, and though I couldn't see it anymore, I knew it was still there.

In that same way, so are we, all of us.

And somehow, that's enough.

ABOUT THE AUTHOR

GREG F. GIFUNE is a best-selling, internationally-published author of several acclaimed novels, novellas and two short story collections. Working predominantly in the horror and crime genres, Greg has been called, "The best writer of horror and thrillers at work today" by *New York Times* bestselling author Christopher Rice, "One of the best writers of his generation" by horror grandmaster Brian Keene, and "Among the finest dark suspense writers of our time" by legendary bestselling author Ed Gorman. Greg's work has been published all over the world, translated into several languages, received starred reviews from *Publishers Weekly*, *Library Journal* and others, and is consistently praised by readers and critics alike. His novel THE BLEEDING SEASON, originally published in 2003, has been hailed as a classic in the horror genre and is considered to be one of the best horror/thriller novels ever written. Two of his stories (HOAX and FIRST IMPRESSIONS) have been adapted into short films, and his novel LONG AFTER DARK is set to begin production as a feature film in 2021. Greg and his wife Carol reside in Massachusetts with their dogs, Dozer and Dudley. Greg can be reached online at gfgauthor@verizon.net or on Facebook, Twitter and Instagram.